WHERE

Destiny

LIES

WHERE

Destiny

LIES

E.G. TUDOR

✦ ★ ★ ★ ★ ★ ★ ✦
Inlustris

First published in the UK in 2023 by Inlustris Publishing, Wales
Text © E. G. Tudor 2023

Edited by Emma O'Connell ©
Cover designed by Inlustris Publishing ©
Interior formatting and design by Inlustris Publishing ©

A CIP catalogue record for this book is available from the British Library.

Paperback ISBN 978 1 915950 11 6
E-book ISBN 978 1 915950 12 3
Hardback ISBN 978 1 915950 13 0

For all those who find themselves at rock bottom
and find their way back up... and to those who
reach out a hand to help.
This is for you.

I was supposed to have the perfect life — I was supposed to have it all with my pick of a noble partner, powerful parents and beautiful home. But instead, my mother was banished to the shadow realm of Fog because of my best friend, who now has everything... while I have nothing.

Prologue

Three Years Ago

"Eva, darling!"

I rolled my eyes at the sound of my mother's voice, and pushed up off my bed. "Sorry, Wen. I won't be a moment." *I hope.*

My best friend, Ceridwen Moonshade, gave me an understanding smile and went back to feeding frostberries to our mothlings, Lunara and Aruna.

I gracefully padded across the plush black carpet of my large bedroom and opened the door looking out into the hallway. With a sigh, I carried on along the marble tiled floor and into my parents' room.

My mother sat at her dressing table, her full, lustrous, gold-blonde hair pulled up into a neat chignon. In the mirror, her bright blue eyes speared my grey ones.

"I have to go out tonight, I'm sorry," she said, not looking at all sorry.

"But, Mother, tomorrow is the Choosing…" I

trailed off as she pouted.

"Now, Eva, darling. You have nothing to worry about. You are a Celestri, daughter of the current Fated Pair. I'm certain you shall be chosen, and whoever is chosen from Sol will be equally as noble. Together you shall rule the Twin Realms as wonderfully as your father and I do."

Though her words rang with a haughty certainty, I had my doubts. Just because my mother, born in the sun realm of Sol, had been paired with my father, a noble of the realm of night, Nos, to rule our Twin Realms, did not make it a cert that I would be Chosen. The Fates could be tricky, and sometimes they chose the least expected candidates.

My mother rose on her black spiked heels and straightened her silver dress to walk over to me. "I have business in Sol, but I shall be back for the Choosing." She gave me an arrogant smile.

"All right," I said, knowing it was pointless to argue. "Can Wen sleep over then?"

Her blue eyes flashed with something, and then it was gone. "Not tonight, darling. You both need to be fresh for the Choosing tomorrow. I know how you girls get."

"Will Dad be here?" I couldn't believe she wanted me to be *alone* the night before potentially the biggest and most important day of my fifteen years.

"Oh, I don't know. He's around… somewhere." She frowned, and I resisted the urge to roll my eyes again.

"Fine. I'll see you tomorrow, Mother."

I made to flounce away, but she gripped my shoulder, her long silver nails digging in.

"Do not take that tone with me, young lady. *Act* like

you are already the next Fated ruler, even in private," she said tightly.

"Maybe I don't want to be." I shrugged off her hand and felt a momentary sense of triumph.

She turned me to face her, her eyes narrowed on my face. "I am going to pretend I did not hear that, Eva Celestri, and you had best hope the Fates did not either." She gave me one long look before gliding from the room.

I scowled after her. I was not afraid of the elusive Fates, the ethereal, mystical forces that oversaw our Realms from their lofty palaces in the sky. I let out a sound of derision. *If they even exist.*

A rumble of thunder rolled across the sky, and I jumped, letting out a squeal of surprise. My mouth dried up, but I let out a laugh and went back to my room, making a stop on the way.

I brandished the bottle at Wen. "My mother has gone out," I told her with a grin.

"Eva," Wen warned. "Your parents will *kill* you if they find out you've been raiding their cellars."

"Oh, don't worry so much – live a little!" I told my gentle friend. "They haven't found out yet." My parents ran a mead-making business, and one of the perks was sampling the wares. Sometimes the gentle buzz made the nights bearable. Rattling around Celestri Manor got boring at times.

I offered her the bottle, but she shook her head. "I really shouldn't. We've got the Choosing tomorrow."

With a shrug, I took a long drink, until Wen grabbed the bottle off me. She stared at me in sympathy. I took in her silver eyes, mass of black-

and-silver curls, and serious expression, and my cruel streak emerged.

"You can't really think *you'll* be Chosen, Wen. I mean, you're not the best at training…" I trailed off as her eyes turned enormous in her pale face.

She thrust the bottle back at me and stood. "Come, Lunara," she called softly, and her purple mothling fluttered over to her shoulder.

The mead turned bitter on my tongue. "Wen, I—"

"Don't worry about it, Eva. I'll see you tomorrow at the Choosing," she said quietly. I blinked, and she had gone.

"Damn," I muttered, stalking into my bathroom and upending the rest of the bottle over the sink. I watched with satisfaction as the golden liquid swirled down the plughole. If only I could pour away my bouts of nastiness as easily.

"Eva?"

"Damn," I said again as I heard my father calling me this time. I thrust the bottle into the bin and ran the tap to clear any residue. Exiting my bathroom, I pasted an innocent smile on my face as my father waited in the doorway of my room.

"I thought Ceridwen was here?" he asked.

"She went home. She wanted an early night, ready for the Choosing," I said lamely.

His silver eyes lit with affection. "How about you? Early night – or would you like to spend some time with your old dad?"

I blew out a huff of a laugh. "You're not *that* old," I teased.

He raised one black eyebrow. "Is that so? Come on, then – how about a bit of sparring? I'll show you old."

I let out a proper laugh, my scrunchy feeling dissipating. "You're on!"

I grabbed my fingerless leather gloves from my dresser. Training had always been an outlet for me, but with the Choosing approaching I had found the training yard more and more stifling, and even the Nos Candidate's mentor, Meuric, had noticed. Thankfully, he hadn't told my mother. Fates knew what she would have had to say about that. So I relished in this chance for a good bout in the privacy of our own training studio – although I didn't know if my dad would take it any easier on me than Meuric did. Lord Cosimo Celestri might be my father, but he was the current Lord of the Twin Realms and one of the best fighters I'd ever seen. I grinned, anticipation zinging through me.

"Ready?" Dad asked, and I slipped on my gloves and gave him a nod.

I followed him down to the basement of the manor, which he had turned into a smaller version of Nos's training yard, complete with climbing wall, sparring arena, weapons rack and dummies.

"You pick," Dad said, with a gesture at the weapons, and I perused the wall.

I was great with a staff, but then so was Dad. Should I play to my strengths, or expose his weakness? He didn't really have any weaknesses that I knew of, but still, I made my decision. With a slow smile, I withdrew two swords, enjoying the way the metal sang as they were released from their holders.

Dad's silver eyes widened. "Swords, huh?" He tossed me a leather body protector.

I handed him a sword and said, "What about

you?" He hadn't put on any protection.

He grinned. "I like to live dangerously."

Perhaps he still thought me not as adept with a sword, but my friend Maxen had been giving me and Wen lessons.

I lifted my sword, and he mirrored my movement. The blades met with a clash, and I quickly sidestepped into a pirouette and brought my weapon down. I was gratified to see Dad's eyes widen in astonishment as the sword came within an inch of his side.

I pulled back.

"Perhaps I will put one of these on," he said wryly. He shrugged into a leather body protector and pulled the straps taut.

I laughed, feeling lighter than I had in a while, and the next half hour passed in a blur of clanging metal and races up the climbing wall.

"I wish Wen had stayed. She could've done with some extra training without everyone's eyes on her," I said as Dad and I sat on top of the wall, legs dangling down.

I felt awful for what I'd said to her, but I wasn't completely wrong. She *wasn't* the best at training. In reality, I thought the true reason was because she hated everyone looking at her and critiquing her, and that made her clumsy. But she certainly didn't need her best friend pointing it out.

"She's having a rough time of it, is she?" Dad asked. His tone was sympathetic, but I thought I detected an underlying tension there too. I looked at him, but his eyes were open and interested.

"Yeah, especially with Gus. He enjoys tormenting her," I told him.

Dad scowled. "Ah yes, his father was the same. He always said it was 'encouragement', but I think most people, Ceridwen especially, could do without that type of encouragement."

"Don't worry, Maxen and I have her back." Guilt wormed its way into my mind, but I was determined to be a better friend to her. If I was Chosen, I'd make sure she wouldn't have to train again, and then she wouldn't have to deal with the likes of Gus any more.

My thoughts wandered to who would be Chosen from Sol, and to Wen's friend, Malakai Ostara. A horrible idea made me frown. What if *he* was Chosen, and I was too? Would that cause a rift between me and Wen?

I shook my head. No, I didn't feel anything for him, despite my mother's pointed comments in that direction. The Ostaras were an old noble family, and she would love nothing more than to see the houses of the Celestris and the Ostaras joined. But surely if he *were* my Fated Partner, then I would have sensed it. I had suspicions that he was Wen's, but if she thought the same, she certainly hadn't confided in me.

I looked up to see Dad watching me with an amused smile. "Nos to Eva," he said.

"Sorry, I was just thinking about tomorrow."

He gripped my hand. "Are you nervous? Remember, whatever happens, your mother and I will be there for you."

I grimaced. Dad might, but *the* Salomé Celestri? I didn't think she would be happy if I wasn't Chosen. She practically had my name etched on the moon-shaped stone on the Celestial Bridge already.

"Perhaps I should go to bed now," I said, suddenly not wanting to discuss it.

Dad gave me a scrutinising look. "All right. But how about a toast first?"

My mouth filled with a bad taste. "A toast? Ah, no thanks, Dad," I said, trying to cover my wince. I'd already had the equivalent of a couple of toasts.

He leaned into me, with a nudge. "Don't worry, I won't tell your mother." He gave me a wink before rappelling down the climbing wall.

I laughed weakly and followed him down, stopping him as he went to pull out a bottle of their finest year from the cold box. "Really, Dad. I'm just going to go to bed."

He replaced the lid on the box. "All right, if you're sure?"

"Absolutely," I said with certainty. I gave him a swift hug and sauntered away. "Not bad for an old man," I added, and was rewarded by his chuckle.

How was I to know that was the last time things would ever be normal – for Wen and me, for me and my parents. For so many others. The next morning, everything changed. Horribly, irrevocably, painfully...

The scream rent the air, and I could do nothing but watch my best friend collapse to the ground. Frozen, my mind warred with my heart. Wen had been Chosen. *Wen*! I hadn't gotten over that shock, or the horrified disappointed look my mother had aimed at me, before Sabra, the Sol Candidate's mentor had declared that the Choosing had gone wrong. That Wen and her Fated Partner – Kai – were actually Fated for a different destiny... one of them would have to kill the other.

I felt sick. I stumbled away from the other Candidates, looking for comfort, for escape – anything to be rid of the nightmare unfolding before me. But I had only taken a few steps when firm hands grabbed my shoulders, the long nails digging deep.

"Hold your head up," my mother hissed.

"Wh-what?" I asked, my throat raw, as if it had been I who had screamed and not Wen.

"Stand up straight and school your features, Eva Celestri."

Right at that moment, I *hated* my mother – hated that she appeared to have no heart. Granted, there had never been any love lost between her and Wen, but did she have to be so cold? Now, of all times? Now, when I needed her comfort the most!

Disdainfully, I pulled myself up to my full height, almost eye-to-eye with her, and snapped, "I am going to Wen."

My mother's blue eyes froze over. "No. You are not. You will stand with me and your father and the other Council members, and face this situation like a noble."

I was so tempted to pull away from her, to simply run across the bridge and leave her standing there before everyone. But I didn't.

Instead, I watched my unconscious best friend be carried from the bridge while her Fated Partner was dragged away, calling desperately for her, by his Candidate friends and mentor.

I turned away from the anguish and grief I saw etched on his handsome, tanned face. I wished I could give free rein to my own pain, but I could not. Not when my mother had commanded me otherwise.

Instead, I shaped my face into an impassive mask, hiding everything I was feeling from everyone around me, even my father. I would hide it until I was alone. Then I would allow the fear to be released.

The fear that I would lose the sister of my heart.

One

Present day

I stood alone on the Celestial Bridge, staring down into the swirling, shifting mists. I swallowed back the sob that wanted to force its way free.

I had lost everything. The events of the day before were still so raw, still so unbelievable. The true identity of my best friend's parents had been revealed, and she had been reunited with her Fated Partner. But in securing her own future, my own had been wiped away. I wanted to be happy for Wen, I did. Of *course* I'd wanted her to live and find happiness. But now it felt as if I was the one who had died, and she had stepped into my life. Assuming the role that had been destined for me.

I had nothing left. There was nothing left for me in the Twin Realms.

I took one step closer to the edge and hefted my bag. But I could do *one* thing. I could rescue my mother from Fog.

I moistened my lips, nervously scanning the mists. She was down there, somewhere, taken by Taranis as recompense for the deal, Sabra – my aunt, I now knew – had made with him. Taranis, the Fate who lorded over the lower realm of Fog and whatever dwelt within it.

My mother, it appeared, had been no innocent victim. She had worked with her sister and mother to manipulate the Choosing when she and my father had been 'Chosen'. Manipulated it so that it would be they who were Chosen, despite my father being truly Fated for another – Wen's mother, Alys. Wen was my sister. Not just the sister of my heart, but one in truth. And I had turned away from her. Turned and fled as she reached out to me.

Because… what if I was no better than my mother? I had, after all, tried to steal Wen's Fated Partner – admittedly, I'd been drunk, but that was no excuse – just as my mother had stolen Wen's mother's true Partner.

How could I look Wen in the eye, when not only had my mother stolen her birthright, but also conspired to kill her? The sob broke free, startling me as it echoed around the area. *No!* I wasn't like my mother – I couldn't be. But still, despite all that she had done, I could not condemn her to die a horrible death in the realm of Fog, in the domain of the Shadowwraiths. Whatever she had done, she was still my mother.

She was all I had left.

My father had his new family now. I couldn't blame him if he wanted to erase all memories of my mother – but did that have to include me? Was I to be relegated into the past, erased as if I had never been born? But then, I *shouldn't* have been born! I'd been created through lies and deceit. Pain sliced through my chest at the thought of never seeing my dad again, never joking with him or sparring with him. Everything had changed, and I was powerless. But I could do this one thing.

I dashed away the tears before zipping up my leather jacket and making sure my knee-length boots were tied tightly. I slipped the dagger from the holster on my hip before locating the metal rungs of a ladder cut into the side of the cliff. I took one look over the Celestial Bridge, steeling myself, before walking over it and towards the ladder.

One hand on the top rung, the other clutching the dagger, I was just readying myself to climb down further when a shout stopped me.

"Eva!"

For one bright, shining moment, I thought it was my father. That he had come to wrap me in his arms and tell me everything was going to be all right. That we would rescue my mother together, and that everything would go back to the way it was.

I turned, but the person emerging through the mists was not my father. Of course it wasn't. He had a new family to be with, and I, the daughter that should never have been born, was forgotten.

"Max, what are you doing here?" I took in my friend's black, braided hair, long leather coat, and the bag slung across his shoulders. My eyes narrowed. "Don't try to stop me."

His grey eyes flickered with sympathy, then cleared. "I won't," he said. "I'm coming with you."

"Max," I said carefully, not liking the stony

expression on his face, "this isn't your fight."

He let out a harsh laugh. "This isn't your fight either, Eva. The Council should have done something. Stopped Taranis."

I shook my head. "What could they have done? You know they're ruled by fear; just look at how easily they fell in with the prophecy, because they were afraid. No, they won't help. Not then, and certainly not now." I met his eyes. "Go home, Max."

He scowled. "There's nothing for me there."

Oh, so that was how it was. I let out a humourless smile. He sounded exactly like me, but for me it was true. At least Maxen had his family in Nos; all that was left of my family was somewhere beneath my feet.

"Look, I know you hoped for something more with W—"

I broke off, in part because I suddenly could not even say her name out loud, but also because of the murderous look in Maxen's eyes.

"Don't," he ground out.

I shrugged. So we were both angry and in pain. Good. Pain and anger I could deal with.

"Whatever," I said. "I'm going. I have no choice. I can't stop you from climbing down the ladder, but I am doing this on my own. You'd be better off going back… before it's too late."

"Just climb," Max said.

My stomach gave a sudden clutch as I set my foot on the rung once again. Mist tendrils snaked around my boot, and swallowing down my nerves at descending into obscurity, I started climbing down. The mist rose above my head, and for one suffocating moment I thought I couldn't breathe, but I forced a few deep breaths and realised it was just fear overriding my senses.

I had stopped and laid my head against the cold metal, but I could hear Maxen above me. Not wanting to get my head stomped on by his size tens, I kept going. This was it; no turning back now. I had chosen this path, and now I had no choice but to follow it and see where it led me.

The climb seemed to go on forever. After a while, with only the muted sound of my own breathing and the soft clangs from above as Maxen climbed down after me, everything took on a nightmarish quality. I felt as though I was caught in the space between life and death, the shadow between night and daybreak. A shiver of foreboding trickled down my spine, and I suddenly needed to hear another voice.

"Max?" I called up.

I sensed him pause. "Yes?"

"Thanks for coming," I said quietly.

I could hear the grin in his voice. "No problem. I couldn't leave Fog to your wrath, now, could I? Anyway, you're like a sister to me. What kind of brother would I be if I didn't help you when you needed me?"

The smile that had grown on my face slipped away, as insubstantial as the mist cloaking me. Wen had been like a sister to *me*. Wen *was* a sister to me. Fates! I felt the tears spring up in my eyes again. *No.* I would not cry on a stupid ladder, caught between the Twin Realms and Fog. I would not cry and let my wits leave me. Who knew what we were climbing down into?

I sniffed, and said awkwardly, "Thanks."

At his muffled grunt, I started climbing again. I had only gone a few rungs when I felt something hook around my ankle. *What the...?* I tightened my grip on the rung, but whatever had me gave a hard tug.

"Uh, Max?"

His reply was lost to me as with a sudden yank, my legs were pulled from the ladder and I lost my grip. My dagger flew from my hand. With a yell, I found myself falling until I hit something firm. Something that gave a groan as I came into contact with it.

"Eva!"

Max's shout came from above me, but in the dim light I could only concentrate on the amused pair of green eyes staring at me. The person they belonged to was pinned beneath my body, but did not seem unhappy about it.

With a sound of disgust, I scrabbled backwards, but I had to go a long way before I pushed myself off his long, slim frame. I stumbled back and into Maxen, who had just jumped off the ladder. He put his arms out to steady me as the young man pushed up to his feet, the amused look still on his face.

"Stay back," Maxen said, and slowly withdrew a sword from the bag he carried and unsheathed it.

"Oh, relax! If I'd wanted to hurt you, I could've done it already. I swear I thought you'd never get down here. That little chat was most touching." The man grinned at me with a flash of white teeth, and my stomach did a funny flip-flop.

Annoyed at myself, I said, "So, what, you're just going to let us waltz into Fog?"

The young man stepped forward. In the eerie glow

coming from the white-green rocks dotted around the floor, I saw that his long, braided hair appeared to be different shades of grey, ranging from light to almost black. His skin had a curious glittery sheen to it, pale as the moonbeams in Nos. "Now, I didn't say that," he said slowly.

"Come on, Eva, let's just go back home," Maxen said pointedly. His eyes flicked to my dagger, just to his left, near the ladder.

"*Eva*, is it? What a beautifully Nos name," the man said with a sneer, though his eyes told a different story. Was he actually checking me out? I did *not* need that right now.

"I did not give you leave to use my name," I snapped, then I winced as I realised how much I sounded like my mother.

The man's head fell back, exposing the lines of his throat above his high-necked, long grey leather coat, as he let out a laugh. "Well, we have got a regal one here. I am sure my lord Taranis would be most pleased to make your acquaintance."

While he was distracted by his mirth, I knelt and snatched up my dagger. He looked up just as I straightened, and his eyes narrowed. He strode to me, and then like a misty blur, he had me pinned back against his chest, his hand clutching my wrist that held the dagger, then easing it from my grip.

Maxen blinked. "What the Fates?"

"Nothing to do with the Fates, mate. These talents are entirely man-made."

I could feel the hard lines of his chest through our jackets, and a shiver of awareness rippled through me. He smelt of woodsmoke and leather.

This would not do. I plunged my elbow into his solar plexus, but that only made him pull me tighter to him. Perhaps it wasn't his chest I felt, but armour.

"Let me go," I hissed, pulling against his hold.

"Ah-ah, ask nicely," he whispered against my hair, his breath blowing the loose tendrils of my long braid.

I scowled. "Let me go, *please*," I said in my sweetest tones.

Immediately, he released me, and I turned, holding out a hand for my dagger. He was inspecting it closely. My stomach clenched as he said, "I'll be keeping this."

"That was a gift!" *From my father*, I wanted to say, but his name on my lips seemed strange to say now.

"Is that so? Well, whoever gave it to you had excellent taste. This is exquisitely crafted." The man's unusual green eyes roved over it, and I huffed an impatient sigh.

"So, can we go while you make friends with my dagger, or...?" I said snippily, and he raised his eyes to mine.

"Sorry, lovely. I have to take you in. Orders, you know."

"She is not your lovely," Maxen ground out, and the other man stepped back, his hands up.

"Sorry, mate. I thought as you two were more like *brother and sister...*"

Maxen gave a smile which didn't meet his eyes. Uh-oh. "Max, no," I said, but it fell on deaf ears. Maxen lunged forward.

The man blurred and was instantly out of reach. He laughed, and Maxen let out a growl.

"Come on, Max. It's not worth it," I whispered. "If he's going to take us in, then perhaps we can find out where my mother is."

Maxen blew out a breath. "Fine."

"Very well, you can take us in," I said with as much dignity as I could muster, and I saw the surprise light the other man's eyes.

"Well, that was easy," he said, but I heard the suspicion in his tone. "I'm Bladen, by the way," he carried on as he gestured for us to walk before him. I tossed him a look over my shoulder, fully intending to tell him I didn't care what his name was, but his eyes captured mine. He let out a slow grin and lifted my dagger. "But you can call me Blade."

I smirked. "Well – *Blade*, is it? – I'll be having that back before this is all over," I told him, nodding at my dagger.

"A challenge. I like it," Blade said.

"No." I stared at him. "A promise." I turned away to hide my grin as his mouth fell open.

"*Who are you?*" I heard him mutter, but I didn't think he actually wanted me to answer.

Instead I turned to look at the terrain before us. The mist hung in a thick, heavy cloud above, but before us was a narrow stone walkway sandwiched between the two cliffsides that bordered Nos and Sol. The strange white-green rocks lit our way. We emerged from the narrow pass into a vast landscape of rock and stone, all of it grey. In the distance was a walled city.

I stopped dead. Maxen stopped too, his eyes widening as if he could not believe what he was seeing. I understood how he was feeling; despite Blade's appearance, I had never imagined a whole other realm down here – not simply a dwelling for the Shadowwraiths, but a place for people to live too. I'd heard rumours, yes, but this was a lot to take in.

"Come on, keep going. It's not pretty, but it's home," Blade said, gesturing us on.

Home, I thought. Where would I make my home now? I couldn't live at Celestri Manor. Not now, not after everything that had happened. Perhaps, when I had rescued my mother, we could go to Sol, where she had been born. I'd miss the cool, starry skies of Nos, but I wouldn't miss the inevitable pitying looks and whispers that would follow me everywhere I went.

"Are you all right?" Maxen asked, and I gave him a jerky nod.

Sensing Blade's eyes on me, I lifted my chin haughtily. If he was looking for a weakness, then he could keep looking. I wouldn't make it easy for him.

"So what are you – a guard?" Maxen asked him.

"I am indeed. Bladen Stone at your service. I'm a captain in the Fog Guard." Blade gave a mocking little bow, and I had to fight to keep the smile which wanted to creep across my face hidden. "And you two are?"

Maxen looked sideways at me and shook his head. I understood that he was warning me from revealing my surname. As daughter of the last Fated Pair, I would make a lucrative prisoner.

"Looking for someone," I said smartly.

Maxen let out a surprised snort, adding, "We're just Max and Eva. That's all you're getting."

"Fair enough, mate, but it's not me you need to be telling anyway. I'm sure Taranis will have a way of getting it out of you." I wondered at the way Blade's eyes lingered on me, as if he felt genuine regret over what might befall me.

I didn't have time to ponder on if for too long.

"Bloody Shadowwraiths!" Blade exclaimed. He grabbed me and whirled me behind a large boulder. "Get down!" he shouted at Maxen.

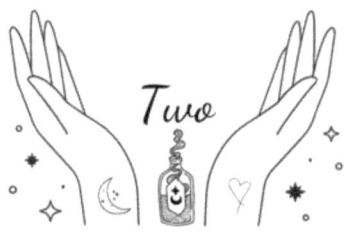

Two

Blade's attempt at hiding me was futile. I screamed as five misty figures materialised around me and instinctively reached for my dagger. *Damn!* Blade had it, I remembered belatedly, before sliding my back down the rock and scissor-kicking my legs, spinning away from the nearest Shadowwraith and giving myself time to get to Maxen's side.

"Go for the throat," I reminded him breathlessly.

"Working on it," he said through clenched teeth, and thrust out his sword. I ducked as a whip cracked next to my cheek. I *really* needed my dagger.

I glanced around, and my mouth almost dropped open as I watched Blade fight three Shadowwraiths. One minute he was in one place, then *blur*, and he was in another. He dispatched two wraiths with clean strokes before raising his head, an eerie gleam in his eyes.

"Eva, run!" Maxen's sudden shout attracted my attention, and I saw another group of wraiths aiming for me.

"Blade, I could really use my dagger right about now," I shouted as I sprinted past him.

He spun, slicing at the one remaining Shadowwraith, and then with a blur he appeared at my side. "My lady." He gave a quick bow, and my dagger was in my hand.

I gave a fierce grin, twisting away to meet the first Shadowwraith with a pirouette and a lunge. It vanished at my fatal strike. *Next*, I thought grimly.

As one, the Shadowwraiths converged on me, as if they sensed my intent to slay them all, get my mother, and get the Fog out of there.

"Uh, Max!" I shouted, sparing him a glance. Breathing heavily, clutching his sword arm, he raised his head and looked at me. I saw the horror curdling in his grey eyes, and he set off at a limp towards me.

I turned and ran, aiming for a cluster of rocks. I slipped in and fought to regain my breath amongst the shadows. *There are too many of them.* The fear threatened to overcome me, but a sudden steely resolve filled me. I was not going to die like a coward. I was Eva Celestri of Nos, and I *could* do this.

I sensed something above me; a cold trickle rasped against my neck. Looking down, I saw a foggy tendril like one long bony finger caressing the skin above my collar. *Ick!* I wrenched away before the wraith it belonged to could fully materialise and throttle me.

I erupted from the rocks and was swiftly encircled by ten wraiths, their feet cloaked by a blanket of mist.

"Eva!" I heard Maxen's shout over the

thundering of my heart, but I couldn't see him; the wall of Shadowwraiths made it impossible. And where was Blade? Had he decided we were too much trouble, and abandoned us? I wouldn't be surprised.

I stared at the wraiths, waiting for them to make their move. I turned slowly, searching for any sign of motion, but they waited. Were they waiting for me to initiate? I took a deep breath and stepped forward, then let out a surprised breath as the Shadowwraith I had chosen disappeared in a hiss of vapour. Blade stood in the space where it had been. The wraiths all turned to look at him.

"Sorry, mates. Was that a friend of yours?" he said, then darted forward and grabbed my hand. A tingle shot up my arm at his touch, but I didn't have time to wonder why – we were already running.

"What about Max?" I shouted.

"Don't worry, we have a plan – we just have to give him some time," Blade threw over his shoulder as he tugged me around a boulder.

We landed backs first against the rock, elbows brushing. "You... and Max... have a *plan*?" How had they managed to get so pally in the middle of a Shadowwraith attack?

"What can I say? I make friends easily." Blade flashed me that knife-sharp grin, and I stared at him. His eyes dropped briefly to my lips, and I abruptly pushed away to look around the boulder.

"Um, well, whatever the plan is, I suggest you do it now." The Shadowwraiths were almost upon us.

"On it," Blade said, and I heard the clink of a bottle.

"What are y—?" My question broke off as he loosened the stopper on the black glass bottle he held and launched it over the top of the boulder.

"Close your eyes," Blade urged, and instinctively I did. I heard the tinkle of the bottle as it hit the stone floor and saw a bright light behind my eyelids, which then increased. "That should do it," he said with satisfaction.

Warily, I opened my eyes to find him standing extremely close to me. I swallowed and tried to move back, but the rock was behind me; there was nowhere to go.

Blade gave a grin and stepped away, his hands up, allowing me to move around him. Rounding the boulder, I surveyed the area. A puddle on the floor next to the shattered black glass bottle gave off the bright light. The Shadowwraiths had all vanished. I looked from the light to Blade and then over to Maxen, who limped over carrying an identical, unstoppered black bottle.

Anger fused with suspicion. "Where did you get those?" I asked tightly, slotting my dagger back in its sheath.

Maxen reached me and grimaced. "Before I came to the bridge, I bumped into Alys and your father. I told them what your letter said. Alys gave me a few supplies."

So my father knew, and still hadn't tried to stop me? I raised my chin.

Maxen watched me warily. "Your father looked terrible. He said to tell you…"

Good, I thought, and interrupted my friend before he could continue. "I don't care what he *said*." I wanted my father's actions, not his words. I wanted him to come after me, and… My thoughts trailed off before the tumult I felt overwhelmed me. I turned my pain into anger and aimed it elsewhere. "Alys, though, Max – really? We could have managed without *her* concoctions." I knew I was being spiteful, but I didn't care. I needed someone to blame. I knew who I *should* be blaming, but then that would make this whole rescue mission futile. No, anger would keep me focused, however displaced.

"Not to interfere or anything, but whatever that weapon was, have you got more of it?" Blade spoke the words lightly enough, but I could see the interest in his green eyes.

Maxen gave me another look. "Perhaps," he said. "Why?"

"Because Taranis's little pets are a pain in the a—" He looked at me and amended, "*behind*. Out here, anyone caught by them is fair game. I've lost good men and women because Taranis is a tyrant who doesn't care about collateral damage."

I stared at him, surprised out of my own worries. "But surely Taranis is Fog's Fate. Don't you have to supplicate to him?"

"What, like you do up there to your precious Belenos and Arianrhod, with your places of worship and conceited Fate's Day?" He let out a snort of a laughter, and my cheeks flushed. The way he said it made it sound as if we were all little pawns to the whims of the Fates. *Well, aren't we?* a little voice asked.

I rolled my eyes and turned back to Maxen. "Have you got anything in your bag that will help with that?" I gestured at the cut on his leg.

Wary again, he said, "Alys gave me healing tonics and salves too." He correctly interpreted to look on my face and added, "Eva, don't be stubborn. We're going to need them."

"Sure," I muttered and walked over to a rock and perched on it, looking out over the landscape and towards the walled city. My senses were still on high alert, braced for another wraith attack.

After a moment, Maxen came over and gingerly lowered himself onto the ground next to me. He rifled through his bag, withdrawing a cobalt-blue pot. With a sigh, I held out my hand, and smiling, he dropped it into my palm.

"I don't suppose you have a clean cloth in there? We should clean it first," I said.

"I do," Blade said, without a trace of his previous arrogance. He crouched down next to us and withdrew a small pack from inside one of the pockets on his long coat. He unrolled it and offered me a strip of clean linen.

I raised my eyebrows. "My, my, aren't we prepared," I said, but I tempered the usual bite in my tone. He didn't *have* to help us.

"Spend enough time here, and you would be too," Blade said softly, but his eyes were fixed on the walled city.

Maxen and I exchanged a look. Quietly, I set about pouring a bit of water from my flask on the cloth. "It would be easier if you took them off," I said, and my friend stared at me.

"*Eva*," he said in strangled tones.

I laughed. "What? It's nothing I haven't seen before. You spent enough time at my pool," I pointed out.

"That was different," he said in dignified tones.

He whipped the cloth from my hand and cleaned his wound as best as he could through the slash in his trousers.

I sensed Blade's gaze on me, and I looked up to see him studying me and then Maxen with a frown. Disconcerted, I opened the salve and dipped my fingertips in, then spread it over the gash on Maxen's thigh.

"I am sure he's more than capable of doing that," Blade observed.

What's his problem? "I dare say he could, but I have smaller fingers and can make sure every piece is covered." I smiled at him sweetly.

"Hmm. Well, I hope I get offered the same treatment if I'm ever in the same situation?" Blade flashed his grin at me.

"Don't bet on it." I capped the jar and tossed it back to Maxen, who stowed it in his bag. "Hadn't we better get moving? We don't want to be caught by another attack."

Blade leaned back against a rock, and stretched out his legs. "What's the rush?"

"Uh, *Shadowwraiths*?" I said pointedly.

"We're safe for now," he said, and lazily gestured up. "We can catch our breaths for five."

I lifted my eyes and felt them widen. "Is that the sun?" I stared in shock as weak sunlight filtered through the blanket of fog above us.

"Mmm-hmm," Blade murmured, sounding bored. "We get one hour where Sol's sun hits us at just the right angle. The Shadowwraiths don't venture out then."

"So what's the deal with the Shadowwraiths,

anyway?" Max asked.

Blade shrugged. "Not much to tell. Taranis creates them to keep Fog residents in check, and to scare you lot now and again. Just to keep you on your toes. Doesn't want any curious Twin Realm citizens finding their way down here."

I gaped at him. "As if we would *choose* to come down here." I shuddered, looking around at the bleak landscape.

"And yet, here you are," Blade pointed out with a mocking grin.

"Yes, well, there's a reason for that," I said awkwardly, a flush burning my cheeks.

Blade straightened, his green eyes suddenly intense. "Indeed? And *what* might that be?"

"Eva," Maxen said warningly, but I needed to find out where Taranis was keeping my mother. Blade was not only a captain of the Fog Guard, but the only person we knew here. Perhaps we could forge an alliance. There must be *something* he wanted.

I shot Maxen a look which I hoped conveyed to him that I knew what I was doing. "I need information. Perhaps we could do a trade? There must be something we can offer you in exchange."

Blade's gaze lingered on my face. The blush burst back on my cheeks, and I was thankful for the low light. What was happening to me? Usually *I* was the poised, assured one. I was the one who flirted and teased and left my admirers disconcerted. I had the distinct feeling that I had met my match.

After a long moment, Blade jerked a head at Maxen's bag. "Give me a few of those light-bottle-weapons, and I might be interested," he said.

Maxen blew out a breath and shrugged, so I took the initiative. "If I needed to rescue someone who had been taken here, where would I go?"

Blade looked at me for a long time, as if weighing up my words. Weighing up whether they were worth answering. "That," he said finally, "would depend on *who* the prisoner was."

Maxen's gaze burned against the side of my face, warning me, but I was too invested now.

"Let's say, oh, I don't know, a very important prisoner – a Fated Lady of the Twin Realms, for instance."

If I hadn't been watching Blade closely, I might have missed his reaction. But my words definitely resonated with him. A tautness seemed to overcome him. His eyes narrowed on me, and he stood abruptly. "Change of plan," he said.

"What?" I said, following suit and standing.

Blade flicked me a glance. "I know exactly who you are now, Eva *Celestri*, daughter of the Un-Fated Pair."

He bowed, and I flushed angrily. Was that what they called my parents down here?

"I'm not going to hand you over to Taranis now. Fates! He'd love having three generations of you. And don't even think about a rescue. There's no way you are getting anywhere near enough to even *attempt* one."

My mind whirled. *Three* generations? That must mean my grandmother was still alive. What was I going to do now? I wondered if Blade meant to let us go free. Well, I certainly wasn't going to just turn tail and go back to Nos. "How do you know who I am?"

"Never mind that," he ground out, not meeting my eyes. My curiosity rose.

"So what are you going to do with us? Let us go, I hope," Maxen said.

"Sorry, mate. No can do," Blade said with a shrug.

"Look," I said, striding to him so that we stood toe-to-toe. A slow smile worked its way across his lean face as he looked down at me. "You've just said you're not going to take us to Taranis. So just get us inside the city and let us go, and you can have your light weapon."

"Sorry, lovely, there are more important things at play now. You'll just have to trust me."

I ignored the term of endearment, frowning over his sudden disinterest in the Shadowwraith deterrent. What could be more important to him than saving himself and his comrades from an attack?

"Trust you?" I demanded. "I don't even *know* you!" I focused on that, and certainly not on the strange cadence my heart was beating at his proximity.

Blade grinned. "Well, that's all about to change. You two are coming home with me."

Three

"Absolutely not," Maxen said, standing with only the merest of winces. "Eva, a word?"

I stepped back from Blade and turned to my friend. I gestured for him to step out of earshot of the intriguing Fog guard. *Intriguing?* I shook my head in consternation.

"I think we should go," I said.

Maxen shook his head. "Are you out of your mind? We have no idea what we would be walking into! What if it's a trap?"

"Max, it's better than being taken to Taranis, like he was originally planning. At least this way we have a chance. I don't care what he says, there has to be a way I can get my mother out of here." I thought of my glamorous, sun-loving mother. She must be absolutely miserable down here.

Maxen paused, and I could see indecision in his eyes. Finally, he blew out a breath. "You're right. We'd never get into the city without him. We'll have to take our chances, I suppose. But I don't like it. Something feels off."

I chanced a look at Blade. He wasn't looking at us, but his shoulders tensed, as if he was alert to everything we were saying.

"Of course it feels off. We're in *Fog*, Max, with very little plan and resources. It's time we take a leap of faith." For some reason, my gut – and every nerve-ending, if I was being totally honest with myself – was telling me we could trust Blade, or at least take a chance on him.

I sensed that Blade had swung his gaze to us, and I met his eyes. The air seemed to crackle between us, and I put a hand dizzily to my head. When was the last time I had eaten? Probably yesterday before the Ceremony, I realised. Fates. No wonder I felt strange. I stumbled, and Maxen put out his hands and gripped me.

"Eva, what's wrong?"

"Just lack of food," I told him wearily, and he put an arm around me and helped me sit.

"Here." He rifled around in his bag before thrusting a bread roll stuffed with cheese at me. I nibbled on it. Despite the sudden gnawing pangs in my stomach, the food tasted like sawdust, but I forced myself to eat it.

"Drink?" Blade offered me a square-shaped metal flask.

"What is it?" I asked suspiciously. I felt that we could trust him, but I wasn't going to go all in. Not yet, anyhow.

"It's what you lot would call cider – if we had any apples or pears down here, that is." A teasing glint entered his eyes.

I had to repress a shudder. I didn't want to think about what it was actually made of, but it wasn't just that – it was the memory of the last time I had taken a drink. Shame curled through my stomach, hot and dark, as I remembered.

Me, collapsed on a bench at the Fate's Day ball, and a pair of warm, strong arms helping me up, promising to find my friends. And then me – *stupid* me – almost ruining everything by trying to kiss him. Kiss Kai, and in front of Wen, no less. I didn't even fancy him, but my mind had been so torn up with what my mother had planted in my head, and over what was going to happen at the Fate's Day Ceremony, that I had latched on to the first bit of comfort shown to me. Fates, I really was a terrible friend, and I'd be a terrible sister too. I couldn't be what Wen wanted… what she *deserved*. The cheese and bread sat heavily in my stomach at that thought. I had severed our bond, and I didn't know if I would ever get it back, or if I should even try.

"No thanks. I don't drink," I said quietly. I didn't even look at Maxen. I could feel the surprise rolling off him in waves, and it just added to my shame.

"What, not even a little bit?" Blade asked. I speared him with my most haughty look – one I'd learned from my mother.

"She said no," Maxen said, obviously seeing I was at breaking point.

"Suit yourself," Blade said, easily enough, and took a sip himself. I noted that he barely concealed a wince as he swallowed.

Good. I hope it rots his stomach, I thought sourly. I grabbed my water bottle and took a long drink, trying to wash the bitterness from my mouth.

Blade cast a glance up, stoppered his flask, and straightened. "Time to go," he said.

I noted that the weak sunlight was dissipating, and didn't fancy fighting another bunch of Shadowwraiths. Especially in my fatigued state.

Maxen stood and hefted his bag, and I followed. "Lead on," I said, and Blade gave a bow.

I rolled my eyes at his back and caught Maxen giving me a quizzical look. "What?" I asked, suddenly feeling defensive.

"Nothing," he said, lightly, and started walking behind our self-appointed guide.

I hurried after him. I didn't want to be left behind out here, especially as the gloom was deepening. A prickle of unease skated down my back as I looked up at the swirling fog above. It danced and wisped about almost hypnotically, and the uneasy feeling left me for a moment. There was a kind of ethereal beauty to it.

I looked around me, really *looked*, at the varying shades and sizes of the rocks, and saw that some had a glittery surface, some smooth and reflective, light from the white-green rocks bouncing off them. It really was quite atmospheric – but still I longed to see the stars, watch the moon arc overhead and listen to the sound of the waves in the distance.

I sighed. *You can't have it all, Eva.* But I'd believed that I really *did* have it all. My pick of a partner, a huge house, anything I wanted, and two parents who had spoiled me. But it had all been a lie. A fake existence. I had been on borrowed time, and had never even known it. What a fool I was. Well, the Fates were laughing at me now – forsaken and abandoned. Perhaps it was best that I was down here and out of their reach, hidden from their censorious and pitying gazes.

I had to hold back a derisive laugh as I remembered arrogantly declaring that I was not afraid of them – of Belenos and Arianrhod. I shouldn't have been concerned with them punishing my blasphemy; I should have been more worried about them smiting me out of existence, because I wasn't even supposed to have been born! But then, they weren't Taranis. They seemed more benevolent, but I didn't believe they wouldn't wield their power when it was required of them.

I stumbled over a rock, and Maxen shot me a look. Yes, I thought, swallowing down bile, perhaps it was for the best, being down here. Perhaps this was where I belonged. Where I deserved to be.

Just like my mother.

Blade stopped in front of us and held up a fisted hand. Maxen and I immediately stopped. "Evening, Warne," he said.

Another man melted out of the shadows. A bow and quiver of arrows were slung across his back over his long grey leather coat, identical to Blade's.

The newcomer's gaze slanted over us. "What's this, Blade? I didn't even think you were on duty tonight."

I saw Blade's shoulders tense, and Maxen and I exchanged a look. "I swapped with Dag," Blade said. "I'm just taking these two in."

"I'll take them," Warne offered, and it was my turn to tense. I slowly slipped my hand down my thigh to my dagger's sheath.

"Ah, no worries, mate. I'll do it. I'd rather finish the

job," Blade said.

Warne stared at him for a moment, before giving a shrug. "Fine. Any Shadowwraith issues out there?"

"Nothing I couldn't handle," Blade said, and I noticed the arrogance was back in his tone.

"Right, well, have a good night." Warne turned a cold look on Maxen and me.

I didn't like the way his pale green eyes lingered on me. I'd seen that look before, and it usually ended with me planting my fist in the offender's face or a knee to the crotch. I resisted the urge to repay the favour of his insulting gaze in my kind of way. I probably wouldn't get away with that here – I didn't have the Celestri name to protect me. Here, my name would more than likely shine a spotlight on me. Especially as my mother had probably been shouting it from the rooftops in outrage. *Don't you know who I am?* I could hear her screeches now.

I didn't realise I was smirking until Warne stepped up into my face. "Something funny, Nosian?" he demanded.

Disgust filled me as I felt his breath on my skin. I sensed Maxen move beside me, tensing. "Would I be terribly rude if I said… you?" I asked him sweetly, fluttering my eyelashes. "I don't know the customs down here."

Maxen groaned, and Blade turned a laugh into a cough. Warne looked sharply at him.

"Sorry," said Blade, "obviously this one is no lady. Probably a bit Fog-touched. First time being down here, and all."

I gaped at him and he flicked his eyes briefly to mine, amusement flashing in their green gaze. No, I certainly wasn't a *lady* – I grimaced – but I was one of the best fighters in my class. Perhaps I should show these two Fog guards just who they were dealing with.

Warne turned back to me, his arms crossed. "Just *why* are you two down here?" His tone held a steel edge to it.

"Stupid dare," Maxen blurted. "You know what it's like."

Warne sneered. "No, I *don't* know what it's like. I am not some pampered Nos noble with nothing better to do than to dare each other to mess about in a realm they have no business being in."

How did they all seem to know so much about Nos and Sol, when we in the Twin Realms knew next to nothing about Fog? As far as we were all concerned, it was simply a realm where the Shadowwraiths dwelt, and a place that should be avoided at all costs. But here we were, conversing with people of the realm before the gates of a massive walled city.

It appeared that my mother was not the only one who had been keeping secrets.

"Sorry. We'd be happy to be on our way and leave this realm we *have no business being in,*" Maxen said. His face held an open, amiable look, but I knew him, and knew he was preparing to fight our way out if necessary.

Blade stepped between us and Warne. "Too late for that, mate," he said. "Come on. See you around, Warne."

He didn't wait for Warne's response, ushering us to the tall, steel-grey gates set into the massive stone walls that bordered the city. The back of my neck prickled, and I turned my head to see Warne watching us go, a thoughtful expression on his face. I repressed a shudder. We'd have to watch out for him.

Blade whirled on me, and I backed up at the look on his face. "What was that back there? Do you *actually* have a death wish?"

"Easy," Maxen warned, but I didn't need his protection. My anger settled over me like a cloak. I took a step forward, determined not to be intimidated by some *Fog-touched* guard.

"How dare you?" I hissed. "I may not be a Lady of Nos, but I am a Nosian lady, and a little respect will go a long way."

Blade took another step, closing the gap between us, and my blood began to thrum in a strange, heated beat. "Is that so, my lady?" he said, deadly quiet. "Well, respect is earned, and *my* respect is hard to come by." He smiled, sharp and lethal, like the weapon he was named for. "So… I wouldn't hold your breath."

I sucked in an outraged breath. "Thank you for the heads up. I'll be sure to remember that. I like breathing too much to waste time holding it."

I rolled my eyes and stepped away. The second I did, goosebumps rose up beneath my leather jacket as my heated blood cooled.

"Then you'd do well to bite that smart tongue of yours, especially around the likes of Warne." The anger had melted from Blade's eyes, and his tone held a genuine warning.

"He does have a point, Eev," Maxen said, and I threw a hurt glance his way. He shrugged apologetically. "I just mean we don't want to antagonise anyone and jeopardise why we're here."

He gave me a meaningful look, and I let out a resigned sigh.

"I hate it when you're right," I said with a pout, giving him a shoulder bump.

"Ha – it's not often you admit it when I *am* right," Maxen replied with a grin.

"Right, well, if you two are finished chatting again?" Blade said, a sharp bite to his tone.

His eyes flashed as I stared down my nose at him, but I resisted, this time, coming back with a retort. I was getting tired of this back-and-forth. What I really wanted was a bath and a rest, but I doubted I'd find either of those things soon.

"Just follow my lead, and *act* like you're my prisoners, ok?"

Why did he look at me *when he said that?* I thought, disgruntled. I was doing my best in very trying circumstances.

I steeled myself as Blade lifted the heavy knocker on one of the gates and dropped it. The sound echoed around the area, before the gate was wrenched open with a long creak.

Four

"Captain Stone, with two Nosian prisoners."

"Straight to the Tower with them. Taranis's orders." The curt voice came through the opening, and Blade turned to give me a warning look.

What did he think I was going to do? Cause a scene? I lowered my head, pretending I was afraid, as Maxen and I followed him through the open gate and inside. Once past the guard, I lifted my head and got my first look at the city spread before us.

Tall, narrow grey stone buildings stretched up towards the fog blanket in circular streets. They twisted away from the main cobbled street, which looked to comprise of taverns, shops and a forge. In the centre of the city, a tower rose in a pointed finger of rock, the tip of it vanishing into the fog. No doubt that was the place from where Taranis lorded over his dominion.

I tried not to stare at the people we walked past, but they were fascinating. I had only ever seen Nosians, with their pale skin, varying shades of black hair, and grey or silver eyes, and the tanned Solians, with blue eyes and hair ranging from white-blonde to golden-yellow. The citizens of Fog looked otherworldly to me, with their smoke-grey hair, silvery skin and green eyes, and tall, slender figures.

"Ooh, what we got here, Blade, my boy?" An exceptionally tall older man sauntered away from the wall of the tavern where he had been leaning, a tankard in hand. His bright green eyes roved over me and Maxen, and I could practically see coin symbols shining in their depths.

"Nothing for you, Da," Blade said.

Da? I looked closer and saw the resemblance.

"Come on – we could make good coin from them! Especially this one." The man's eyes turned on me. I sighed. I really did not want to hurt Blade's dad.

Blade gripped his father by his tunic. "She – *they* are not for sale, Da. Now go and finish your drink." He released him and patted his father's shoulder.

"You're getting above yourself, *Captain*," the older man said with a sneer.

For a moment, an uneasy silence filled the street as a few other patrons turned to watch with interest. I frowned. If it was this hard going halfway up a street, how would we traverse the rest of the city, and how would Blade be able to hide us?

"Night, Da," Blade said, and we all started walking again. "Sorry about that," he said awkwardly, then fell silent.

"Don't worry about it," Maxen said. "We didn't expect it to be easy infiltrating the city." He tried for a jokey tone, but it fell flat.

"Left here," Blade said, and we turned down a

narrow alley. "I'd put those up if I were you." He gestured to the hoods on our jackets. With a sliver of apprehension, I pulled the wide hood up over my head, and tucked my long, silky black braid out of sight. I pulled the rim of the hood down, so it shadowed my eyes. Maxen did the same with his long braided hair, until in the gloom we looked like three Fog citizens going for an evening stroll.

Muted sounds came from the run-down houses surrounding us, and I put my hand up to cover my nose at the stench of rotting food. Even the poorest areas of Nos would seem like the most affluent in Fog, if this was anything to go by.

"Stay close to me," Maxen whispered from behind. I had no inclination to forge on ahead. Fate knew what would await us if we got separated.

Blade turned and looked at us. "Down here," he said, slipping into an alcove. We followed. He rapped three times on a door, and after one long moment it was pulled open.

"Blade! What are you doing here?" a female voice asked.

"Hi, sis. Sorry to barge in like this, but I've got company," Blade said apologetically.

A long sigh snaked out of the open doorway. "You'd best not be bringing trouble here; Kane won't like it."

"It's not for long, I promise. Can we come in?"

"Fine."

Blade gestured for Maxen and me to follow him into the small, narrow abode. Inside, I noticed that the occupants had tried to make it homely, with a knitted blanket in muted tones thrown over the back of the old sofa set before a small fireplace, well-worn rugs covering the floorboards, and a vase of strange white-grey flowers displayed in a squat stone vase on a small side table. Beyond the living area was a kitchen/dining space with a round slate table and wooden chairs.

"Welcome to my home, friends of Blade," the young lady said, and I turned to get my first proper look at her. Withdrawing my hood, I noted that she looked similar to Blade, with her light green eyes and varying shades of grey hair, though hers was pulled into an intricate side plait. Perhaps they were twins.

She gasped as she took in my appearance, then turned her gaze to Maxen, and her eyes widened fully. "No, Blade, just no! Kane will kill you for bringing them in here."

"Relax, Brienne. He's on duty tonight, isn't he? He'll never know they were here," Blade insisted, and added to us, "He's a Major in the Fog Guard."

Before I had the time to digest this, Brienne said in low, incredulous tones, "You're asking me to lie to my Fated Partner?" Her green eyes narrowed as she crossed her arms over her apron.

I blinked in surprise. "You have Fated Partners down here?" I blurted out.

Something flashed in Blade's eyes. He damped it down, but Brienne let out a sarcastic laugh. "Oh, you think it's only the lofty Twin Realms that can have their soulmates, that can indulge in the luxury of true love?"

I flushed. "N-no, of course not," I said lamely, wishing the ground would open up and swallow me. "It just took me by surprise."

Brienne tilted her head, as if taking my measure, and

I couldn't help but raise my chin. I'd been taught never to show weakness. But it was getting extremely hard to keep up the façade.

Maxen, thankfully, interceded. "Thank you for your hospitality, mistress."

"Hmm, well, at least this one has pretty manners, Blade. Sit, I'll make you some food." Brienne turned to the kitchen area.

Feeling like I needed to redeem myself, I flicked a look at Blade, set my pack down next to the sofa, and followed Brienne. "Can I help?" I asked her. "I'm Eva, by the way, and that's Max."

She didn't even spare me a glance. "You can chop those," she said, pointing to a bundle of strange, long vegetables of some sort, resembling the leeks we had in Nos.

Very well. I unzipped my jacket and hung it over one of the chairs, then pushed up the long sleeves of my tight-fitting black top and looked at the vegetables. I set them on the marbled stone chopping block and topped and tailed them, before cutting them into slices.

"So, I assume my brother won't tell me, but what is a girl such as yourself doing down here?" Brienne said quietly, chopping up what looked to be potatoes.

I chanced a look over my shoulder, but Blade and Maxen were conversing, Maxen showing Blade the weapons he had brought with him. *Typical Max*, I thought fondly. Brienne was Blade's sister, but how much should I tell her? She obviously also had loyalty to her Fated Partner.

I decided to be honest. "I'm looking for

someone, but I don't think it's wise to tell you any more than that. I don't want to get you into trouble. I appreciate the risk you're taking in letting us stay here."

This time, Brienne did look at me. "Fair enough," she said simply. "But what I don't understand is why my brother didn't take you straight to the Tower. I know what the new orders are. Kane told me Taranis wants to deal with any absconders from the Twin Realms himself now."

I couldn't answer that, but I knew that as soon as Blade had realised *who* I was, his attitude had changed. Perhaps I should ask him what his plan was. "I don't know. Perhaps he doesn't agree with Taranis's way of doing things?"

Brienne sucked in a breath, her eyes turning wary. "No one goes against Taranis or his Council. Not unless they want an appointment with a Shadowwraith. My brother always was reckless," she added under her breath.

Hmm. Maybe that was why Blade had been interested in Alys's weapon. I cast a covert look in his direction, but this time he was watching me and Brienne. I aimed a smirk at him. He had his secrets; let him think I had some too.

I turned back around, the smile still on my face, and caught Brienne's speculative expression. The smile fell from my face. "Anything else I can do?" I asked lightly.

"No, that's it, thank you." Brienne scooped up the vegetables I had cut, along with hers, and slid them into a large pot bubbling on the stove – a broth of some kind.

I looked around, suddenly feeling awkward. I had never had to ever lift a finger at home; we'd had an army of servants, and my mother thought it demeaning for me to help. She'd never even baked a cake with me. That was why I had so enjoyed sneaking off to the cottage and spending rainy afternoons with Wen and Alys. An overwhelming wave of grief hit me like a punch to the gut as I saw us laughing in the small kitchen, covered in flour, as the scent of bitter chocolate and frostberries scented the air and we futilely tried to stop Lunara and Aruna from stealing all the berries. I let out a gasp, closing my eyes against the pain, as the vision left me.

Fates above. I would never have those moments ever again.

"Everything all right?" Brienne asked. I opened my eyes to see her standing before me, shielding me from the living area.

Grateful, I let out a shaky smile. "Yes. Just tired and hungry."

She didn't look as though she believed me, but she let it drop with a nod. She wiped her hands on her apron and turned to pick up a stack of stoneware bowls.

"Let me," I said, taking the bowls from her.

She smiled her thanks, but I almost dropped the bowls as a piercing cry filtered down from the opening in the ceiling to the side of the room, where a ladder protruded.

"What's that?" I asked in alarm.

Brienne let out a laugh at my ignorance, but immediately went to the ladder.

"I'll get her," Blade said, eagerly stepping past his sister and disappearing up into the area above.

"Her?" I asked, setting out the four bowls on the kitchen table.

"Yes. This is my niece, Miss Arianne," Blade said in the softest tones I had yet heard from him. He carefully turned from the bottom of the ladder, cradling a tiny baby.

My stomach did funny things at the juxtaposition of his strength against the softness of the baby in the blanket. I swallowed. This man was a mystery – a contrast to everything I'd assumed him to be. But I would *not* let my mind go there. I had to stick to my plan. Get my mother, get back up the Celestial Bridge, and make some semblance of a life in Sol.

Despite my resolve, I couldn't help but walk forward and take a peek inside the bundle. I let out a soft sigh as the tiny baby stared up at me with sleepy green eyes. Her silvery-grey hair stuck up in swirling tufts as one glittery, pale fist pushed its way from the white blanket.

"She's beautiful," I breathed out softly, and for one moment our gazes met and held.

"Beautiful," he murmured back, his eyes on me.

My heart started beating a strange rhythm. Flushing, I stepped back as Brienne moved past to take her baby in her arms.

I turned away and saw Maxen watching me with a look of resigned frustration on his face. I knew what he was thinking – knew that he thought I was a terrible flirt and I gave my heart away too easily. But he didn't know the truth: that ever since Wen and Kai's Choosing, I had lost all faith in the premise of Fated Partners. From the age of fifteen, after that horrible Choosing, I'd wrestled with that question: how could it be that they, who were so obviously meant for each other, had been forsaken? And on top of that, I had grown up watching my parents' version of what it was to be in a Fated Partner Union, which had just seemed wrong to me. So I had searched and searched for it, looking to see it in others, to see if it was *real* or just a fallacy created by the Fates to keep us hopeful and biddable.

Then yesterday, I had finally seen the strength of it in action as Wen and Kai had fought *for* each other, and triumphed – but in doing so, they had revealed the dark truth of a deception that went back to before I had even been born. My father had been Fated all along to be with another. I was sickened to my very bones by the whole thing, and the thought of being Fated to be with someone turned my blood cold now. What I had witnessed so far, I wanted no part of. It only brought pain in the guise of *true love*.

I joined Maxen, who looked meaningfully at Blade and said, "We don't have time for distractions."

My distaste for the route my mind had taken brought out my cruel side. "Oh really, Max? Well, perhaps you should have thought of that. You've been in a constant state of distraction for the past three years."

Maxen stared at me as though I had just taken out my dagger and stabbed him in the heart. "That was a low blow, Eva, even for you," he said softly, before walking away from me.

"Max," I called after him, but he slid up his hood and left the house. "*Damn!*"

Blade looked at me, a question in his eyes, then shook his head and went after Maxen.

I bit my lip as I realised that I had just unleashed an angry Max on a strange city full of people who would stop at nothing to do Taranis's bidding.

I could have just signed my friend's death warrant, all because of my stupid mouth.

Five

"Come — sit and eat."

Brienne shifted the baby in her arms and nodded at the table. "I'm sure Blade will return with him soon."

I swallowed down the burning in my throat and made my way over to join Brienne. Sitting, I put my head in my hands.

"My Partner has a hot temper too," Brienne said quietly, taking a seat opposite me.

My head whipped up in denial. "Oh no — Max and I are not... we're like brother and sister!" I managed.

Brienne grinned. "All right, sorry. I just thought, as he had come all the way down here for you..."

"No, truly, he's just a good friend, that's all. Far better than I deserve," I added in an undertone. I groaned. "Everything is just all messed up, and now I'm pushing away the one person that has been there for me all along."

"Sometimes we lash out in fear. But then we see

who truly cares for us. He'll be back, I guarantee it." Brienne gave me a bolstering smile before lifting the ladle in one hand, holding a babbling Arianne one-armed.

"Let me," I told her, taking the ladle to dish up the soup into our two bowls. Curiosity got the better of me while I anxiously waited for Max to come back. "Are you and Blade twins? You look remarkably alike."

Brienne rubbed her hand on Arianne's back in a little circles and smiled. "No – you would think so, but I'm older by two years. But sometimes I *feel* a lot older. Our mother died when Blade was three, and our da, over the years, just gave up, so I had to care for Blade." She must have seen the question in my look because she carried on, an amused twinkle in her green eyes, "He's twenty."

"Ah, right," I said. That would make him two years older than me – *not* that it mattered, I reminded myself firmly, but despite that, knowing more about his tragic past made me feel a strange kinship with him. Our situations were worlds apart, but still I understood that neither of us had the mother we needed.

Silence fell as we ate the meagre, yet surprisingly tasty, fare. The warmth soothed my insides, so that when Blade and Maxen re-entered the house, I felt strong enough to stand and face my friend.

"Max, can I have a word?"

He stared at me impassively but moved to one side, out of earshot of the siblings.

"I can be bitchy, you know that, and I am feeling extra on edge at the moment, but it doesn't excuse what I said. Max, you're my best friend, it's always been us" – *and Wen*; the words hung like a ghostly spectre between us, but I forged on – "and I am so sorry for lashing out at you like that. It was unforgiveable, but still, I'm asking you to *please* forgive me. Because I need you, Max. I can't do this without you."

Maxen watched me as I spoke, his grey eyes unreadable, until finally he let out a huff and pulled me into his brotherly embrace. He kissed the top of my hair. "We can't turn on each other down here," he said.

I breathed in his familiar, comforting scent of black pepper and tobacco soap, and immediately felt at ease. Maxen had that way about him. He deserved to find someone who was his – someone who could appreciate him. My friend deserved love. I just didn't believe I did.

"I know," I agreed. "Go and eat." I pulled back, and he gave me a searching look before nodding.

"I am starving," he admitted.

"You're always starving," I teased, and just like that we were back on an even keel.

He grinned and made his way over to the table where Brienne, holding a now-slumbering Arianne, and Blade sat paying close attention to their bowls of food. I wasn't fooled. Blade had that alert look about him, and I knew he had been extremely aware of Maxen and me.

He looked at me as Maxen took a seat, then rose on his long, rangy legs and took his bowl over to the sink. Leaving the others to finish their soup, he sauntered over to join me.

"Trouble in paradise?" he said for my ears only, jerking his head in Maxen's direction.

"Don't be an idiot," I said with a roll of my eyes.

"I told you, he's like my br—"

"Brother – yeah, you said, but that little scene didn't seem very brotherly."

So he *had* been watching, I thought, smug in the knowledge that my instincts had been correct. At least I knew I could rely on them.

"What does it matter to you anyway?" I asked, then wished I hadn't, as his gaze landed lightly on my lips. Well, maybe I'd asked for that. "Never mind," I muttered. *Smooth, Eva, real smooth.* "Anyway, what do you plan to do with us? We can't stay here; we're putting Brienne and Arianne at risk."

Blade raised one eyebrow, as if my concern for his family came as a shock to him. Did he actually think I was so self-absorbed that I wouldn't care about them getting caught in the crossfires of *my* family drama?

"I hadn't planned to bring you here, but it wouldn't be safe to take you to my house now Warne is expecting me to take you in. Don't worry though, we'll be moving on again just before morning. We'll just have to keep a low profile until I get you both to our destination."

"And just where *is* that?" I asked, hating to be at the mercy of someone else's plan. I was starting to think it might be in our best interests to sneak out and try and break into the Tower after all. I knew that was where my mother would be – though knowing her, she had more than likely talked her way into Taranis's quarters rather than a jail cell. She always was good at falling on her feet.

A sudden dark thought filled me. Perhaps I should just leave her to it. Would she come all the way down here? Risk her life for *me*? I sorely doubted it. But...

didn't I want to prove that I was nothing like her, that I wouldn't make the same decisions she had? By that reasoning, I *had* to rescue her.

Torn, I sat heavily on the sofa, completely forgetting that Blade and I had been in the middle of a conversation. He took a seat next to me, and I felt a frisson of awareness as his knee bumped mine, jolting me back to my senses.

"I *said*." Blade smiled. "That I am going to take you and Max somewhere safe. Somewhere that you can gather important intel that might help both our causes."

I frowned. "What do you mean by that?" *I knew he had secrets.*

"Look." He leaned forward, his green eyes intense. "Not everyone likes how things are done down here. You and Max turning up with that fearsome weapon might be exactly what we need."

I lowered my voice. "Are you talking about some kind of *resistance*?"

He grinned at the hushed awe in my voice. "You could put it like that. But don't mention it to Brie, ok? Her man is good to her, but he's a bit of a follower of the rules. She'd be honour-bound to tell him. You know, Fated Partners stuff, and all that." He said the last words easily enough, but I noted the interested way he looked at me, as if gauging my reaction.

I couldn't help the wince that broke free.

"What, you don't believe in it?" he asked.

"It's not that I don't believe in it, exactly," I said tightly, feeling my heart begin to pound uncomfortably. "I just don't believe there's a 'Fated

Partner' for everyone. Or at least, I don't believe it's in everyone's best interest to put much stock in it and search for it." I couldn't believe I'd actually said all that out loud. *Damn your stupid mouth, Eva.*

"Who was he?" Blade murmured.

"I beg your pardon?" I said sharply, straightening.

"Whoever hurt you. Whoever made you stop believing in love." His eyes swirled almost mesmerically. I could feel myself falling into them, and for one heady moment I did not want to stop myself.

"No one," I said, "there's no one." And the last little sliver of my broken heart slipped away to shatter at his feet.

He looked as though he didn't believe me, but I was not about to convince him that it hadn't been *one* person – that instead it had been many who had broken me… and *I* was one of those that had. I didn't know if I could ever be fixed. If I deserved to be fixed.

I gave an unconcerned Eva shrug and stood. "Is there anywhere I can wash up?" I asked without meeting his eyes.

Silence lingered, until he seemed to make the decision to humour me. "Brie, can Eva go and wash up?"

I shivered at the way he said my name. It was like a caress.

"Of course. Follow me – you can have my room tonight. I'll sleep on the folding bed in Arianne's room," Brienne said and stood, holding the baby against her shoulder.

"No, I couldn't take your room," I said, horrified.

"I insist," Brienne said with a smile. "You boys can bunk down here," she directed firmly at Blade.

Blade flashed a smile at his sister, then at me, with more of a suggestive quality. I had to bite back a smile of my own. He really was an incorrigible flirt. A bit like I used to be.

Focus, Eva, I thought, and waving goodbye at Maxen, who was finishing up what looked to be his second bowl of soup, I hefted my pack and followed Brienne over to the sloped ladder. She deftly manoeuvred the baby before climbing up. I heard Blade explaining to Maxen where the downstairs facilities were as I ascended.

Up the ladder, I took a look round at the cosy area, split into three small rooms. The heat from the downstairs fire had created a warm little nook, and I could feel myself becoming drowsy.

"Washroom and toilet is through there, Arianne's room is this one here, and you can have my and Kane's room tonight. He won't be back until noon tomorrow."

I nodded. "Thanks for this, Brienne. You don't have to help us."

"I'm not doing it for you," she said, but her smile softened the words. "I'm doing it for my brother."

I nodded again. "Well, thanks anyway. Goodnight." I stepped into the wash room, closing the door on her quiet goodnight.

Alone, I took care of my needs before splashing water over my face. I undid my braid and massaged my head through my silky waterfall of hair, then located my brush in my pack and brushed out the strands until they gleamed.

...Ninety-nine, one hundred. There, look how it shines... I closed my eyes against the vision of my mother

brushing out my hair when I was a little girl. Every night, she had done so until she deemed I was old enough, or perhaps conditioned enough, to do it myself. She'd always prided beauty above everything else.

Rebelliously, as I looked at myself in the small mirror, I stopped brushing at ninety-nine. To me my hair never looked any different, whether I kept going to a hundred or not. Sometimes at home I even stopped at ninety, and she never knew. But it allowed me to wield some power. To have some semblance of control. *Fates, I sound pathetic.* The only control I had over my own life was how many brush strokes I completed. I tossed the brush down with a sneer, and it clattered into the metal basin.

I gripped my hair almost painfully and twisted it up into a bun on top of my head. For some reckless reason I had a sudden urge to cut it all off, so that it was almost as short as Alys's. A grim satisfaction came over me. What would my mother think about *that*?

A half-laugh, half-sob wrenched out of my mouth and before I realised it, I was sliding down the washroom door to collapse on the floor. I finally gave into the tears. The tears of pain, of betrayal... of loss. All of it. I embraced it, embraced the way my heart pounded, my chest tightened, and my throat turned raw. At least I was feeling *something*!

Anything was better than the bitter numbness.

I came back to awareness to find myself curled in the foetal position, my hands claw-like in my hair, clutching at my now throbbing head. I pushed myself up.

You are a Lady of Nos... you will stand tall... you'll show everyone what you're made of… My words to Wen, words I only realised now had been echoed from my mother, came back to haunt me. *Oh, Wen.* My thoughts trailed off as tears once again streamed down my face. *What have I done?*

Only the thought that I was hogging Brienne's washroom forced me into staggering to my feet and helped me to focus enough to manage to splash water on my face again. Fates, I looked a mess. But strangely, it helped to settle me. No one would recognise me. Here I could reinvent myself. I wouldn't have to be the fallen princess; I could just be Eva.

Eerily calm, I shoved my things back into my pack and slowly opened the door. I paused on the threshold as I heard gentle singing coming from Arianne's room. Brienne was singing of an immortal who loved his mortal bride, and somehow managed to forge a lifetime of love with her, filled with many children. I listened for a moment with a pang to my heart.

My mother would never have sung to me.

Six

I couldn't sleep.

Despite the squashy comfort of the mattress and the warm knitted blankets I had wrapped myself in, my mind kept racing with thoughts of the man who had captured us, and whose sister's house we were currently hiding in.

With a huff, I kicked my legs out of the blankets and pushed myself up to a sitting position. I then carefully crept across the room, padding across the floorboards in my socks and the shorts and vest top I had slept in. If I went to get a drink of water, it might settle my mind.

I found my way to the ladder using the light from the strange white-green rock set into a glass jar on the landing and descended. Snores met my ears; I grinned. That would be Maxen. Camp-outs with Max and Wen had always resulted in me and Wen moving our camp beds further away to at least try and get some sleep.

Only a dull ache hit my chest as I thought of Wen this time. Perhaps if I forced myself to think of her, I would grow immune to the pain until I could cope with it. Fates, if this was what I was feeling, how must Maxen be coping? And then I had gone and rubbed his face in it. *Damn*. He was a far better friend to me than I ever was to him.

I paused, listening as his snores filled the air, and smiled sadly this time.

I turned to locate the sink, then faltered at a sudden blurred motion. In the time it took me to suck in a breath, I found myself pinned against the sink, a cool hand over my mouth. I was tempted to bite it.

"Careful, there – for one moment I thought you were a Shadowwraith come to attack us in our sleep."

"Well, technically, you aren't sleeping," I pointed out quietly once Blade had withdrawn his hand. "And you'd be dead meat if you tried that with an *actual* Shadowwraith."

"True. I found myself somewhat distracted," he said, and in the low light his eyes gleamed.

Don't ask, don't ask. "About what?" *Damn it, Eva.*

"Not what," Blade said, his voice low, "who."

My mouth completely dried up. I could really have used that glass of water right then. To prove to myself that I wasn't intimidated, though, I gave him my best cat-like smile.

He raised one grey eyebrow and settled each hand on the basin either side of me, caging me in with his lean yet muscular arms. Belatedly, I realised his chest was bare; his strange, pale skin glittered. I itched to run my finger over it.

"You, Eva Celestri, are not what I expected," he

said.

It was my turn to quirk an eyebrow. "And were you... expecting me?"

His eyes flashed before they hooded over, hiding his reaction. *Hmm, interesting.* Why had he been waiting beneath the Celestial Bridge? Was it merely coincidence that he'd been patrolling there?

The arrogant, flirty smile was back on his face. "I just meant, I expected a noble of Nos to be more stuck up, self-absorbed."

I nudged him backwards, and he released me from my 'cage'. "Maybe I am," I muttered, breaking the intrusive eye-contact.

"Nah, you wouldn't risk your pretty little neck down here if that was the case," Blade said.

Anger flared. "You don't know anything about me, or what made me come down here. But right now, I wish I hadn't," I hissed.

For one moment Maxen's snores ceased, and I held my breath. But the next instant they resumed and I shot Blade a glare. Why was I letting him get under my skin?

"Easy, love, it was just an observation." Blade stepped back, hands raised in surrender.

"You know what you are? *You're* the snob, laughing at us because you believe you have the monopoly of suffering under the tyranny of a Fate. Well, you couldn't be more wrong." To my horror, I felt tears rise in my eyes. *No, no, no.* I would not cry in front of him.

Before I could even will the tears back, Blade had stepped to me and pulled me into a hug.

Shocked, I stood stiffly in his embrace, breathing in his unique scent, until I finally succumbed and leaned into him. I closed my eyes. I had never felt more safe and secure than I did in that moment. My head seemed to fit perfectly against his shoulder, and I could hear his heartbeat. It was soothing.

"I'm sorry," I murmured at last.

He pulled back, and I stared awkwardly at him. Usually I was so sure of myself when it came to the opposite sex, but I was coming to see that I had indeed met my match, or been spectacularly out-manoeuvred. Whatever game we were playing, Blade had definitely won this round. I felt vulnerable and exposed, like he could see the real me. Not the one I used as a front, the one everyone expected to see because of who my parents were.

He smiled a genuine smile. "Don't be. We all have our monsters to battle. But if you want to talk, I'm the last person who would ever judge."

I let out a humourless laugh. "My story is long and sad, and I don't want to bore you with it."

He straddled one of the kitchen chairs, his arms loosely hanging over the wooden back. "Try me."

But I was telling the truth; I had no desire to tell him. Especially not my part in betraying my best friend – my *sister* – or of what my mother had done to Wen and her family. For some reason, I didn't want him to think poorly of me. Suddenly, his opinion of me mattered. I could not, for all of the Twin Realms, figure out why.

Can't you? a sneaky little voice asked.

"Why, Captain Stone, we've only just met," I said teasingly, doing what I always did and turning away from dealing with the deep emotions. "You can't expect me to tell you all my deepest, darkest secrets."

For one moment disappointment shone in his green eyes, but he gave me an easy-but-with-a-hint-of-predator smile. "Well, perhaps we should get to know each other a little better then."

Fates, he was good.

"*Perhaps* we should get some sleep," I said. "And no, that wasn't an invitation to join me," I added, before he could even open his mouth.

"Spoilsport," he murmured, and I laughed, feeling a bit better.

"Good night," I said, and walked over to the ladder, completely forgetting that I'd actually come down for a drink.

Halfway up I heard, "Good night, Eva Celestri."

His husky voice did strange things to my insides. Who would have thought I'd have to leave the Twin Realms to find someone I could be myself around? If I believed in destiny, I would have ascribed it to that. But I didn't, so perhaps it was merely that I was more like the citizens of Fog than I ever would have imagined.

With that strange and troubling thought filling my mind, I slid back into the bed and fell into a fitful slumber.

I walked along the Celestial Bridge in a dress as black as midnight, my hair in an intricate mass of braids and waves. I wafted a hand through the misty tendrils snaking around me, and noted that my nails were talon-sharp and slicked with a polish so dark red it appeared black. I stared at them dispassionately. It was a colour my mother favoured.

As if my thoughts had called her into being, she materialised before me, but she was not alone. A figure with hair that wisped around his long, pointed face like smoke impaled me with his eyes of dark pits.

"Darling, we shall rule. You and I and Taranis." My mother draped one long-nailed hand over his shoulder, and I shuddered at the intimate gesture.

I stumbled back, but my silver heels were so high that I lurched off balance. A bony hand gripped my wrist and righted me before I could tumble over the side of the bridge.

"Just come to me freely. Join us, and you shall have your pick of consort." Taranis waved his other hand in front of my face and I saw Blade kneeling before me in supplication, his face wooden and adoring. Nausea rose up inside me. I didn't want him like that.

But you do want him? Taranis's voice whispered sneakily in my mind.

No!

I wrenched free of his grip and stared accusingly at my mother. "Don't join him, Mother. Come home with me. *Choose me!*" I pleaded.

She only smirked, a falsely puzzled look on her beautiful face. "But why would I return there, when here I can be queen? And you, my darling, could be a princess." She stalked towards me with perfect balance on impossibly high heels, wearing a dress that shimmered and shifted like the fog itself. Her blonde hair looked white in the eerie light, but her eyes – her blue eyes – had taken on a green-grey tinge.

"You could have it all, Princess Eva…"

"Come on, princess, time to wake up."

My eyes shot open, my heart in my mouth as I stared around the small room. With a sigh of relief, I realised I was still in Brienne's home.

I struggled out of the blankets and met Maxen's amused gaze. "Rough night?" he asked.

"You could say that," I muttered, the nightmare and late-night encounter with Blade still fresh in my mind.

"Blade says we're leaving in ten minutes. So if you want to eat, I suggest you get dressed quickly."

I groaned. "Ten minutes?" It would have taken me ten minutes back home just to slather on my daily moisturising cream.

Blade's voice floated up the ladder. "Nine now."

I rolled my eyes at Maxen, who shrugged helplessly and left me to my basic ministrations. I hustled and made it down the ladder with two minutes to spare.

I stopped self-consciously as I saw Blade at the table, filling a pack with supplies. The nightmare version of him adoringly kneeling at my feet caused my cheeks to burn hotly.

He turned and I tore my eyes away.

"Good morning," he said, and I heard the amusement in his tone. Fates above, I would never be able to look at him again!

He offered me a hot pastry filled with some kind of berry, and I took it without meeting his eyes.

"Thanks," I murmured.

"Eat on the move," he said, hefting his pack.

Brienne rose from her seat on the sofa. "Take care, Blade," she said, and flicked a worried glance in my and Maxen's direction.

I wanted to reassure her that I wouldn't put her brother in danger, but I didn't. "It was nice to meet you, Brienne, thank you for letting us stay."

She nodded her head. "You too," she said quietly, though her eyes said otherwise. I couldn't blame her. She had a baby to worry about, and a brother who was knowingly assisting two Nosians who should, by rights, already be sequestered in the Tower.

I felt Blade's eyes on my face as Maxen took his leave of Brienne, and taking a deep breath, I finally met them. He watched me for a second, and I felt relieved that I was able to return the gaze without burning up into a flaming crisp. *There, the hard part's over.* Hopefully I could leave the nightmare behind me, and put it down to it being simply that. Just a nightmare.

Maxen and I followed Blade out of the house and into the narrow alleyway. I didn't know how Blade could tell that it was almost morning; the light looked the same to me. That eerie low light that painted everything in a murky shade of grey-green – like a giant bruise across the landscape – never seemed to change much.

"Hoods up, voices down, and stick close," Blade whispered. We followed his instructions to the letter. I had no desire to find out what would happen if we were caught now. Blade, for certain, would be in as much trouble as us.

In single file, with me slotted between them, we kept to the shadows of the alleyway until we reached a metal ladder on the side of a building. Blade turned around, his green eyes glowing beneath his grey hood, and with a jerk of his head indicated that we were to climb.

He went first. Giving him a few rungs' space, I

started up after him, Maxen following. We climbed for what felt like forever, until my jacket was sprinkled with water droplets from the fog cloud and the sounds of the city waking up below were diminished.

A ghostly hand suddenly appeared above me, and Blade said, "Grab it."

I took his hand, and he pulled me up through the mist, which swirled out of the way at the movement. I looked around and saw that we were on a flat roof.

"Where are we?" I asked, as Maxen clambered up to join us.

"Old Grenda's," Blade said, as if I should know what that meant. He cast me an unreadable look before adding, "She's a Seer."

"I don't put a lot of stock in Seers," I muttered, thinking of Sabra. What she had 'seen' on the Celestial Bridge three years ago had changed everything, and caused a lot of pain for everyone involved. Me included.

Maxen put a hand on my shoulder and gave it a comforting squeeze.

"Well, Grenda is the real deal," Blade said, "and if you want intel, she's the one you go to."

"But why would she help *us*?"

"Let's just say, perhaps she'll have a vested interest in it," Blade said cryptically.

He turned on his heel and squatted down to haul on a metal ring set into the floor. He pulled open a hatch, and a waft of herb-scented heat billowed up.

Immediately, I was transported to Alys's kitchen; I almost doubled over with the strength of the longing and the force of the memory...

"Go on, Alys," I wheedled, "just one more batch of your super-duper lavender face mask. I want to surprise Wen with a relaxing girls' night."

Alys's harried look softened. We both knew how much stress Wen was under. "Very well," she relented, but looked at me mock-sternly. "But you, young lady, will be my helper."

I grinned. "Of course!" I hated helping around the manor, but here in the cottage, it was different. Helping had meaning, a warmth, and it wasn't just about getting something done – it was about strengthening connections and making memories. I knew this one would be special... because it was for Wen.

"There you are," Alys said when we were done, handing me a large cobalt-coloured jar.

I took a big inhalation of the herby lavender scent. "Perfect!" I set the jar down and threw my arms around my friend's adoptive mother in a quick hug. "Thanks, Alys." I let her go and retrieved the jar.

"My pleasure. Oh, don't forget Max's soap..."

The memory disintegrated like bitter ashes on the wind, and I met Maxen's eyes. I couldn't go in there and be assailed by an aromatic reminder of my betrayal. It evoked too many memories. Such happy memories that they *hurt*.

"What is it?" Blade asked at my hesitation.

"Max, I can't," I whispered, and he knew, he *knew* exactly why – because I could see it in his eyes too.

Seven

Maxen took a deep breath, as if battling his own pain.

I was once again reminded of his strength.

"Eev, we have to carry on despite it all. There's no going back, only forward, ok?"

"Fates, Max, you're better than all of us," I managed.

He let out a humourless grin. "Not at all, but I am here for you and to help you follow this through."

Now it was my turn to give him a comforting squeeze. I had no idea what was going on behind his grey eyes, but through the flashes of pain he mostly kept hidden, I understood it was enough to rival my own.

"Come on then, let's go forward – together," I said decisively.

I met Blade's eyes, and this time there was no mocking smile. He simply said, "After you."

I steeled myself against the scented air and stepped onto the wooden step leading down, carrying on into the eerie light that was becoming strangely familiar. I waited in the corridor for Maxen and Blade to join me, noting a vent in the wall where the herby air seemed to drift from.

Blade pulled the hatch down after him, moving past me and Maxen to push open a metal door at the end of the corridor. It opened onto a stairwell. We went one floor down before Blade pushed open a door, leading us out into another corridor. The walls were a dingy grey, and the floorboards were splintered and rotted in parts.

Blade hunched his shoulders slightly, and I wondered if he was embarrassed at bringing us here. Old Eva might have sneered. Old Eva might have refused to step foot in a place like this, but this version of me couldn't afford the luxury of condescension now. *Oh, how the mighty have fallen…*

Fallen all the way to Fog.

Blade stopped at a door and tapped it in a pattern of knocks. Was he serious? Was all this cloak-and-dagger stuff really necessary? The door was pulled open a crack, emitting more herb-scented warmth, and a small face peered through, wary suspicion in its pale green eyes.

"Blade!" the little boy exclaimed, unlatching the chain and pulling the door open.

Blade leaned over and ruffled the boy's short pewter hair. "Hi, Flint. Grenda in?"

"She's just making breakfast. Come in." Flint watched me and Max with wide eyes as we stepped past him into the small entrance area. They widened even further as I withdrew my hood to reveal my long black braid.

"Ah," he breathed out in a strangled voice. "*Nosians.*" His fingers twitched as if he wanted to touch my hair, and I hid a smile.

"Hello, Flint. I'm Eva, and this is Max," I said to the boy, who looked to be around ten years old. He flushed.

"Hi," he mumbled back, and fumbled to close the door behind Blade.

"Lock it," Blade said.

Flint stared up at him for a moment, then gave a swift nod of understanding and slid across the three bolts.

"Flinty, my boy, who is it?" a voice called out.

Flint set off down the short corridor, and Blade indicated that we should follow.

"It's Blade, and he's brought—" Flint began with ill-disguised excitement, but the old lady with pale grey hair in one long braid, wrapped around the crown of her head, had already turned from cutting up herbs at the long wooden counter.

"If it's Blade, then I know *exactly* who he's brought." Her milky green eyes impaled me, and for one moment I felt as though she could see into my very soul. She gestured to the table, which was already set with five bowls and spoons.

I exchanged an uneasy look with Maxen. It appeared she had been expecting us.

Blade rounded the table and pressed a kiss to Grenda's paper-thin cheek. "Morning, Mistress Grenda," he said.

She swatted him with a tea-towel. "Aren't we in high spirits this morning, my boy!" She levelled another look in my direction, and the back of my neck prickled uncomfortably.

A smile crept across Grenda's face, and she nodded.

I felt distinctly uneasy, like she knew everything about me and that she'd already foreseen my every action. It was disconcerting, if not downright intrusive.

"Sit, Eva Celestri and Maxen Mercurius."

I jolted, and Maxen's mouth dropped open.

"I am a *Seer*," Grenda said, "but I am only shown the things I need to see. I can also show others things they need to see."

I realised what she was offering. I wanted the 'intel' Blade had said I could obtain, but I didn't trust this way of getting it. I took a seat and smiled politely. "While I thank you for your hospitality, Mistress Grenda, I must decline your offer."

Blade shot me a look of impatience and took a seat beside me on my left, while Maxen sat on my other side. "Eva," Blade said, "this is what you need to do. You have nothing to fear from Grenda. She's the best at what she does. You can trust her visions."

I shook my head, my hands gripping the side of the chair beneath the table.

"Blade," Grenda said warningly. She set a steaming pot of what looked to be porridge in the centre of the table, and a smaller bowl of green berries beside it.

"Mistberries! My favourite!" Flint exclaimed as he sat beside Blade and leaned forward to scoop up a heap.

I had a sudden lurch in my stomach as I thought of my beloved pet Aruna and her love of Nosian frostberries. I wondered what she would think of these lurid green berries. *Fates*. I hoped she was all right and that she was being looked after, and that she would in time forgive me for leaving her behind. There was no way I would have brought her down here; it was too dangerous for her. *But not for you?* my inner voice asked. I shrugged it off. I didn't care what happened to me, but Aruna was much too important and innocent to be caught up in my poor decisions.

"Flint." Grenda's laughing tones brought me back to the present. "Save some for our guests."

"Oh, sorry," Flint said, and offered me his handful of berries, a flush staining his glitter-pale cheeks.

"That's all right, Flint. You have them," I said with a smile. The boy pulled his hand back and dumped them in his bowl, topping them off with a hefty scoop of porridge.

"I'll try one," Maxen said, and picked one up from the bowl and popped it in his mouth. I watched him for his reaction, but his eyes clouded with pleasure. "They're really good, Eev. Like frostberries, but slightly sweeter."

"Frostberries. I haven't had them since I was a little girl," Grenda said, a reminiscent smile on her lined face.

"You have frostberries here?" I asked in surprise. I'd thought they only grew in Nos.

"No, actually, we don't," Grenda said. She caught my look and added, "You are not the only one who has left their realm in search of something."

I sat back and took a good look at the older lady. "And did you find it?" I asked, so softly that it was almost a whisper.

To my surprise, Grenda reached across the table and took my hand. "I did" – she squeezed my hand – "and it was so worth it."

Emotion welled up inside me, taking me by surprise. For one second Blade leaned forward in his chair as if he wanted to say something, but the moment passed. Grenda released my hand, while Blade grabbed the ladle and scooped up some porridge.

I felt at a loss, alone, surrounded by people who seemed to know the next moves, while I had no idea what my role was. So I did the only thing I could: I took a portion of porridge and ate.

As I looked around at the mismatched group, a group that still seemed to make sense somehow, it filled a hole I'd never known I had. A hole perfectly shaped for family life; one I'd never experienced.

But that's not strictly true... Knees bumping and elbows brushing as we ate thick sandwiches together, crowded around a small kitchen table: me, Wen, Alys and my... my father. *That* was the family I had been missing. My spoon clattered into my bowl as the food congealed in my stomach, but I paid no heed to the porridge I'd clumsily splashed onto my jacket.

All eyes turned to me, and I flushed, coming to my senses. "I'm so sorry," I said, "I'm so clumsy."

You're so clumsy... My words to Wen came back to haunt me once again. I stood and pushed back my chair; Blade followed suit, his eyes searching mine.

"I need to..." I trailed off. What exactly *was* it that I needed?

Grenda stood and seemed to say something to Blade without words, because he sat back down. "Come with me, Eva," she said gently. Flint watched me with curious eyes.

"Are you all right?" Maxen asked, and I nodded, but I looked at Grenda, finally giving in to what I'd known was inevitable the minute I stepped through her doorway. The herbs infusing the air were like an omen. An omen that I was in the right place at the right time, and Grenda could help me.

Wordlessly, I followed her out of the kitchen area and into a small room at the back. I saw that it was a pantry of sorts, with shelves and shelves of jars and bottles, bunches of strange-looking herbs and dried flowers hanging from an overhead rack. It was so similar to Alys's that I wavered. *Keep going forward*, I reminded myself. A small table was set in the middle of the room with a chair either side of it.

"Take a seat," Grenda said. I sat on the chair facing the doorway which we'd come through.

She picked up a small, cloth-covered bowl and set it on the table before sitting opposite me. She looked up at me then, her eyes intense.

"You must put your trust in me, Eva, for this to work. Destiny has a funny way of twisting itself if you don't allow the threads to fully coalesce and knit together. Do not reject what comes to you. Trust in it, and you will see."

"But I don't believe in destiny," I said miserably.

She removed the cloth and dipped one finger in the mist hovering in the bowl to set the tiny cloud aswirl. She pushed it towards me, and as if compelled, I looked into the bowl and felt myself falling. Her softly spoken words penetrated my mind before I fell fully into the vision.

"No? Well, my girl, it believes in you."

My mother sauntered across an elegant room;

gossamer-thin grey drapes billowed at the windows, where the eerie grey-green light glowed. But the numerous candles set in pewter candlesticks and delicate glass containers gave off the illusion of it being a boudoir in Sol.

"Why has she not arrived yet? You promised me my darling Eva would be here by now, Mother."

A cold, disembodied voice filtered from behind my mother. "Patience, Salomé. When have I ever steered you wrong?"

"Oh, I don't know – perhaps when you and Sabra promised me Cosimo? Look how that turned out?" My mother pouted and tossed back her long mane of hair.

Something unpleasant crawled into the pit of my stomach. She was speaking of my father as if he had been something to own.

"You still had him, though, didn't you? It is not *my* fault you couldn't keep him."

The unpleasantness intensified. Now I understood why my mother was like she was.

A flicker of hurt crossed my mother's face. She stalked away to stare out of the window, and in the vision I could see that she observed the whole of Fog from a lofty vantagepoint. I knew where she was now. She was indeed in Taranis's Tower.

The vision blurred and I thought it was over, but it shifted into something different. Something that had my blood thrumming and my breath catching. A tenderly smiling Blade leaned over me, his eyes holding mine – and I? I reached up to take his face in my hands before pulling him down to me, knowing that I had never felt so complete—

I pushed back with a vehement, "*No!*" The chair clattered to the floor, and the mists settled.

Over the roar of my heart, Grenda said, "You will have to make a choice, Eva Celestri. Separate the truth from the lies, if you want to find the love you deserve."

I laughed, but it sounded more like a sob. "Love? I don't believe in that either." The words didn't come out as assured as they'd sounded in my mind.

I suddenly became aware of a pair of green eyes watching me from the shadowy doorway, and my breath hitched. Blade stepped forward into the room, and for some reason I wished I could take the words back.

The Seer looked from me to Blade and back again. "Hmm. We shall see about that, my girl, we shall see about that."

"I just wanted to check you—" Blade began, but I couldn't take any more. I rushed past him through the rest of the house – ignoring Flint and Maxen's startled looks – and pulled open the bolts on the front door before wrenching it open, vaguely aware of being followed.

"What did you see?" Blade called after me, as if he needed to know the answer.

I didn't stop until I reached the stairwell. I gripped the railing, sucking in breath after breath, but I couldn't get enough air, it seemed.

"Eva!" Blade had followed me out. "What did you *see?*" He turned me around to face him and gently gripped my forearms, searching my face.

Everything within me rebelled against him and what he represented, but I couldn't pull away. I didn't want to pull away.

"Get your hands off her!" Maxen shouted as he came though the doorway. He roughly shoved Blade away. Blade stumbled back against the metal rail and hissed out a breath.

"He's not hurting me, Max," I said wearily. *Oh, but he might*, my heart said. *Or I might hurt him.*

"Regardless, he shouldn't have his hands on you!" Maxen frowned.

"Why, because you'd rather yours were there, Nosian?" Blade snapped.

Was Blade *jealous*? He didn't have that right. He barely knew me!

"Max, no!" I said, seeing fury blaze into his grey eyes. Blade squared up to him, and I saw my friend's hands curl into fists.

I stepped between them. "Fates above! Men, always thinking with their fists or their..." I trailed off as Blade looked at me, a spark of humour in his green gaze before he stepped back.

"Sorry, mate," he said gruffly, offering a hand.

Max stared at it, then, with a look at me, took it and shook it grudgingly. "What is your problem, anyway? You've only known her a day."

Something haunted filled Blade's eyes. "A day, yes... but I've known *of* her for a lot longer."

I stilled. What in the Twin Realms did he mean by *that*?

Eight

I dared not ask, but Maxen had no such qualms.

"You'd better start talking. How have you known about Eva?" he demanded, worry etched across his face.

Blade huffed out a breath, and for one moment he looked so vulnerable that I had to resist the urge to go to him. What was *happening* to me? He gestured towards the door leading to Grenda's hallway.

"You... saw me?" I asked tentatively.

His eyes met mine in a searing clash of green and grey, and the intensity almost made me stumble. Had he seen me in the same way that I had just seen him? I flushed and broke the contact.

No. I refused to believe it. No one's destiny was set in stone, least of all mine. I refused to be its pawn.

"Am I missing something?" Maxen asked, glancing between us.

"Not at all," I said firmly, ignoring Blade's expression. Just because we'd seen something in a cloudy bowl did not make it true. I was the mistress of my own life, and I had bigger things to worry about.

"You Nosians are so uptight. I know what you two need," Blade mused. "You need to lose some of that intensity. How about I give you a proper welcome to Fog? A night on the town later is just what you need."

I gaped at this about-turn, and Maxen's eyes flashed at the teasing insult.

"Uh, in case you hadn't noticed, we don't exactly blend in." Maxen gestured at his black braids and at my shining midnight-black hair.

"Don't worry, we have ways." Blade grinned and gestured us back through the doorway into the hallway.

I balked at going back to Grenda's and having to apologise. I really was not showing myself in the best light down here. But instead, Blade knocked at a door opposite Grenda's.

"This had better be worth me getting up to open this Fog-damned door," a cross, feminine voice snapped.

"Don't worry, Niara's bark is worse than her bite," Blade said with a slow smile.

The door opened. A slender girl with silvery hair down to her waist and flashing green eyes stood before us in shorts and a vest top, one hand fisted on her hip. She was stunning, and looked as if she knew it.

"Blade!" She pulled him towards her and smacked a kiss on his cheek which had my figurative claws extending.

Fates alive. Blade was right, I was strung tighter than a bow. Perhaps a night out would be a good idea.

The girl surveyed Maxen and I. "Ooh, gifts," she said. *What?*

"Don't worry, Niara is a Glamour-Shield. She just means she can practice on you," Blade said reassuringly.

I gave him a narrow look. "No offence, but that does not sound any better."

"I like her," Niara commented, and one long-fingered hand snaked out to pull me into her apartment.

I looked around at the sparse but neat living area. The sofa was covered in a velvety blanket topped by patchwork pillows in muted colours. Candles dotted the room and gave it an inviting glow.

"I'll do you first," Niara said, once everyone had entered and she'd locked the door behind us.

"Pardon?" I asked, exchanging a shocked look with Maxen.

"Oh, relax, it won't hurt a bit." Niara rolled her eyes and directed me to a chair.

Giving in to whatever awaited me, I sat, and Niara studied me critically. With one quick jerk, she pulled the tie off the end of my braid; my silky hair unwound itself to swing around my shoulders, almost to my waist.

"So pretty," she murmured. "Such a shame to change it. Are you sure, Blade?"

I met Blade's eyes, and he stared at me for a moment before nodding.

"Very well," Niara said.

I held my breath.

Niara's eyes gleamed impossibly green, and she waved a hand across my face and down my hair. I felt a strange ripple of air around me, but just as Niara had promised, there was no pain.

She clapped her hands together and grinned. "Fates, I'm good."

"You can say that again," Blade said, eyes wide, while Maxen blinked mutely.

"What?" I stood up to walk over to the mirror propped on a shelf, then almost stumbled back as I took in my appearance. My hair was now a mass of soft grey waves, swept to the left, while tiny braids were intricately woven with silvery cord on the right side of my head, disappearing into the waves. My eyes had taken on a green tinge, while my skin glowed like pale moonbeams through mist. I looked like a warrior queen. I kind of liked it.

I turned around with a grin and took in Maxen's new look. Niara had kept his braided hair, but now the colour ranged from white to charcoal grey. It looked very effective with his green-tinged eyes.

"Put this on, and you'll fit right in." Niara threw me a shimmery silver top made up of numerous straps. "You can change through there." She pointed to a doorway covered with a curtain. With a nod of thanks, I pushed my way through and found myself in a small bedroom.

I shrugged off my leather jacket and swapped my black top for the strappy one. It barely covered my midriff and left my arms bare, with the straps hardly covering the rest of me. I looked down at myself. The top wasn't *completely* dissimilar to what I might have previously worn on a night out... but even I could admit that it was more revealing than Nosian fashions. I felt a little of my old Eva recklessness come over me and left my jacket on Niara's bed. I made sure I had my dagger in my holster, strapped to the thigh of my tight black leather trousers though. My trusty calf-length boots added to the warrior queen look.

Taking a deep breath, I left Niara's bedroom and found three sets of eyes on me – two appraising, one full of brotherly concern.

"Uh, Eva, we're not supposed to be drawing attention to ourselves," Maxen said.

I took in what he was now wearing. "Speak for yourself," I retorted with a smirk.

A red tinge coloured his glittery skin as he looked sheepishly down at the skin-tight grey top with two slashes across the chest.

"It's a friend's top," Niara said. "He won't mind, I'm sure. Where are you off to tonight?" She looked at Blade, who seemed to be unable to take his eyes off me.

I fought the urge to cross my arms over my body, and instead owned the recklessness, sauntering over to perch on the arm of the sofa as if I wore this kind of clothing every day. I thought of Kari, the dressmaker of elegant Nosian attire, and knew she would have had a fit if she could see me right then.

"I thought I'd take our new friends for a bit of Fog hospitality later, before they finalise their plans," Blade said. "You in?"

Niara pursed her lips. "You know I'll have to if you want to keep them in disguise."

Blade nodded and turned to me and Maxen. "A Glamour-Shield can change others' appearances and maintain them as long as they are within the vicinity."

"That is incredible," I said, in awe.

"It would be better if I could change my own too, but I don't have that ability," Niara admitted.

"Are there many like you, or others that have different skills too?" Maxen asked.

Niara shot a look at Blade, who, after a moment, gave her an imperceptible nod.

"Not as many as there used to be. We're either dying out or being wiped out – comes down to pretty much the same thing. Years back, Grenda said there were loads of Glamours, Glamour-Shields, Weather-Wards, Seers, true Healers and others, but now it's getting rarer for one to be born." Niara's lips flattened into a thin line. "Taranis doesn't seem to like us having power – any type of power. He's always fearing an uprising."

Blade pushed off from his position leaning against the wall, and Niara stopped talking. She bit her lip as if she had said too much and threw him an apologetic look.

"Can I ask something?" I began, and Blade quirked an eyebrow. "You speak of Taranis as if he rules over you – I mean, from *within* the realm. Does he not..." I waved my hand, thinking of Belenos and Arianrhod. "*Poof* in and out? Our Fates keep to their own domains and can only appear in corporeal form on Fate's Day."

"Ah, but you're forgetting one thing about Taranis," Blade said. I frowned. "He doesn't play by the rules."

It seemed like he certainly didn't. He struck deals with mortals, and punished them when it didn't go to plan; he'd meddled in the lives of so many with merely the lifting of his finger, and now my family were paying the price.

"Then perhaps he needs to be reminded of

them," I said softly, but I could feel the anger bubbling beneath. My hand strayed to play with the hilt of my dagger.

"And you think you're the one to do that, do you?" Blade demanded.

I stood. "Well, obviously you're thinking along the same lines, otherwise you would have taken us straight to the Tower," I snapped. The air crackled between us as our gazes clashed. "Or perhaps you still intend to?"

"Woah, no fighting in my house, please," Niara said, stepping between us.

"Sorry, Niara," Blade said, before directing at me, "Of course I'm not going to give you in. I wouldn't have gone to so much trouble, risked so many, if that was the case." He waved a hand at me, encompassing my disguise. "Don't underestimate Taranis, though. At least with your Fates, you can expect them to do what they've always done. Taranis is dangerous, in that he does what he wants when he wants, and it appears he answers to no one, not even your Fates."

"Fine." I would give Blade the benefit of the doubt… for now. But I still couldn't believe he wasn't planning *something*. And that something involved me. "But our Fates are not so benevolent as you think. They allow a lot to happen in our realms under the guise of mortal free will."

I almost spat the last words. If only Arianrhod had stood up to Belenos for the good of Nos, she could have prevented all that befell her people. Or if Belenos himself had stepped in and stopped Sabra, my mother and grandmother from striking deals with Taranis, then things would have been different. *But then you wouldn't have been born*, that sly voice whispered. I sat back down heavily on the arm of the chair.

"All right, Eev?" Maxen asked.

I looked up at him blankly. What could I say? That cunning voice was right once again. In saving my family and friends from much heartbreak, I would have been the sacrifice: the child that never should have be born. The lie born of a fake love. What a twisty mistress fate was. But at least I could do something constructive with my life. Perhaps I had not only come to save my mother; perhaps, I could help the people of Fog rid themselves of Taranis. Maybe it was time to find my mother and discover if she knew what Taranis's weakness was.

But first, it appeared, we were to have a night on the town. Niara said we could spend the day at her flat, and if I was being totally honest with myself, I was actually looking forward to going out with her and Blade. Max and I had been running on full speed since scaling the ladder from the Celestial Bridge, and a moment – just a moment – of normality would be welcomed. If I wanted to get to know Blade a bit better, see if I could figure out his agenda, then a casual night out would be the perfect place to do it. I had seen my mother charm enough people to know I could get the information I wanted if I tried.

The thought of acting like my mother gave me pause and left a bad taste in my mouth. I swallowed it down, looking up at Niara with a smile when she asked if I wanted to help her make some sandwiches.

A few hours later, Niara shimmied her way

through the doorway of the smoky bar. Linking her fingers through mine, she pulled me after her. With a laugh, I followed, taking in the long stone bar, tables and stools filled with Fog citizens, and a group of musicians playing hand drums and strumming long stringed instruments. On a small dancefloor, people danced and appeared to be having a good time. Niara let me go and danced over to a group of girls.

Now this was my kind of place – well, it used to be, I corrected myself. I gazed longingly at the bottles behind the bar, before decisively turning away. My gaze landed on Blade as he stepped up close to me to speak over the music. "Drink?"

"Just water for me," I said. He raised an eyebrow, before turning to Maxen and asking him the same thing, then heading off to get our drinks.

"Come on," Maxen said. He pulled me into the corner where a shadowy table sat empty, and we sank into it. I watched Niara laugh and dance with her friends with a pang. I would miss doing that – being carefree and only worrying about where to spend the evening or whose house the next party would be at. Now, I didn't even have a house to call my own. I was as untethered as a wisp of smoke.

Blade returned and set four glasses down. I toyed with my water, sipping it with a grimace. It had a smoky taste to it, not like the clear, crisp taste of Nosian water.

Blade noticed me watching the dance floor. "Would you like to dance?" he asked me, his voice causing goosebumps to rise on my skin.

The recklessness reared its head. I smiled. "Sure, why not?" I rose. "Max, you coming?"

He shook his head. "No, you two go on."

I shrugged and allowed Blade to lead me onto the cramped dancefloor. He hooked his hands loosely about my hips, and I draped my arms over his shoulders. We moved to the tune, but as my eyes locked onto his, it was as if all the sound diminished and we danced instead to our combined heartbeat. My blood sang, and I couldn't pull my gaze away. It was an intoxicating feeling, right and wrong all at the same time.

Don't deny what you know to be true. Embrace it, that inner voice said.

And I almost did. I almost surrendered myself to the mysterious Fogian. But at the last moment, as his lips hovered above mine, I wrenched myself away.

No. I would not submit to my emotions this time. I would not mask my pain in a fleeting moment of madness. Fates, all I'd wanted was a brief moment of normality, but perhaps it was better to feel nothing. My eyes trailed longingly to where the others' drinks waited. I stepped to the table, throwing a teasing look over my shoulder at Blade to hide my sudden discomfiture at the almost-kiss. I was a mess, I thought in disgust.

I grabbed one of the drinks, not caring what it was, before downing it. *Now* I was acting normal. Now I was acting as everyone expected of me.

"Eva, no!" Maxen said, and snatched the cup away, but it was too late – I'd already emptied it.

I gave him a dazzling smile. "Fates, Max, I think you need one of these!" Whatever the drink was, it was coursing through my veins, smoothing away my frazzled nerves and leaving me with a confident buzz. This was what I'd wanted. For my worries to just fade away.

Maxen opened his mouth, but I leaned over and pressed my fingers to his lips, halting his protests. "Just relax, Max." I lifted another cup and offered it to him.

Just like old times.

Nine

Maxen refused the drink.

With a shrug, I knocked it back as Blade joined us.

"Um, I thought you didn't drink?" Blade said in wary tones as Maxen ran a hand across his face. "That's Fog whiskey – pretty potent, love."

"Tonight I do," I told him. Maxen groaned.

Blade crossed his arms and gave me a shrewd look. Was he *judging* me?

"Why don't you have one, Blade?" I cocked a hip and slid the remaining drink his way. He couldn't very well judge if he was joining in. "No?" I carried on when he didn't make a move to pick up the drink. "Then why don't we resume our dance?" Looking at him from beneath my lashes, I moved towards him.

His gaze turned wary. "Now, love, I'd be happy to dance with you, but perhaps we should take a breather…"

I frowned. Wasn't I supposed to be doing

something? Oh yes – finding out *all* his secrets. Ignoring Maxen's disapproving look and enjoying the easy-going feeling the whiskey was giving me, I placed a hand on Blade's shoulder. His eyes widened fractionally, causing my breath to hitch at the interested gleam he couldn't hide.

"Eva—" he started, but we were interrupted by Niara.

"We have a teensy problem," she announced. She looked me up and down as I stepped back from Blade with a slight wobble, before pointing at a figure weaving through the crowd. "Kane."

"Oh! Isn't Kane Brienne's Partner?" I said loudly. Blade clapped a hand over my mouth. "*Rude*," I mumbled.

Blade settled me into the chair. "You don't know Brienne, ok?" He looked at Maxen. "Don't let her say anything," he warned, then turned to face Kane.

The handsome man was broad for a Fogian, and his grey hair was shaved close to his head except for one long braid down the side. His shrewd green eyes focused on Blade. "Aren't you supposed to be on duty?" he said, then noticed Niara and frowned. "What have I told you about being in here?"

Ooh, drama, I thought, and placed my elbows on the table, my fuzzy head propped on my hands to watch.

"Aww, Kane, stop being so protective," Niara complained. "I'm only letting off a bit of steam."

Kane's eyes narrowed. "You're glamour-shielding, aren't you!" he hissed, and grabbed her elbow, pulling her deeper into the corner. "What have I told you about *that* as well?"

"Kane, she's fine—" Blade started, but Kane shot

him a look.

"I didn't ask you, *captain*. Now, why aren't you on duty, and why have you dragged my little sister into this dive?"

"Ah, *sister*! Now that makes sense," I piped up, nodding sagely, and everyone turned to look at me.

Blade made a strangled noise, but Kane's eyes focused intently on me, and even through my inebriation I could see that he would make a very good guard. Definitely a pedant for the rules, this one.

"Who are you two? I don't recognise you," Kane said, straightening.

I tried for my best smile, but Kane's lips thinned. I wobbled to my feet, holding out a hand. "I'm—"

Who was I again? Oh, yes, I'm in *disguise*. My befuddled brain wanted to let out a laugh at the absurdity of it all.

"I'm Larissa," I announced proudly, coming up with the name of my friend from Nos. When Kane didn't shake my hand, I instead clapped it onto Maxen's tense shoulder. "And this is Gus."

Maxen turned murderous eyes my way, and I grinned at him.

Blade intercepted smoothly. "They're friends of Grenda's from the outer circle. Niara and I are just showing them around."

"Is that so? Is that why you're shirking your guard duties?" Kane asked, crossing his muscular arms.

"I'm not shirking them, Kane. I swapped with Dag," Blade drawled, but Kane didn't look reassured.

"You're supposed to run any shift swaps with me, Blade. Just because you're my brother-in-law, don't think the rules don't apply to you."

"Oh yes – Fate forbid you'd put family before the rules, Kane," Niara said bitterly.

"Niara," Kane said, uncrossing his arms and putting out a hand to her, but she shrugged away.

"I'm getting a drink," she said.

Kane tried to stop her as she flounced off, but with a huff, she elbowed her way through the crowd and hollered at the barman, Kane following.

"Family drama is everywhere," I announced to no one in particular, and Maxen shot me a look.

"*Gus*? Really, Eva?" he said disgustedly, and I let out a giggle.

"Well, I could have said Kai, but I thought that would go down like a rock thrown from the Celestial Bridge." I blinked. *Damn.* "Oops – sorry, Max." And that was one of the reasons I didn't drink. *Damn my loose mouth, and even looser braincells!*

He gave me a narrow-eyed look. "I'll put that down to the whiskey," he said shortly, and turned away.

"Who's Kai?" Blade asked, looking between the two of us.

Maxen stood abruptly. "I'm getting a drink," he said, and followed Niara and Kane.

"But there's one here," I called after him, lifting the remaining cup. He didn't look back.

"Who's Kai, Eva?" Blade repeated, and I let out a sigh.

"He's—" Fates above, did we have to do this now? "The Fated Partner of my..." What? Best friend, ex-friend... *sister*? I suddenly felt sick. I toyed with the cup, watching the dark liquid swirl almost mesmerically.

"I thought you didn't believe in Fated Partners," Blade said lightly.

"I don't," I said vehemently, "but *they* do, and that's all that matters." I was suddenly close to tears.

"Hey," Blade said in concern, setting a hand on my arm. "We're supposed to be having fun."

"I used to be fun." I sniffled. The drink beckoned to me, and recklessness fought to overpower my sadness. "In fact," I said slowly, "now seems as good as any time to rediscover my fun side."

"I'll admit I'm kind of intrigued." Blade took the cup off me and sipped slowly, his eyes meeting mine over the rim.

"You'll like this version of me, I promise, Captain Stone." I flashed him my most Eva smile, before retrieving the drink and downing it. I stood up just as an up-tempo song began to play. Perfect.

I crooked a finger at him teasingly, and he followed as I strode over to a table next to the dancefloor, pulled myself onto it, and started dancing. I hadn't taken years and years of dance classes for nothing. I gave myself to the beat and the feel of my limbs going looser with each movement, revelling in the hollers and whistles.

This Eva was impenetrable. Hurt and pain bounced off her veneer.

"I think you should get down." The easy smile had vanished from Blade's face as he stared around at the tavern-goers watching me. His hands reached to lift me down, but out of nowhere a fist appeared, hitting him on the cheek.

"She's not going anywhere, Stone. Leave the

pretty lady to dance." A tall Fogian stared up at me.

The first stirrings of unease wormed their way through my bleary head as I saw Blade turn back, his eyes glinting. Oh Fates!

Dimly, as Blade launched himself at the other man, I saw Maxen heading back towards me, a look of horror on his face. Something didn't look right. His hair was black.

His hair was *black*.

"Nosians!" someone shouted, and all Fog broke loose.

The band stopped playing. I was stuck up on the table, surrounded by a crowd of angry-looking men and women from a realm Max and I clearly didn't belong in. Someone grabbed at my leg, and I kicked it away. My balance off from the drink, I stumbled back, almost falling from the table.

"Eva!" Blade shouted, and suddenly he was up on the table beside me. "When I say jump, jump. Get to Max and get outside."

"I am not going to leave you in the middle of a tavern fight," I said, trying for indignation, but it sounded more like excitement to my ears. Fates, my blood was suddenly *pumping,* and my head unexpectedly cleared.

"Damn. Should have warned you. Fog whiskey gives you a bit of an adrenaline hit too," Blade muttered, kicking out a leg at his eager assailant.

Nice.

"Let's dance," I said, a wide grin creeping across my face as I reached down and pulled out my dagger.

Blade's eyes widened. But with a whoop, I launched myself off the table and faced down a group who were approaching Maxen. He'd slipped on a pair of Nosian knuckle gloves and stood his ground.

I gave him a hip bump. "Just like old times, eh?"

He sighed and rolled his eyes, but I saw him grin as the fight began.

I didn't plan on using my dagger, hoping the sight of it alone would deter opponents. But I did use what else I had in my arsenal: pirouettes, jetés and arabesque kicks. One landed neatly in Blade's attacker's stomach, and the man collapsed to the floor.

Blade looked askance from me to the man, and, seeing an opening, grabbed my hand. "Come on, Max!" he shouted, and ducking and diving through the throng, the three of us burst out into the street. The sounds of the fight continued behind us.

Blade pulled me on, and Maxen followed us down an alley. "Come on, the Guard will be here in a moment. Where's Niara?" Blade shouted.

"That's what I was coming to tell you when the fight started. Kane made her go home," Maxen explained, taking off the metal-knuckled gloves with a wince as we stopped to lean against the wall and catch our breaths.

"Ah, that's why the shield broke," Blade said. "Damn, I should never have brought you both here. Now Niara's in trouble with Kane, and I think our cover *might* just be blown."

I couldn't help myself – my blood was still zinging. I leaned over, hands on my thighs, and burst out laughing. "You think?" I managed.

"Fates, Eva, what were *you* thinking?" Maxen exclaimed, and I heard the frustration in his voice.

"This isn't Nos, where you have the protection of your important father and mother – where you can do anything you like and get away with no consequences!"

The laughter died in my throat. I slowly straightened, sobering instantly. "I know, Max," I ground out. "I know *exactly* where I am. And I won't ever have the protection of my parents' name again. So excuse me for trying to forget it for a little while."

I pushed off the wall and walked away from them both.

"Eva!" Maxen called after me, but I needed a minute, a *damn minute* alone.

I strode further along the alleyway and found a dark alcove to push myself into. The shadows absorbed me, and I set a trembling hand to my brow. I felt sick and ashamed. How could I have given into the lure of oblivion so easily? I'd made a vow to Wen – a self-imposed vow, but still. Did I have no honour left, or was my subconscious disregarding anything I had promised to her?

Why couldn't I *think* straight? I plunged both my hands into my loose black hair and clutched at my pounding head. I was going to be sick. I stumbled out of the alcove and over to a trio of metal bins. I retched behind one until my throat burned and my eyes streamed. *Fates, what was in that stuff?* I groaned.

I put a hand to my side and lifted my head carefully, assessing my movements, but it appeared the sickness had passed for now.

"Feeling better?" a soft voice asked, and I turned to see Blade leaning against the opposite wall.

"Not really," I said with a wince. "Look, I—"

He pushed off the wall and crossed to me. "Don't

apologise. If anyone's to blame, it's me. I should never have risked bringing you both out. Brienne's always telling me I'm too impulsive and don't think things through."

That sounded familiar.

"Come on, we have to get off the streets." He turned my chin up to look into his eyes. "You were wrong, you know."

"About what?" I asked quietly, falling into his eyes.

"I prefer *this* Eva – vulnerable yet strong. The one who hides her pain, but still goes forward despite the fear there may be more to come. The one who tries to do the right thing."

"I'm failing abysmally though," I said, trying my hardest to ignore the warmth that was pooling in my stomach. "While I appreciate the sentiment, I'm more the other version than this one. It's too ingrained in me." I lowered my lashes and whispered, "But I wish it was the other way around."

"Then you *are* more this version. It's our choices that make us, Eva, and you've chosen to come here, to save your mother, despite the danger." Blade dropped my chin and rubbed a comforting hand down my arm.

"If you knew the truth about me and my family, you would know that I had no choice *but* to come. Please don't mistake me for someone honourable, Blade. You're liable to get hurt." I stepped back. I couldn't allow him to put me up on some kind of pedestal. It would only crack beneath my heavy heart.

He blew out a frustrated breath. "You're wrong,"

he said simply. "I have great intuition, and you will make the right choice when it comes down to it, Eva Celestri."

I tilted my head at him and wondered again what he had seen concerning me. *You will have to make a choice, Eva Celestri. Separate the truth from the lies, if you want to find the love you deserve.*

I pushed Grenda's words away. I was here to get my mother, and pay back Taranis. That was all.

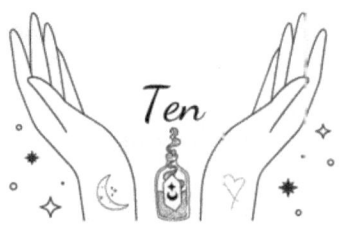

Ten

Footsteps thudded down the alleyway towards us, and I turned to see Maxen jogging out of the gloom. He flicked me a glance, but spoke to Blade. "There's ten guards coming this way."

"Damn. Come on, Grenda's is closest. I can't risk going to mine now." Blade looked around, frowning. Spotting a folded-up ladder attached to the building, he clambered up onto one of the bins and pulled it down. "Follow me," he said, and once again we found ourselves climbing up towards the blanket of fog.

We didn't climb as long this time, soon clambering onto another flat roof. I pressed a hand to my side, working out a stitch.

"All right?" Maxen asked.

"I will be," I said.

"Eev—"

I stopped him with a swift hug. "We really have to stop sniping at each other, Max. We've both been through a lot, and it's understandable, but we just need to get through this."

"I agree. I shouldn't have said what I did. I was just worried," he said, pulling back to ruffle my hair.

"Excuse me." I pouted, smoothing back my hair, and he let out a relieved grin.

"You really are like brother and sister," Blade said, watching us as if only just figuring this out, and I rolled my eyes. *Finally, the guy gets it!*

Maxen gave him a funny look, then turned to survey the rooftop. It was set lower down than the ones surrounding it, with walls towering up away from us and more ladders visible through the mist. I shivered and realised I had left my jacket, and my pack, at Niara's.

"Uh, Max, did you leave all your weapons at Niara's apartment?"

He grimaced. "I thought we were going straight back. Everything's there except for my gloves and the dagger in my boot."

"Don't worry about that now. I'll get your stuff once you're safely at Grenda's. It's better I go alone in case Kane is still there," Blade said.

For some reason the thought of Blade going back to Niara's late at night had a little worm of *something* niggling at me. I shrugged it off. He could do what he liked.

"Fine," I said. I thought I had tempered my voice, but Blade still shot me a quizzical look. I gave him a small, unconcerned smile, and he turned to pull down the next ladder.

We climbed up and then traversed two more rooftops before we made it to Grenda's building. By that time, I was shivering uncontrollably.

Blade turned around to say something. He took one look at me before striding over and taking me in his arms. I let out a surprised breath, but as his warmth stole around me, I relaxed.

"Sorry. I forgot you Nosians wouldn't be used to nights in Fog, especially in such – ah – minimal clothing." He swallowed, then said, a laugh in his voice, "Care for a warm-up too, Max?"

"I'm good," Maxen said, and I heard the humour in his response. I smiled against Blade's neck.

"Better?" Blade whispered, his breath stirring my hair, and I nodded. I felt warm from the inside out. He released me, his fingertips brushing my arm, and I fought against a shiver, this one nothing to do with the cold.

I couldn't meet his eyes as he stepped back and hunkered down to pull open the hatch. This time I was prepared for the waft of herb-scented air. Gratefully, I made my way down into the corridor and waited for the others to join me.

"Stay here, I'll check it's clear." Blade moved along the corridor and pulled open the door to the stairwell.

"We're going to have to come up with a plan, Eev. I don't know what Blade's angle is, but he's put himself in danger now. I don't think he'd do that just for a girl he barely knows," Maxen mused.

I pointedly ignored the last part. "Perhaps we're the spark, Max. There's more than just my mother to rescue," I said softly, thinking of how Taranis had everyone in Fog under his control.

"What did Grenda show you?" Maxen asked. At my hesitation, he added quickly, "You don't have to tell me if you don't want to."

I sighed. "I saw my mother at Taranis's Tower. She was speaking to my grandmother about… me." I didn't mind sharing that much, but everything afterwards was private. Even if I didn't put much stock in it.

"Your *grandmother*? What were they saying?"

The door opened, and I shot Maxen a warning look. "Later," I said quietly, as Blade re-appeared.

He gestured to us and we followed him through the door, into the stairwell and down into Grenda's corridor. We passed Niara's door and went straight into Grenda's. Blade bolted the door after us, and showed us through to the living area, where Grenda sat in a cosy knitted robe.

"Eventful night?" she asked. "I don't need to be a Seer to see that." She let out a laugh and indicated the sofa.

I took a seat nearest to her. "I'm sorry for running out earlier, Grenda, it was incredibly rude of me."

She leaned over and patted my hand. "Do not worry, my dear. I understand. First visions are always shocking, and sometimes hard to believe."

I sat back. *Extremely* hard to believe, I thought, and accidentally caught Blade's eye as he perched on the arm of Grenda's armchair. There seemed to be a question and an answer combined in his gaze, and for one long moment I could not pull away. I wanted to explore it. Figure out the possibilities. But I feared I would not like the conclusion.

"Hmm," Grenda said, and I pulled my gaze away sharply to see her watching me innocently.

I wanted to squirm, but I forced myself to sit still. Maxen settled himself next to me. Grenda spared him a smile, then her gaze sharpened.

"Interesting," she murmured. "Maxen, you shall see your future before you leave."

He jolted in his seat. "What?"

Grenda stood and leaned over me to pat his arm. "Do not be afraid. It is up to you to accept it, and not turn away because of stubborn pride." She smiled at Maxen again, then walked over to the kitchen and set the kettle on the stove, leaving him with his mouth slightly open.

Blade shot him a grin. "You'll get used to her, mate. It's easier to just go along with it. It makes the visions easier to accept."

"I think I'd rather not know," Maxen said slowly.

On that we were in agreement. Surely it must be easier to *not* know what the future held. It wouldn't weigh on you then, barrelling towards you with no way of avoiding it. Instead, you could experience a dash of possibility with a bit of unknown adventure thrown in.

Grenda returned with mugs of steaming, aromatic tea. "Flint is in bed. I'm sure you three can make yourselves comfortable in here. There are extra blankets and cushions in the box there." She indicated a carved wooden trunk.

"Thanks, Grenda." Blade set his mug on the small side table. "I'm just going to go to Niara's and get Eva and Max's things – and check she's ok."

"She's a good girl," Grenda said. "But glamour-shielding can tire her out. Make sure she hydrates and rests."

"Will do," Blade said, then turned to Maxen and me. "I'll see you soon – get some rest yourselves.

Max, lock the door after me?" He was gone, Max trailing after him, before I'd even had the chance to say anything.

I sat and pensively drank my tea.

"I added a few extra herbs in yours," Grenda said on her way towards a curtained doorway. "Fog whiskey will give you sickness and a pounding headache if you're not used to it." She slipped through the curtain and I stared after her.

I gave a bemused shake of my head and drained every last sip of the tea. I really did not want to wake up with a hangover. If what I'd already experienced was any indication, the after-effects wouldn't be pleasant. I really needed my wits about me; tomorrow, I was going to go on a scouting mission. I wanted to see what the Tower looked like up close.

Feeling better now that at least I had a plan, I smiled at Maxen as he returned and opened the box to toss me a cushion and blanket.

"Take the sofa, I'll be fine on the floor," he said.

"You sure?" I said through a yawn.

He looked at me in amusement. "Absolutely. Eev, we need to decide what we're going to do, and we need to finish our talk about your mother and grandmother."

Another yawn took over; my eyelids felt so heavy that I fought to keep them open. Apparently the healing herbs were doing their work. "In the morning," I said sleepily. I unlaced my boots, kicked them off, pulled the blanket over myself, and gave in to the comfort of slumber.

I awoke to the sounds of snoring and whispered voices. I sat up and saw Maxen still asleep on his side on the carpeted floor next to the sofa. I grimaced as I noted his position; he was bound to have a cricked neck when he woke up.

Flint and Grenda were in the kitchen making breakfast. Blade was nowhere to be seen, though, and a distinctly uneasy feeling filled my stomach. Had he not returned?

I swung my legs around without thinking, and inadvertently caught Maxen on the shin. He awoke abruptly.

"Sorry," I said, and he sat up and scrubbed a hand over his face.

"Don't worry about it." He pushed the blanket off himself and stood with a wince, then rolled his shoulders back and rubbed at his neck, confirming my prediction.

"Good morning," Flint said enthusiastically, seeing we were awake. "Granny and I made breakfast!"

"Good morning," Maxen replied, walking over to take a seat at the table. I padded behind him in my socks and sat.

"Where's Blade?" I said in an undertone, when Flint had turned around to grab a platter from Grenda.

"Perhaps he's still at Niara's," Maxen said. "He said not to worry if he didn't come back." He took one of the mistberry pastries from the platter as Flint set it down.

"He spent the night there?" My voice came out a squeak.

Blade's amused voice came from behind me. "Why – jealous?"

I flinched, a flush burning the back of my neck and cheeks, but thankfully Flint and Grenda seemed too intent on finishing the breakfast preparations to be listening to our conversation. I swivelled around in my chair to retort something smart, but the intense look in Blade's eyes made my mouth dry up.

He sauntered over to me. "She'd be more interested in you than me."

Oh. "Ah, right." How had I misjudged that so spectacularly?

Blade reached past me, his arm brushing mine, to grab a pastry. "She's like a sister to me," he said with a wink, and Maxen barely concealed a snort.

Well played, Captain Stone, well played, I thought as I shot Maxen a quelling look.

Maxen turned his attention to his food, but I noticed that he frowned as Grenda took a seat beside him. A look seemed to pass between them, and I wondered about her declaration the night before; that he would see his future.

"How was Niara this morning?" Grenda focused on Blade, who sat between me and Flint.

"She's fine. The more she glamour-shields, the quicker she rebounds, it seems," Blade said between bites.

Grenda nodded. "That is true for a lot of us, but she still must take care of herself."

"Don't worry, Kane had given her strict instructions to rest. He's coming to check on her later and might even call here. I said Max and Eva were friends of yours from the outer circle," Blade told her. "But he thought they were called Larissa and Gus. Unfortunately, their disguises were blown after Kane took Niara home, so he'll know they're actually from Nos once he goes on duty."

"Oh dear," Grenda said. "I sensed something had gone amiss. So the Guard know you are harbouring them?" Her eyes turned wary, and she cast a concerned look at Flint.

Blade nodded. "We'll be moving on after breakfast. I have no desire to endanger you and Flint."

"Where will you go?"

"I would say it's best not to tell you," Blade said, "but I know you have ways of finding out."

Grenda's worried look cleared, and she chuckled. "That I do, my boy, that I do."

We ate, but I noticed Flint picking at his food. I hoped he wasn't worrying because we were there. I hated that our presence was causing the boy distress.

He looked up abruptly and said, "I want to help," a mutinous twist to his lip.

"Now, Flint. It's not safe…" Grenda began.

He shot flashing green eyes her way, and I gasped as rain seemed to burst from the sky, soaking us all.

"Flint!" she cried, and immediately the rain stopped. The boy stood, his fists curled at his sides.

"I can help," he said, but quieter this time.

"Let me talk to him," Blade said, and with droplets dripping off his hair, he took the boy and led him out of the room and along the corridor.

Maxen and I looked at each other in shock while Grenda stood and gathered some cloths from a shelf. She handed them out, and Maxen and I dried ourselves. Grenda pressed a cloth to her own face and stood with it covering her features for a moment, as if she needed to gather herself. She withdrew the cloth and looked at us.

"Let me show you something."

Curiously, Maxen and I followed her through the kitchen and into her pantry, where she opened a concealed door to reveal what appeared to be an inside garden of sorts. Plants, vegetables, fruit, and herbs grew in abundance.

I let out an exclamation of surprise, and Grenda looked at me. "Indeed. This is *not* common for Fog. Our atmosphere doesn't suit a bountiful harvest. I can only maintain this because Flint practices in here." She paused, then said, "He's a Weather-Ward."

At our blank looks, she elaborated. "He can create weather. It is a rare skill, and I have tried my best to protect him." Tears sprang into her eyes. "After what happened to his mother – my daughter – I tried to find a way to bind it, but how can I bind an intrinsic part of him? And so he practices in here, and it helps him to control it. At this age it's mainly emotion-based, as you just saw."

I digested this information. "What happened to your daughter?"

Grenda swallowed; anger flashed across her lined face. "Taranis, that's what happened. His Council have been incrementally tightening the laws around using skills for years. One day, it was suddenly illegal to use them in public – but it was just an excuse to round everyone up. He took my Tora and her man, Caelum, and locked them up in his Tower with the others."

I looked at Maxen. I was right! If they were still alive, we would have more than just my mother to rescue.

It seemed we would be the spark that ignited the kindling beneath Taranis's mist-shrouded feet.

Eleven

"I'm so sorry about your daughter and son-in-law," I said to Grenda.

"Thank you, dear. It was lucky Flint was with me and none knew of his skills. Now I never leave without Niara, if I have to go out. She hides me in plain sight." She dimpled out a semblance of a smile. "We are self-sufficient here, but I fear the day is coming when Flint won't be content to stay hidden. He wants to do something to help his parents, but I try to make him understand that it won't help if he gets caught."

I recognised the boy's frustration and admired his determination to rescue his parents, but I knew it was futile for him – for us – to act alone. We were mere mortals against a Fate…

…But we were mortals with *free will*. My mind whirred. Surely that meant something? *It is our choices that make us…* Blade was right. Did the citizens of Fog choose to allow Taranis to rule over them as he did? What if they rebuked him – what then? He couldn't lock them *all* up.

I needed to think it through, but first, I decided I was long overdue for that scouting mission.

"Eva? You've got that look," Max said, bringing me out of my reverie. "The one you get before you take me down in a staff fight." He pressed a hand to his side, as if in remembrance of the cracked rib I'd once given him. But he was right – I was feeling the same sort of determination.

"I need to find Blade," I said, heading back through the pantry and kitchen.

He was in the living area, his wet hair slicked back. "Flint's fine. He just wants a few minutes alone," he told me as I looked around for the boy.

"It must be hard to have a skill that you have to keep concealed for the most part," I said, and Blade looked at me sharply. Had he read something unintended in my comment? I remembered the blurred way he had moved so fast out in the wastelands and filed that away for another time.

"Yeah," he said, almost a grunt.

"I want to have a look at the Tower. Is that something you can help me with?" I asked, getting straight to the point. Sitting opposite him, I watched the emotions ripple across his face.

"I could, but I won't," he said bluntly.

"Fine," I said. I grabbed my boots from the floor, shoved my feet into them and laced them up tightly. Standing, I looked around for my other things, hoping Blade had brought them back with him from Niara's.

Blade stood and caught my arm. "What are you doing?"

I gave him a flat look. "I'm going to have a look

at the Tower. If you won't take me, I'll find my own way."

"No way, Eva."

I shrugged his arm off, then caught sight of my jacket and pack in the hallway. I rifled through my pack and found a dark purple long-sleeved T-shirt. Blade whipped it out of my hand, and I huffed out a breath.

"I am not your prisoner, Blade. You passed up that chance when you didn't take us in." I gripped the T-shirt and pulled it back. "So, if you wouldn't mind—"

"I do mind, actually," he said through clenched teeth. "If you get caught, that's it. You'll be Taranis's *prisoner*. You'll be caged up in a dungeon, Eva. I'm willing to bet you wouldn't like it one little bit."

"Well, come with me and make sure I don't get caught then." I grinned triumphantly, waggled the top at him, and slipped into the small washroom.

I let out a surprised squeak as he followed me in and closed the door behind him. The room really was not big enough for two people; he crowded me against the wall. "What are you doing?" I hissed.

"*Fates!* You are so frustrating," he ground out. "Why are you risking yourself?" He propped one arm against the wall next to me and leant in. "You could get hurt." His voice softened as his eyes glinted in the gentle light.

My breath hitched. "Maybe that's what I want... what I deserve," I whispered, then felt my eyes widen at the admission that seemed to have come from somewhere deep inside me. I hadn't even been aware of what lurked there. "You don't know what I've done. What my mother has done. Her blood runs in my veins." Tears tracked their way down my face.

"Eva, *no*," Blade said, using one gentle thumb to

catch my tears and smooth them away. "We are not our parents. All my da does is try and make quick coin at the expense of other people. Brienne and I long ago learned to forge our own way. Don't take on your mother's guilt and make it your shame, love."

"I don't have your strength, Blade. I did nothing but run. I ran from Nos, and everyone I cared about. I was too cowardly to face it, face the truth of her lies." A sob burst out of my mouth, and I pressed a fist to my mouth as if to shove it back in.

"Come on. Lean into me," Blade murmured. Once again I found myself in his arms, and once again I fitted perfectly. He let me cry out my shame until I was hollowed out inside.

"I have no idea why I keep doing this to you," I sniffled, pulling back.

"Don't you? Don't you feel it?" Blade asked intently, his eyes roving over my face as if he could never tire of looking at it.

I froze. My mouth wanted to say yes. *Yes, I feel my blood pumping to your heartbeat, yes, I feel our gazes connecting like the key in an ancient lock – one that was exquisitely crafted for just you and me. Yes, I feel my soul singing a song that your soul wrote.* I wanted to say all that, but I did not. I couldn't risk myself. If I said the words, I wouldn't be able to leave and hide away in Sol. Leave him.

The unspoken words hovered between us, and I was tempted for one minute to selfishly take what he offered. Take the comfort his lips would provide. But it would be an empty comfort, for it could never become anything more, and I was not so far gone that I wished to cause him pain.

I carefully disentangled myself, and I felt his disappointment like a tangible thing. "What I *feel* is that we have been thrown together in exceptional circumstances. In times like that, emotions can become heightened and—"

"That's crap, Eva," Blade burst out. "But" – he held up a hand – "I'll humour you for now. We *will* be revisiting this conversation." He yanked open the door and shot me a look. "Get ready. I'll take you to the damn Tower." He very deliberately pulled the door closed behind him with slow, measured movements, as if containing a tempest.

This was starting to get complicated. I needed to stop falling into his arms – it wasn't healthy for either of us. But I was like a little mothling fluttering around him. I stared at myself in the mirror and admonished myself. *Get a grip on yourself, Eva.*

I splashed water on my face and changed out of the strappy top into the purple one, tucking it into my leather trousers. Then I finger-combed my straight hair before braiding it in one fat plait from my crown all the way down my back, securing it with a tie I found in my trouser pocket. There, that was better.

I finished my ablutions, and taking a deep breath, opened the door. Blade was pacing the living area; of Maxen, Grenda, and Flint there was no sign.

"Where's Max?" I asked.

Blade's head whipped up as if I'd startled him out of deep thoughts. "Grenda's got him," he said with a small smile.

"Ah. I thought he didn't want to know?" I said, bending to pick up and shrug on my trusty hooded leather jacket.

"Apparently whatever Grenda said convinced him… I wonder if he'll believe what he sees." The words were said innocently enough, but I couldn't help but feel they were directed at me.

"What is *that* supposed to mean?" I demanded, finally looking Blade square in the eye.

"Nothing. Just some are more open and *accepting* than others."

There – that was definitely aimed at me. But I didn't have time to reply; as soon as Blade had said the words, Maxen stormed through the kitchen area and stopped dead. He looked white as a ghost.

I immediately went to him and gripped his arm. "Max, what is it?" His muscles were bunched tight.

He stumbled to the chair and lowered himself down.

"What did you see?" I asked him in fascinated terror. Surely it couldn't have been as disconcerting as what I'd seen, but it had certainly knocked the wind out of him.

"No. I'm not even going to entertain it by giving voice to it. It is just so ludicrous – *preposterous*! No way is that my future." He let out a harsh laugh that turned almost hysterical. Was he having some kind of breakdown? I knew I shouldn't have let him come down here with me. I had broken my friend.

I looked up helplessly at Grenda as she came in the room. She gave me an innocent look. "He has had a bit of a shock," she conceded.

"A bit?" I exclaimed.

Blade sat beside Maxen. "Look, mate, they can take a bit of adjusting to, but generally they are the outright truth. Perhaps you'd better find a way to come to terms with it. You can't fight against destiny."

"You have no idea what I saw, how abhorrent it is," Maxen said through clenched teeth, and while I quailed at the vehemence in his words, I was relieved to see a bit of colour come into his cheeks.

"Max, I saw things that… disconcerted me." *I am not going to look at Blade, I am not going to look at Blade.* Damn, did my eyes flick to his? "But… I believe that fate, destiny, whatever you want to call it, isn't always definite."

"Do you truly believe that?" Blade asked quietly, and I sensed Grenda's attention on me.

"Someone said to me recently that it's our choices that make us," I returned, equally as quietly.

I saw a shutter come down in Blade's eyes, and a sense of loss filled me. Had his question has a hidden meaning? And had I just given the wrong answer?

"You'd better be right, Eev, because I do not *choose* that future for myself," Maxen growled, then noticed I had my jacket and boots on. "Where are we going?"

"Taranis's Tower." I hefted my pack.

"What?" Maxen and Grenda said at the same time.

"Don't worry, Gren, I won't let them get caught. It's just a scouting mission." Blade stood and hugged the older lady.

She squeezed him. "Please be careful, all of you." When she released him, her look included me and Maxen too. "And if you ever need me, you know where to find me."

Blade nodded. "Say goodbye to Flint for me. If he wants to talk through anything, Niara will know how to get a message to me."

"Thank you, Blade. Goodbye, Eva, Maxen."

"Thanks for letting us stay, Grenda," I said, and Maxen said, "We appreciate it." But his face still looked pinched from the revelations he had just been given.

He grabbed his jacket and pack, and together we moved to the door, Grenda bolting it behind us.

In the corridor, Blade turned to us. "We'll go over the rooftops again – safest that way. I can't risk Niara again, so just keep your hoods up, and stick close, ok?"

"Aye, Captain," I said, earning myself a grin from him. I was glad we seemed to be all right, despite the loaded moment a few minutes before.

As Blade went on ahead to check the stairwell was empty, I laid a hand on Maxen's arm. "I'm not going to pry," I said – Fates knew I was keeping what I'd seen about my own supposed future close to my chest – "but if you ever want to talk, or vent, or anything, I'm here – no judgements, ok?"

Maxen looked at me for a long moment. I thought he was going to confide in me, but he just gave a jerky nod. "Thanks," he said gruffly.

Blade's voice floated in through the doorway. "All clear."

Up on the roof again, I realised I was getting used to the strange, gloomy Fog light; my eyes seemed to be adjusting to it, as I could see Blade moving ahead of me across the rooftop more clearly than the day before. I kept my hood up, glad of my jacket; the damp air seemed to cling to me. We kept moving at a steady pace across the rooftops, hopping over gaps and climbing down ladders, until the Tower loomed tall and many-windowed in front of us.

"This is far as I dare to go right now," Blade whispered, gesturing for us to lie down on the roof and peer over the edge.

Carefully, I looked over and saw that the base of the tower was set into a large, circular courtyard comprised of a mosaic of light and dark grey stones. Massive gates were set into a smaller circular wall that encircled the Tower's courtyard, while the Tower itself boasted thick grey metal doors. The building we were lying on, and every other building that bordered it, was too far away to let us climb onto the wall.

I pointed at the doors. "Is that the only way in?"

Blade nodded. "The Council convene every week, but are escorted in by the Fog Guard, and other than prisoners no one else goes in. Taranis's staff live in, and supplies are taken in by the Guard the same day as the Council meetings. There's an arena at the back, but the entrance is separate."

"Hmm," I said, thinking all that through.

"Eva?" Maxen said. I blinked and focused on him. "You've got that look again."

I smiled thoughtfully before letting my gaze track up, and up, and up the Tower until my vision blurred. My mother was in there. My grandmother was in there. But what I really needed to know was how *I* was going to get in there.

My eyes drifted back to the ground, where two Fog Guards were dragging a young man towards the gate.

It appeared there was only one way I was going to get into Taranis's illustrious Tower.

I would have to get caught.

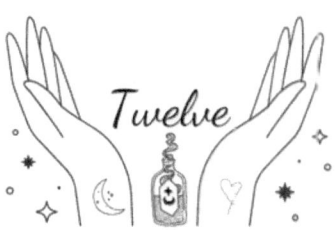

Twelve

"No way, Eev," Maxen said, at the same time that Blade snapped, "Absolutely no way in Fog are you giving yourself in."

I let out a frustrated breath. "I won't be giving myself in. I'll be going undercover. I'll just march up to the gate and demand an audience with my mother."

"Still no," Blade said.

I tried a different tack. "I saw my mother, in Grenda's vision. She's expecting me; my grandmother told her I would come."

Blade narrowed his eyes on me. "I thought you didn't believe."

"It's our choices, Blade," I reminded him. "Perhaps it *is* all laid out before us, and we must choose which strand to pull on." I shrugged, not knowing if I was just saying it to win this argument or if I was coming to understand how it all worked. But then... if I followed that belief system, then I *could* choose to accept the future I had seen that included Blade.

Nope. Not going there, my mind said, while my heart purred at the thought.

"Anyway," I continued, "my mother obviously believes, so perhaps I should take advantage of that. I need her on side if we're to help your people, Blade. Taranis seems to hold her and my grandmother in some esteem, as she doesn't appear to be languishing in a jail cell. We can use that." I didn't know exactly when my focus had shifted, but I really wanted to help the people of Fog now. It gave me a sense of purpose and filled that void.

"Eva, I don't mean to insult your mother, but she was always good at manipulating you, and getting *you* on side," Maxen said, bracing himself.

I gave him a humourless smile. "You're right, Max. I know what she is. I've had eighteen years of it, but what happened a few days ago opened my eyes to what my future could have been like. I don't want that for me, but I can't just leave her here – she *is* still my mother. And if I can help Blade's people, Grenda's family, and so many more besides, then I can't sit back like the pampered princess I was and do nothing." I looked at Blade. "Let me *do* something."

He stared at me for a long moment, then flipped onto his back on the roof and gazed up at the fog blanket.

"Please tell me you're not considering this madness," Maxen said to him.

"I don't like it," Blade said, and I felt a thrill of anticipation as I sensed him weakening. "But she does have a point."

Maxen groaned and dropped his head down to the

roof's edge.

"Look, Max, my mother won't hurt me, and if she's favoured by Taranis, then he won't either. What could possibly go wrong?" I attempted a jokey tone, but Blade turned his head and impaled me with his stare.

"Do not underestimate Taranis or his Council. They are no pampered nobles – they're hardened and shrewd and dangerous. Some are ex-Fog Guard commanders, and not easily fooled."

I tossed my head in a perfect imitation of my mother. "Don't worry, Captain Stone. I learnt devious machinations from the best. I've got this." I grinned confidently, and he swallowed as he stared at me.

Maxen groaned again, but did not lift his head. "This is a bad idea. Bad, bad, bad idea."

I patted Maxen on his shoulder. "Have faith, Max. When have I ever led you wrong?"

He did lift his head at that, to gape at me incredulously. "Oh, I don't know – how about when you tried to climb down here on your coming-of-age party for a dare and me and We…" he trailed off, then rallied, "…had to stop you, or how about the time—"

"That was you, was it?" Blade said with interest, and Maxen and I both stared at him. "I was on duty with Dag. We heard a commotion above and thought we saw a bunch of kids through the mist."

"Bunch of *kids*?" I said icily.

"Well, you were acting on a dare. Not very grown-up behaviour, is it?" Blade laughed, and I pursed my lips.

"He's got you there, Eev." Maxen grinned.

"Hey, you're supposed to be on my side!" I swatted Maxen, and he shrugged.

"I'll always been on your side, you know that."

A silence fell. I did know that. Maxen had always been there for me. Been there for both me *and* Wen, but now everything was different. Now there was someone else there for Wen, and Max and I only had each other.

I gave him a smile of understanding, and he nodded.

"Right, well, before we go along with your plan, Eva, I'm going to take you somewhere safe where we can firm out the details." Blade pushed back from the edge of the roof, and Maxen and I did the same.

Keeping low, we made our way back the way we had come, and I wondered where Blade was taking us this time.

He took us over a few more rooftops, before indicating that we should follow him down a ladder. One by one, we dropped into a narrow, dingy alleyway.

A shout echoed after us. Blade turned and peered above us. "Damn. Get back and follow my lead."

"What is it?" I whispered.

"Warne," he bit off, then pushed me and Maxen into a darkened, set-back doorway and walked away from us.

I made sure my hood was pulled up, and that we couldn't be seen by the guard we had encountered when we had first arrived at the city.

"Been looking everywhere for you, Blade. Where's your friends?" Warne dropped effortlessly to his feet in the alleyway and adjusted the bow and quiver on his back.

"I've been around," Blade said lightly. "Which friends?"

Warne laughed. "Oh, you know the ones. The ones you were supposed to take to the Tower – the ones that caused a tavern fight yesterday. Those friends."

"Can't say I know what you mean. Now, if you'll excuse me—"

"Don't think so, Blade. I've got my orders. I've got to take you in. So it would be best if you told me where they are – or they'll get it out of you at the Tower." Warne shrugged. "Your choice."

I bit my lip, reaching for my dagger. This wasn't the plan; *I* was supposed to get taken, not Blade.

Before I realised what I was doing, I was creeping out of the alleyway, making good on the dance training that afforded me lightness of foot. I crept up behind Warne. For a moment I thought I was going to have the element of surprise, but at the last second he whipped around, already reaching for his bow. I ducked and kicked out smoothly, taking the guard's legs out from under him. I pounced, dagger to his throat, and he stared up at me with hatred in his eyes.

"Hello," I said, "looking for me?"

He struggled beneath me, but I kept my knee pressed to a sensitive part of his anatomy and held the dagger close.

"I'm not the only one," he said through clenched teeth. "You won't get far, Nosian."

"Perhaps I don't want to," I quipped, and was gratified to see the confusion dull his eyes. "Now be a good boy and hold still. There's rope in my pack,"

I called over my shoulder, and heard the noise of a zip being undone.

"I'll enjoy taking you in," Warne spat, and I grinned my cat-like grin.

"I don't think so." I eased back as I felt Maxen binding his feet and hands. I stood and sheathed my dagger, while Blade and Maxen dragged Warne over to the side of the alleyway. He shot me a dirty look as I waggled my hand at him. "See you around!"

"I wouldn't antagonise him," Blade warned, but I shrugged, unconcerned. I was used to young men like Warne.

Blade knelt over Warne and slipped his bow and quiver from his back. "I'll just keep these safe for you."

Warne scowled. "You damage them, and I'll take great delight in damaging you, Blade."

"Noted." Blade settled the bow and quiver across his shoulders. "Come on, we need to get off the streets before more come along."

Leaving Warne to be discovered at a – hopefully – later point, we followed Blade down the alleyway and paused at a cross section of roads. People milled about; I hoped wherever Blade was taking us was close.

"Hoods up, act natural," Blade instructed. We did as he said, slipping into the crowd and slowly manoeuvring our way across the road and into another alleyway.

"Where are we going?" I whispered as we stopped in the shadows.

"Not far now," Blade said, then a gleam of humour lit his eyes. "I hope you don't mind getting a bit dirty."

"I beg your pardon?"

He grinned and pointed downwards. He couldn't

possibly mean—? "Are you kidding me?" I groaned.

"It's character-building, Eev," Maxen said.

"Really, Max? Thank you for that observation," I said with as much dignity as I could.

"Come on, it's really not that bad." Blade led us to a grate set into the floor further down the alley. He knelt and withdrew something from his pocket – it looked to be a key of some sort. He set it into the hole in the grate and turned it. The grate unlocked, and Blade pulled it open. "In you get," he said. I gestured for Maxen to go before me.

With a grimace, I slid in after him, and he helped me down into the tunnel. Blade followed and pulled the grate down after him. It closed with a click.

"What is this place?" I asked.

"Old sewerage tunnels. Things have been diverted now, but we will have to navigate a few of the newer ones to get to the base," Blade said cheerfully, his boots splashing through the shallow water running along the gulley.

"The base?" I said, stopping dead. "What are you not telling us?"

Blade turned back. "I promise I'll explain everything once we get there."

I exchanged a look with Maxen. "I'd rather know what we're walking into now."

He made his way back to me. "Fine, let's do this now, in the middle of an old sewerage tunnel."

I crossed my arms and waited.

"I am the leader of a rebel group," Blade began.

My mouth dropped open. I'd had my suspicions he was involved in some sort of resistance group, but to be its *leader*? Fates, I had not seen that coming.

"I, along with some others in the group, work in the Fog Guard to keep up appearances, but we also help by letting people go, or turning a blind eye when we can. The people are starving, oppressed, and I'll be damned if I sit back and do nothing!" He stopped, and we blinked at each other.

"That speech sounds familiar," I said with a smile, and he gave me a crooked grin of his own.

"It kind of resonated with me," he admitted.

"So, how many are in your group?" Max asked.

"A hundred or so. We've had a few new recruits recently. Friends of Niara's."

"Niara is involved?" I asked, thinking of her over-protective brother, who had a strong sense of keeping to Fog's rules.

Blade grimaced. "I don't like her being a part of it, but she got us out of a sticky situation once, and I kind of had to let her in."

"What about your sister and Kane?" I said.

"They don't know, naturally, but I know Brienne suspects something, so I've had to distance myself from her lately. I would hate to put her in danger, but the other night I had to get you off the streets quickly."

"I'm pretty sure Kane would have your head if he knew, especially with Niara being involved too," I observed.

"I am well aware of that fact. Kane is a good man — he looks after my sister and niece — but he's misguided if he thinks it won't get worse here. We need to do something about it now, before they start rounding up non-skilled citizens just for the fun of it." Blade ran a hand over his hair and sighed.

"I get it, I do. It's hard being stuck in the middle, but that's when going with your instincts is key." Going with instinct now, I put a hand on Blade's jacket sleeve. "You're doing what you think is best for your people."

"I hadn't planned on blowing my cover so soon though," he admitted. "But when you and Max arrived I knew it was time for action."

The way he spoke made me think there was more to this than just mere instinct. Perhaps this was what he'd been referring to when he mentioned he'd 'known' of me for a lot longer. Had he seen us, and believed we would help, in a vision?

"Then let us help," I said simply. I met his eyes, and he held my gaze for a beat, before nodding.

"Come on."

Thirteen

We followed Blade through the sewage tunnels – navigating a few active ones, where we had to practically shimmy along a narrow ledge to avoid the mire – until we reached a ladder. We climbed up and found ourselves before a round metal door. Blade tapped on it; a spyhole at the top of the door was pulled back, and a pair of lively green eyes peered through.

"Blade! Fates, where have you been?" a masculine voice asked. The sound of numerous locks being undone was heard, and the door opened.

"Hi, mate," Blade said, and leant forward to clasp wrists with the young man. His hair was so pale it was almost white; it stuck up in spikes around his mischievous face. Those bright green eyes took in me and Maxen. "Eva, Max, this is Dagatar – Dag to his friends."

Dag held out his hand. "Any friend of Blade's is a friend of mine." He'd obviously noted that we were from Nos, but didn't seem to react in any way. He clasped Maxen's hand in greeting, before turning to me and sketching a bow. "My lady."

I laughed. "Aren't you a charmer!"

Dag grinned at me, a twinkle in his eyes. Blade, easy amusement on his face, said, "He certainly is," but he turned to Dag, and something in his expression had Dag responding with a raised eyebrow. A clear message was passed between the friends.

I hoped Blade wasn't being so crass as to stake his claim – that was certainly not what this was – but I didn't want to cause a scene. I did, however, give Blade a look to let him know that I had seen whatever that just was. He gave me an innocent smile in return. *Hmm.*

Dag ushered us into the base and locked the door behind us. "So, are you going to clue me in on what's been going on? I swear Warne is after your blood," he said as we followed him down a set of metal stairs and into a large room, zoned off into different areas.

I looked around in interest as Blade said, "We know. We just had a run-in with him." He removed the bow and quiver, and Dag tracked the movement with his expressive eyes.

"Ah," he said.

Blade patted him on the shoulder. "Gather everyone together and I'll explain."

I watched Dag move around each area; there were sofas and chairs set around a low table where people of various ages lounged. A few others sat at desks filled with papers, or congregated in a kitchen area.

Blade directed me and Max to the back of the

room, where there was a large table, and gestured for us to sit in one of the many chairs around it. A free-standing board covered with diagrams and writing waited at the head of the table.

"You did all this?" I asked Blade, gesturing around the whole area.

He shrugged casually. "With help."

We stopped talking as the other members of Blade's group arranged themselves around the table, some sitting, some standing. All eyes were on Maxen and me – curious, mostly, but I sensed distrust in some.

"Afternoon, all," Blade said, standing at the head of the table. I straightened in my chair at his commanding but friendly tone. "You've probably been wondering where I've been, and now who our guests are." He paused to allow the nods and murmurs of agreement to work their way around those assembled. "I met our new friends beneath the bridge. It seems our intentions converge. Eva and Maxen, here, are looking for someone who was taken from their realm of Nos and deposited in the Tower."

"Why would Taranis take someone from the Twin Realms?" Dag asked. "That's not his domain."

"May I?" I spoke to Blade, who nodded. "My aunt made a deal with him, but did not follow through on her end of the bargain. So he took my mother as compensation, to teach my aunt a lesson." That was succinct enough to sum it all up but not have to go into detail.

Blade looked at me sharply, and I realised I had never actually told him any of that. His lips thinned, and I flushed.

"What was the deal?" an older man asked, his pale

green eyes interested. I shot a panicked look at Maxen.

"It related to Eva's family, but it's personal, so perhaps we'd better not go into too much detail," he said, and I smiled at him gratefully. "Suffice it to say that Taranis wanted control of the Twin Realms too, and when he didn't get it, he wasn't best pleased."

"Taranis does like his tantrums," a boy of about sixteen sniggered. Laughter rippled around the group.

"Yeah, but they usually involve him releasing his pets on us," a young woman snapped, and the laughter stopped. She tossed back her long, wavy charcoal hair.

The boy flushed, and Blade walked around the table to lay a comforting hand on his shoulder. "Elianna is right," he said, acknowledging the woman, "but we have a way to stop them now. Max?"

Maxen looked at me, and I nodded. We had offered to help, so we needed to follow through now.

He pulled his pack onto his lap, rifling around inside until he found a many-looped belt filled with the dark bottles. He set it onto the table before him. Everyone leaned forward.

"What is that?" someone asked.

"It's made from essence of moonflower, I believe," Maxen said. "It emits a light so bright, the Shadowwraiths flee from it."

Everyone started talking at once, voicing surprise, or some scoffing at the idea. Blade held up a hand. "Yes, I know it's hard to believe, but it's true; I have seen it in action. It works."

"Is that all you have?" Dag asked, gesturing at the eight remaining bottles. "Can you get more?"

Maxen and I looked at each other, and I felt myself pale. We could... if we asked Alys. I battled with myself. On the one hand I wanted to help these people free themselves from the fear of Shadowwraith attacks, but to face those I had abandoned? I didn't know if I was strong enough yet.

Maxen nodded slowly. "It is possible we could get more, but yes, this is all we have left at the moment."

"That's all well and good, but it's not going to stop Taranis, is it?" Elianna said, and everyone fell silent.

Damn, the girl was right again – but I had an answer. I looked at Blade, who regarded me steadily, almost sadly. "I am going to infiltrate the Tower, and learn Taranis's weakness."

"Girl, are you out of your mind?" an older lady demanded.

I dragged my gaze from Blade and smiled at her. "Perhaps. But I know my mother has talked her way out of a cell and into a plush room. Now, why would Taranis do that if he didn't esteem her in some way?"

"Cloda is right, you're out of your mind," Elianna said, and I turned a frosty gaze on the girl at her scathing tone. "Perhaps he's using her as *bait*. Taking someone from the Twin Realms is just asking for her people to come down here to rescue her, surely. Maybe that was his plan all along."

I sat back in my chair in shock. "If that was the case, then who was he hoping to reel in?" I murmured slowly, my mind spinning. Taranis knew no one else would come after my mother to rescue her, not after what she had done to her own people… but had he known *I* would come? Her loving daughter. Fates, was I still being manipulated, even now?

"You," Blade said, so softly that I barely heard him. "He expects you to strike a bargain with him to get your mother back, of your own free will." His thoughts had aligned so perfectly with mine that I felt the strength of it hit almost viscerally.

"No! I would never be drawn into making a deal with a *Fate*," I snapped, standing. Maxen gripped my wrist in warning, but I carried on. "I've seen how that plays out, and believe me, *no one* benefits."

"The plan is off the table," Blade snapped back, and I reeled back as if he had hit me.

"You do not get to decide that!" I stormed, fully prepared to march around the table and square up to him. My blood was burning, but I couldn't tear my eyes from his.

A silence fell in the room, and finally I became aware of myself. Flushing, I looked around to see all eyes riveted on us. Dag stared from me to Blade, and a look of understanding came into his gaze.

"Give us a minute," Blade said grimly. "We'll reconvene later."

Silently, one by one and in small groups, his team moved away until it was just him, me and Maxen.

Now I did round the table, but Blade met me halfway. "I am going," I hissed, at the same time as he stated, "You are not going."

A pointed cough reached my ears, and I turned to spear Maxen with a furious look. He stood. "When you two figure it out, let me know, ok?" He walked off, heading towards Dag in the kitchen area.

"Come with me," Blade said, and – wisely refraining from touching me – gestured to a door at the back of the room. He opened it and motioned me through.

I strode in and stopped short, looking around at the small living-sleeping area. "You sleep here?" I asked, disconcerted.

Blade leant back against the closed door and crossed his arms. "When I need to," he said.

I thought of everyone who had put their trust in Blade, and the fight seemed to drain out of me. He had so much at stake. Not just himself – his family, everyone in the room beyond, and the ones not here but still a part of it.

"Look," I said, and he raised one eyebrow. "I know you fear something going wrong. You have so much to lose—"

"You have no idea," he said, pushing off the door and stepping closer.

My heart started to thud painfully, and I became aware of every nerve-ending in my body. *Don't do this now,* I thought. My resolve was balancing on a knife-edge. If he asked me the same question he had asked me this morning, I might crumble.

"Please don't," I said, my voice breaking, and he stopped, his hand flexing as if he wanted to reach out to me.

He sighed. "We're just going around in circles here, Eva."

"I know. I'm sorry," I said helplessly. What did he want from me? A declaration, a promise? Well, he would be waiting until Fog froze over before I revealed what was in my heart. He wasn't the only one with much to lose. And I didn't want the pain that would inevitably come with it.

We stared at each other, at an impasse, until I said, "If I promise you that I won't make a deal with Taranis, will you let me go?"

"Let you go?" he said, almost to himself. He refocused and sat on the edge of the bed. "It's too risky. We'll have to find another way."

I blew out a breath. "You're impossible." I strode to the door, leaving him to stew.

I simply wasn't going to find another way. Me going to the Tower, getting my mother to confide in me about Taranis, and getting her to agree to leave with me was the *only* way. I would just have to bide my time and wait for an opportune moment to leave, since Blade seemed to have no intention of letting me go. My heart gave a sudden thud at the double-edged thought. Fates, I needed to leave *soon*.

It was down to me and me alone now.

I joined Maxen in the kitchen, where he offered me a bread roll stuffed with meat and a cup of herbal tea. I listened to the friendly banter as the Fogians accepted me and Maxen – well, everyone except Elianna, who continued to look at me suspiciously. Perhaps she had good reason to. I shrugged to myself. I didn't really care if she didn't like me; I wasn't here to make friends, I just wanted to help in any way I could. And if that meant doing something she didn't approve of, well, so be it. Someone had to get close to Taranis.

Out of the corner of my eye, I saw Blade leave his room, cross the larger hall, and go up the metal staircase.

"He's gone to guard the door," Dag told me,

seeing where I was looking. "We take it in turns." Moments later, a girl with two grey ombre braids descended the stairs and helped herself to some food.

"How often do you switch?" I asked nonchalantly.

"Every hour. Gets tedious otherwise," Dag said with a grimace, popping the remaining bite of his sandwich into his mouth.

I stored that away for later. I would have to find a way out, and it looked like that door was the only way. Then I would need Blade's key, or someone else's key – unless...

"Is the grate the only way in and out? Blade took us through a load of tunnels to get here. I can't get over how amazing this place is." I sipped my tea and looked innocently over the rim of my cup, adding a subtle flutter of my lashes.

Dag blinked, and cleared his throat. "Uh, no, actually. There is another way – just to the right of the door is a tunnel that leads up to the main drain. We have that fixed as an emergency exit. And it would have to be an emergency to use that way," he said, ending on a laugh.

I joined in with the laughter, but inside I wanted to shudder. *Emergency exit it is.* I just had to find a way to get through the metal door. I pondered on that, and noticed most of the group were readying to leave. "What's going on?"

"Oh, patrol, and others have to go home. They have regular lives to maintain too. Don't worry, though, I'll be here," Dag reassured me with a cheeky grin.

I couldn't help but like him, and I hated using him for information. Old Eva wouldn't have cared, but he seemed like a genuinely nice guy, and I felt guilty.

"You guys can take the sofas and have a nap if you like. I'm on door duty next, but I'll bunk in Blade's room after that so I don't wake you up." Dag gestured over to the living area. With a yawn, I made my way over there.

"Perhaps we should get some sleep; it's been a long day," I said as Maxen joined me. I would feign sleep until I could seize my chance. I knew I'd have to leave Maxen behind, and though it didn't sit right with me, I saw no other choice. He would be safe with Blade.

"Good idea," he said. Toeing off his boots, he lay down, facing the back of the sofa.

I watched him for a moment, my insides squirming, then lay down myself, but my mind and my heart raced. Dag moved around the room, covering a few of the glowing white-green rocks to dim the light, and I watched through narrowed eyes, waiting for my chance. I kept my boots on but covered them with my bag, and pulled the hood of my jacket up so it shielded my eyes.

A little later, Dag made his way up the staircase, and a few minutes after, I saw Blade descend. I held my breath as he looked over in my direction. My heart squeezed painfully. This might be the last time I saw him. I trusted my mother not to hurt me, but who knew if Taranis would have other ideas? What if Blade was right, and Taranis wanted me to make a deal with him? What would happen when I refused?

I couldn't think of that. I had to pull on the strand now and see where it took me. Blade headed into his room. Stealthily, I sat up, picked up my pack, and lightly crossed the room to the stairs. I didn't look back. I couldn't.

Dag looked up as I approached. I pressed a hand to my chest, stumbling, and his bright green eyes widened. "What's wrong?"

Show-time, I thought grimly.

"Dag, I need your help," I wheezed, putting a hand up to my chest and pressing on it, before I gave a moan and stumbled into him.

Fourteen

Dag helped me over to the door and propped me against it.

"What can I do?" he blurted.

"I – I think I'm having a panic attack! We're so far underground" – I gasped – "I feel like I can't breathe!"

"I'm going to get help!" Dag turned to grip the handrail of the stairs and slide down them.

I pushed down my self-disgust at the depths I had sunk to and counted to five, giving Dag the chance to run halfway across the room, before I turned to the door. I wrenched back the three bolts, turned the metal wheel in the centre, and yanked it open. I wasted no time in running through and pulling it closed behind me.

I looked along the tunnels and, remembering what Dag had said, sprinted along the right-hand one, not caring what was splashing up my legs. I kept running until my legs burned and the water started to rise, but with every footstep I took, something pulled me back as if I was on an invisible tether. Every fibre of my being told me I was running the *wrong* way, that what I sought was behind me, not in front. I battled the disconcerting sensations and clambered out of the rising sludge, shimmying along the ridge running parallel. I was just reaching up to push up the main drain's grate when I heard it.

"*Eva!*"

The roar echoed along the tunnel. My heart felt like it was being cleaved in two at the raw emotion in it.

With a sob, and a gigantic push, I wrenched the grate sideways and clambered out. I slid the grate back across with my foot, and saw that I stood in the courtyard just beyond the Tower's boundary wall. My chest heaved as I tried to suck in breath after agonising breath.

I staggered forward, my boots and trousers caked in muck, fully ready to draw attention to myself, when I found arms gripping me from behind.

I turned wearily and looked into Blade's livid eyes.

"You used Dag, Eva. You left..." *Me.* The word hovered in the air.

"I *told* you not to believe I was honourable, Blade," I almost sobbed out, trying to inject every ounce of haughty Eva-coldness into it as I could. I had to make him leave before he was caught too. "I make poor decisions, and everyone else just gets caught up in the aftermath. Don't waste your time on me. Just let me go, *please.*" I had no idea why my heart felt like it was breaking, why I suddenly couldn't bear to look into his eyes. I turned away. This was all wrong. But I couldn't stop what I'd started.

Sudden shouts rang out across the courtyard, and I

pulled out of his grip and shoved him towards the grate. Blade took one final desperate look at me and said, "This isn't over." With a blur, he was gone.

Moments later, I was body slammed to the floor.

"I told you I would enjoy taking you in," a satisfied voice said from above me.

My body ached and so did my heart, but my pride would not allow me to be taken in by that weasel. Warne lifted me up, and I let myself go suddenly limp, throwing him off-balance. I sensed him adjust and made my move, dragging my foot down his calf and stamping hard on his foot, before ploughing my elbow into his stomach. I whirled around, out of his reach, as he lunged at me. I let a teasing grin adorn my face, but danced backwards away from him.

Two other guards rushed me; I held up one dainty finger. "I am Eva Celestri, and I have come to see my mother, Lady Salomé Celestri."

The guards stopped as if I had been surrounded by an invisible wall. One of them looked me up and down. I had to admit that I probably didn't paint the picture of a young female noble from Nos, but my name obviously held weight.

"You heard her, Bilt," the taller guard said to the other. "You know what his lordship said."

My ears pricked at that. I *was* expected.

Warne gripped my elbow, and said with a sneer, "Allow me to escort you, my lady."

I pulled out of his grip and stalked towards the gate with my head held high. Two guards behind the gate looked at Warne.

"Prisoner's name?"

"I am no prisoner," I said. "Tell my mother I am

here." I needed to keep up with the haughty act. It was the only defence I had now.

"Oh, I am going to enjoy watching Taranis knock you off your pedestal," Warne muttered, "and then I'm going to find Blade and—"

No one knocked me off my pedestal but me, I thought grimly. "While I would *love* to chit-chat... no, forget that – actually I wouldn't," I said, inspecting my nails. "You're boring me now." I couldn't help bait him. I was spoiling for a good fight.

Warne obliged, gripping my arm. He spun me around and bashed me against the metal gate. I laughed in his face, enjoying the way his eyes narrowed. I waited a moment then lifted my knee towards him, grabbed his tunic, pivoted and flipped him around, so *he* crashed against the gate and slithered to the floor.

"Eva! Stop playing with the help."

I straightened at the cold, disapproving tones.

"Mother," I said, trying not to appear thrown as she stepped from a swirl of fog behind the gates. She was dressed in a slinky grey dress that flashed with green shimmers as she walked forwards. Her mane of blonde hair was pulled back by two sparkling combs.

She looked me up and down, taking in my less-than-pristine appearance, her blue eyes scathing. "What *have* you been doing, darling?"

She threw the guard an impatient look and he immediately unlocked the gate, a look of abject terror on his face. My mother waved an imperious hand at me, and I walked through, blowing a mocking kiss at Warne as he struggled to his feet. The guard locked the gate behind me.

"Oh, you know – battling Shadowwraiths, causing

tavern fights, traipsing through sewerage," I told my mother, and she laughed as if I were joking. I noticed that she kept her distance, wrinkling her nose.

"You certainly took your time. I expected you to come straight away."

"Well, you don't appear to be suffering, Mother," I observed.

She pouted. "You know I don't do well without my daily trip to Sol. It is so gloomy here," she said with a delicate shudder.

"Indeed. Why don't we just leave, then? You appear to have the guards in the palm of your hands." I jerked my head to the gate, testing a theory.

"Oh no, we can't leave." She let out a nervous laugh, a shadow lurking behind her eyes. Hmm – so I was right. She *was* in a cage. A gilded one, to be sure, but a cage nonetheless. "Now, let us get you cleaned up, ready for your audience with our lord, Taranis."

I took a deep breath. *Pull on the strand.* "Lead the way," I said with more confidence than I felt.

I allowed myself one last thought for Maxen and Blade, hoping they would find a way to work together while I did what I could on the inside. Then I faltered, suddenly realising I had no way to contact them if I did find something out. I cursed my impulsiveness.

"Come on, darling. We mustn't keep our lord waiting." My mother cocked a hip as I worked through the realisation. "And then we can catch up. I want to know all about what happened after I left."

I stared at her. She sounded as if she was the one who had been slighted – the victim in the situation she had wrought. I tamped down my incredulity and pasted a smile on my face. "Of course."

She nodded, but then what else had she expected? I always fell in line with her whims and wishes. I could feel myself – the Eva that I had worked so hard to be these past days – vanishing.

With a grimace, Mother tossed her head before placing a long-nailed hand on my grubby arm and clicking her fingers. A cloud of fog enveloped us. For one suffocating moment I couldn't see, but it cleared to reveal the room I had seen in my vision. I swayed, pressing a hand to my head.

I barely had a chance to orientate myself before an older version of my mother strode into view. She wore loose, silky grey trousers and a matching top. Her blonde hair had faded, but her blue eyes still held intellect and strength. She inspected me from head to toe while my mother hovered at her side.

"She is very Nosian, isn't she?" she said dispassionately.

I spoke tartly without thinking. "I *am* Nosian."

Her eyes flashed. "You wouldn't be *anything* if it weren't for me," she said tightly. "*I* arranged for your parents to be Paired, so a little respect and gratitude would be appreciated."

Disgust curdled low in my belly as my mother fluttered her hands nervously. Did this woman really think I should be grateful for what she'd done? Yes, I exist because of it, but I'd had absolutely no choice in the matter. I existed at the expense of years of happiness for the ones she'd wronged.

"Eva has had a long journey, Mother. She just needs a bath, and she'll be back to her best." My mother looked between us both, her eyes blinking a warning at me.

I turned on a smile. "Yes – I'm sorry. A bath would be wonderful."

"Perfect." My mother nodded in satisfaction. "Now, Eva darling, this, as you have surmised, is your grandmother."

"You may address me as Sybilla. I have no time for this 'Grandmother' nonsense." Sybilla stared down her nose at me.

"I am pleased to meet you, Sybilla," I said, trying to correct my earlier wrong footing. I would need to keep both these women on side if I was to survive here and do what I had set out to do. But I was coming to realise that I might only be able to carry out one of my plans. Getting my mother out was looking less and less likely. Sybilla had been in Fog since before I was born. I hadn't even known she was still alive until I'd come here. Taranis did not appear to let his acquisitions go easily.

My mother smiled at me approvingly, and then crooked a finger. Obediently, I followed her into a large bathroom with three arched windows overlooking the city of Fog. A round bath dominated the room, set into the tiled floor, and a wide mirror reflected the flickering candlelight from over a vanity housing a sink.

"There, get yourself cleaned up, darling. You're looking almost feral." She tittered. "I shall arrange clothes for you. The fashion here is rudimentary at best, unless you have friends in high places." She winked at her own joke, and left me alone in the room.

I waited a moment before turning the lock in the door and leaning against it. I blew out a long breath. Fates, what had I got myself into? All I could do was the next thing, and that meant shedding my icky clothes and taking a bath. I was trying to be less spoilt, but even I had my limits, and I was about at the end of them.

I pushed off the door, managed to get my boots off with only the merest of winces, and turned on the taps, adding a heavy hand of hot water – hopefully it would soothe my bruises from my run-in with Warne. I grinned. *Worth it, though.* I drizzled in a dash of whatever the pale, shimmery liquid was, and it frothed up in mass of musky-scented bubbles. Satisfied, I stripped off and slid into the bath, completely submerging myself, letting my hair fan out around me.

I stayed beneath the bubbles, holding my breath for as long as I could, only bursting back up when my lungs burned. Slicking my hair back, I washed bubbles from my face, lay back, and just concentrated on breathing. In and out. In and out. I would not think of him. Of Blade. Not of the way my head fitted perfectly against his neck, or the feel of his hands at my hips, or the way I felt more *me* with him than I ever did alone.

Tears squeezed from my eyes, mingling with the bath water, and with an angry motion I dashed them away. It was no good. I was only tormenting myself.

This is not over… Fates, it had been over before it'd even begun.

I determinedly scrubbed myself until my pale skin pinked, using the musky soap to wash my hair. Then I stayed in the water until my fingertips wrinkled and the water cooled around me.

A knock at the door made me glare at it. "Eva, darling. It is time."

I counted to five. "Coming, Mother," I called, and pulled myself out of the bath. I wrapped myself in one of the large towelling cloths, before squeezing out my hair and wrapping it in a smaller cloth.

In the other room, my mother stood beside the long stone table. On it was a selection of heeled shoes, boots, accessories and clothing. Of Sybilla there was no sign. Good.

"Come and choose what you would like to wear."

I joined her and looked over everything, noting that the clothing was comprised mostly of slinky dresses, similar to what my mother was wearing, in muted shades. I stared at them. A week ago I would have snatched one up and not thought twice about wearing it, but instead my eyes trailed over to a pair of tight grey leather-look trousers and a slash-neck top. I picked them up.

"Oh no, darling, not to meet Taranis. He is most particular about attire."

So much for choice then. I concealed a sigh and picked the most demure of the dresses – a high-necked, sleeveless pale grey dress that looked like it would skim the floor, even on me.

"Perfect. Go and get dressed and brush out your hair. Remember to brush it—"

"One hundred times. I remember," I cut her off dully, but she only smiled and turned back to select me a pair of stiletto heels.

I returned to the bathroom, dried off and pulled the slinky dress over my body. Of course, it fitted perfectly. I removed the towel from my hair and picked up the silver metal-backed brush and dragged it through my damp hair. I didn't even bother to count.

My mother appeared in the reflection behind me. For a brief moment our eyes met, and I saw an echo of our past. A chink in her armour that perhaps I could widen.

"Mother, come home with me," I whispered, yearning in that brief moment for things to be as they had before. When I'd foolishly imagined she did truly love me, and would choose me above all else.

She hesitated, I *knew* she did, but the next instant she seared her armour closed with a blink of her blue eyes and a toss of her head.

"It's too late for that, darling. Come; it is time for you to meet our lord, Taranis." Her tone had a ring of finality to it.

My heart stuttered. Was I to be stuck here too?

Fifteen

Sybilla, my mother, and I walked into the large hall that spanned the width of the Tower.

I covertly looked around, noting the Fog Guard encircling the perimeter of the room, all dressed in smart dark grey uniforms with a lightning strike erupting from a fog cloud emblazoned on their sleeves. These were obviously Taranis's personal guard. Not that he would need protection – he was a Fate – but his arrogance evidently required a little pomp and show. Grey silky banners with the same insignia hung from the walls above the many tall arched windows. The room itself, tiled with grey marbled stone, was lit with the glow of hundreds of the white-green rocks.

A semi-circular table and chairs dominated the centre of the hall set in front of a large, raised dais where three pewter metal chairs sat, one much larger than the others. I repressed a sneer. Taranis's throne.

"Wait here," Sybilla instructed, and I paused before the table as she and my mother carried on to the dais and took a seat either side of the larger chair. I had to hold back my surprise. They seemed at ease, sitting as if they belonged there. Perhaps they did.

Feeling as if I was about to undergo some sort of test, I balanced perfectly on my grey glittery heels and kept my head up. My mother had pulled my hair into a tight twist. It pinched at my temples.

The doors behind me crashed open, and I turned my head to see twelve men and women making their way in. They regarded me openly. I gazed back in a bored manner as they took their seats around the table, facing me.

Once they were settled, a hush filled the room. The back of my neck began to prickle; inexplicable goosebumps rose along my bare arms. The room filled with a pressure, the kind I'd experienced just before a Nosian thunderstorm.

I blinked. A cloud of fog appeared before me and stepping from within it was the imposing figure I had seen before... in my dream. He regarded me from dark eyes set in a long, pointed face. His hair wisped around his face, as if moving in its own personal wind.

Instinctively, I lowered my head and curtsied.

"Charming," Taranis said in a cold, clear voice that sent shivers rippling over my skin.

I raised my head, and he tilted his head as if determining something. I hoped he couldn't read thoughts. I knew little about the Fates, only what we had been told, but even less of Taranis.

"You have come to claim your mother?"

I nodded.

"Brave to venture into my realm... alone." *Does he know about Maxen?* I forced myself not to react. He gave a small smile. "And brave to think I would relinquish what I was *owed*." His voice turned sharper, lightning strikes forking out from the fog.

I had two options; supplicate to him, or stand my ground. It was an easy decision, perhaps a foolish one, but *I* did not lower myself to anyone. Even a Fate. "Technically, she was not what you were owed. You sought a different prize."

I heard the hisses of outrage fill the air, but I kept my focus on Taranis only. He stroked a hand along his chin thoughtfully. "You know, I could blink you out of existence with a mere thought."

I steeled myself.

"I *could* – but unfortunately, I am bound to some tricky little laws set out by myself and those other Fates that you revere so. I have no wish to have Arianrhod storming down here and spoiling my mood." I relaxed somewhat, but his next words made me swallow. "Although you, Eva Celestri of Nos, are a quandary. A child born of a Twin Realm Union... but only through interference from *me*." He reached out one long, pale finger and stroked my cheek. The icy sting made it feel as though he had split my cheekbone open. "So, I could be forgiven for thinking that circumstance offers me a loophole, no?"

"No," I said, then louder and firmer, "No."

"You are intriguing. You have your mother's poise, but there is something different about you. I want to say strength, but it is more than that." Taranis stepped around me, affording me a clear view of my mother. Her smile was frozen in place, but I saw how tightly she gripped the arms of the chair.

I swallowed as Taranis completed his orbit of me.

"Perhaps you have some darkness in you – a darkness wrought from the weight of my magic. A hefty price must be paid for thwarting the will of a Fate, and I interfered in Belenos and Arianrhod's little ceremony... not once, but twice." Taranis seemed to take that as a point of pride.

My aforementioned poise deserted me, and I staggered. *No!* I was a child of the night, but not of the darkness... never of the darkness. Arianrhod would not forsake me; surely she would not blame an innocent child for the schemes of one of her own kind. Starlight glimmered in my veins and the velvet midnight sky kissed my hair. I had felt it, *known* where I belonged when I stood in the temple ruins with Wen and Maxen. Three children of Nos, connected by their heritage and birthright.

What birthright? You had no right to be born, the dark voice inside my mind whispered slyly.

"I..." I could not speak.

Taranis waved a hand. Everything around us vanished.

I stumbled back from him, but let out a scream as my foot found only thin air. Taranis's cold hand gripped me before I fell and pulled me back. The fog surrounding us parted, and I saw we stood on a small circular platform, exposed to the suffocating smog.

I realised where we were; the very pinnacle of Taranis's Tower.

"Now, I have been lenient, *extremely* lenient, in indulging your grandmother to treat your mother, and now you, as honoured guests. It took Sybilla many years to earn that right." Taranis stepped close to me, tiny flickers of lightning sparking in his hair. "If I sense at any moment that the darkness in you is aimed at me, then you shall spend the rest of your gifted existence in the dungeons. Do I make myself clear... daughter?"

I gasped.

"I bestowed life upon you, so you shall be treated as my daughter. A princess of Fog. How would you like that?" Amusement rippled across his face, and I knew he was enjoying my discomfort. But he had presented me with an opportunity... an opportunity to get close to him. *Pull the strand, Eva.*

I schooled my face into an impassive mask and curtsied. "You honour me, my lord."

"*Never* forget it," he said, gripping my arm, and we were back in the hall.

Respectful silence fell as Taranis escorted me to the dais. A chair materialised beside my mother, and he released me so I could sit. I kept my face forward as he took his own seat in between Sybilla and my mother. I felt sick to the very soles of my feet. He had just created a parody of a loving family – all I had ever wanted. But this one was far, far worse than the one I used to have, the one I had always felt was dysfunctional, off somehow, but still believed was true. *Careful what you wish for...* Sometimes those shooting stars arcing across the silken skies of Nos burned up before the wishes even left your lips. That was what I had now: a half-wished-for family that could burn up with one spark.

Was I that spark?

I slowly turned my gaze to my mother, passing

over her wide-eyed look and beyond her to Taranis, who met my eyes. I met them squarely and gave him a wide, accepting smile. *Let's dance*, I thought.

He inclined his head at my supposed acquiescence and turned to his Council, who had swivelled in their rotating chairs to face us. "What news?"

"My lord." A slender man of about fifty stood with a bow and focused his green eyes on Taranis. "We have taken in five more skilled. My son brought in three of them," he added with a touch of pride.

"Is that so?" Taranis said in unimpressed tones. "I would expect nothing less from your family. You have always been eager to please, Magnik. Where is your son? I should like to reward him."

"My lord?" Magnik said in faltering tones.

"I should like to reward your son," Taranis repeated, steepling his fingers in front of his face.

"O-of course, thank you, my lord," Magnik said. He left his seat and hurried through the hall and out of the doors.

I doubted that a reward from Taranis would come without strings. *Never make a deal with a Fate,* I thought, almost like a mantra. But… had I made a deal with him, when I'd agreed to act as a docile daughter? I swallowed down my distaste. I didn't believe so; I hadn't said any such words. I hoped Blade was wrong and that Taranis would see me as nothing more than a mortal toy, not anything that could benefit him in any way.

"Anyone else? What about the rumblings of dissent, have they been quashed?" Taranis looked at the other members, and I roused from my thoughts. Was he referring to Blade's group? I sat up in my chair and watched the uncomfortable emotions flitting across the

Council members' faces. None of them spoke up.

"Well? Do I not allow you, exalted twelve, free rein to run this realm as you see fit, when I am otherwise busy?" Taranis scowled at them all, and a few squirmed in their seats.

He looked up as Magnik re-entered, and my heart skipped a beat when I saw Warne slink in behind him. *Damn.* I should not have poked that particular snake.

His eyes zeroed in on me, and I caught the faintest whisper of a smirk before he focused on Taranis and bowed.

"Name, guard?" Taranis asked, drumming one long-fingered hand on the arm of his chair.

"Captain Warne Caligo, my lord."

"I hear you have been instrumental in detaining three skilled. I would offer you a reward for your service. What do you desire?" Taranis said.

To my horror, Warne's eyes flicked again to me and then swiftly away, but not before Taranis had noticed.

"You desire my new daughter, do you?" he said in a low, intrigued tone, and I almost retched all over my dress.

Warne rose his chin. "Not in that way, my lord. She and I merely have a score to settle."

Taranis turned to me, one eyebrow raised, while my mother let out a murmur of disbelief. "And how is it that she is but newly arrived and has already been making... ah... *friends?*"

Warne's eyes flashed maliciously. Double damn. "She was seen in the company of a guard, who was instructed to bring her in, but did not." *Don't mention*

Maxen, don't mention Maxen, I prayed. "I encountered her again and she… resisted."

"Is that so? Daughter, why is this?" Taranis seemed to float over to me.

I was not my mother's daughter for nothing. I turned my most guileless look on him. "I do not know, my lord. I asked the other guard to show me the way to your Tower, but a fight broke out and we were separated. I was scared and did resist Captain Caligo, as I thought he meant to do me harm." I hoped that wasn't overdoing it. "But I am sure the other guard *intended* to bring me in."

Taranis stared at me for so long that I felt as though I were falling into his dark, fathomless pits. After a moment, he spoke. "Captain Warne Caligo of the Fog Guard, what would you do to my new daughter if I allowed you to settle your score?"

I sensed my mother's outrage, but I forced myself not to react. Taranis was testing me. Testing Warne and I both.

The pause was loaded with promise as I waited to hear what Warne *thought* he could do to me. He had no idea who he was dealing with. I was no pampered Nosian 'princess'. Eva Celestri never backed down from a fight.

"I would only wish to give her the fight she so obviously desired." My adrenaline spiked, and I hoped I hid my exhilaration successfully.

Taranis smiled slowly. "I agree," he said. "I am interested to see what she can do."

"My lord." My mother stood, surprising me. "I thought you had promised a ball in our honour. We do not want to mar Eva's beautiful face with cuts and bruises."

"Then you had better hope she is a skilled and nimble fighter." Taranis dismissed her, turning back to face the front, and Sybilla leaned across Taranis's vacant chair and gripped my mother's wrist tightly, pulling her down.

My mother sat, and I searched her profile. Had she genuinely tried to stop me fighting because it might spoil my looks... or was that her way of protecting me? And a *ball*? That was an unexpected revelation. Probably my mother's idea.

"Captain Caligo, you shall have your reward – a fight with my new daughter."

Warne threw me an exultant look, and I rolled my eyes. I had already bested him twice now; did he really think he would win this round? But the look fell off his face as Taranis continued. "If you win, you shall be promoted. However, if you lose, you shall become her personal guard, and if you allow any harm to befall her, well... I shall get extremely creative with your punishment."

"But... but, my lord, he is a highly trained, efficient member of your Guard," Magnik blustered.

"Then let him prove it," Taranis said, turning his back on him. I noted the strange, almost excited gleam in the dark depths of his eyes.

I didn't know who was more horrified by the thought of Warne becoming my personal guard. If I let him win, he would be promoted and be free to carry on persecuting the skilled Fogians, but if I won – which was likely, I acknowledged to myself – I would be stuck with him, and I could not attempt to contact Blade. *Fates above*. I looked at Taranis. Before he took his seat, he met my gaze, a knowing look in place of the excitement. He knew exactly what he was doing, and had manoeuvred Warne and me exactly into position.

"Now, the hour grows extremely late. Council dismissed. Captain Caligo, I shall expect you in the arena first thing in the morning," Taranis said, waving his hand. Immediately, the Council members stood and bowed, before leaving.

Warne's eyes fixed on mine, and I waggled a mocking wave at him. He turned on his heel and left with his father. I wouldn't let him see that I was torn as to whether I should throw the fight or not.

That was tomorrow's problem.

Sixteen

"Well, I hope you're proud of yourself." My mother paced up and down in front of me, only stopping to wrench her heels off and toss them across the room.

"Salomé, calm yourself." Sybilla lounged back in a grey velvet high-backed chair in the living area of our shared suite.

"I cannot! She has been in the Tower mere hours and already she is making a mess of things." My mother seared me with a look.

"Excuse me," I snapped, everything catching up with me. "I think *you* are the one who made a mess of everything. If you hadn't interfered with Wen's Choosing, we would be in Nos right now." I hadn't intended to bring it up, but it needed to be said.

My mother's face reddened, and she thrust one finger at me. "How dare you? I only did that to save our family. She and her harlot mother had to be punished for trying to usurp us."

I stared at her. She still believed that she'd done

no wrong. "Usurp us, Mother? We were the imitations; *they* should have been Daddy's family."

She let out a brittle laugh. "Don't be so naïve, Eva. I simply took what should have been mine… ours."

Sybilla smiled indulgently. "Your mother desired a noble partner, and I ensured it happened. I didn't foresee the repercussions, but one must make sacrifices for one's children." She gave me a chastising look. Did she think what my mother had done was for me – that I should be appreciative? No, she'd done it for the one person she always thought of first. Herself.

"Oh, Mother," my mother sighed, "I wish you had been there to see that silly girl's face when I pushed her off the bridge. Such a shame her stupid pet rescued her."

My blood ran cold. "You did *what*?" I had been there when she'd revealed she had kidnapped Wen as a baby and left her to die on the Celestial Bridge, but pushing her off as well?

"Hmm?" My mother looked at me. "Oh, yes, I forgot you had your little tantrum and ran off before I enacted my final revenge."

"*Mother*," I breathed out, staring at her. I barely recognised her. Who was this monster with my mother's face?

I stumbled to the other armchair and sat, my head dropping into my hands, the nausea returning ten-fold. What had I done? She was beyond saving. She had *always* been beyond saving, but I had been blind to it, and stupidly come down to Fog to rescue her, propelled by some false sense of justice. *Damn, damn, damn.* And now I was trapped here with her, and with the woman who had created her.

The guilt at leaving Wen to rescue the woman who had tried to kill her multiple times stabbed painfully at my heart. I should have stayed. I should have stayed and faced the ramifications. Wen would have needed me. Needed her *sister* – and I had abandoned her, just like she believed she had been her whole life. The sob burst out of me; I couldn't stop it. Wen had discovered everything she knew about her life was a lie... just like mine. Fates, why had I not recognised her pain? Because I had been too caught up in my own. *Wen, I'm so sorry I left you!* I was sobbing openly now, not even caring that my mother and grandmother were witnesses to a grief they could never understand.

I should leave. Leave my mother and grandmother to their strange and deserved banishment. I had no appetite for ever becoming like them, now I knew what they truly were. And to think I had felt sorry for my mother! I'd pitied her! Now I could only pity myself, and the situation of my own doing...

But, my heart whispered, *if you had never come, you never would have met Blade, the one person who made your blood hum with an ancient knowledge.* I sobbed even harder at that, at what could never be. Even if I'd thought we could somehow have made it work, I had abandoned him too. Just like I did with everyone.

"Good grief, Salomé, is she always so dramatic?" Sybilla's voice snapped me out of my shocked haze.

I stood on wobbly legs. I couldn't look at either of them. "I want to go back to Nos," I said.

My mother and Sybilla fell silent for a moment.

Then the room filled with laughter that took on a hysterical edge.

"You came to Fog of your own free will; Taranis will not let you go now," Sybilla told me.

My blood thundered in my veins. "But I was not taken as punishment – I'm not part of the boon he claimed!" Or had I just been fooling myself? Could I really leave if I changed my mind?

"Oh, my sweet darling child," my mother said patronisingly. "Any citizens from the Twin Realms are immediately imprisoned if they so much as set foot here. Taranis is most particular about keeping Fog for the Fogians. Why do you think he rounds up the skilled? So they can't escape and plot against him." She clapped a hand to her mouth as Sybilla shot her a furious look.

My dismay at knowing for certain I *was* trapped faded in the face of my mother's revelation. Interesting... So Taranis feared them. A Fate feared something? Very interesting. I could use that. Blade and his group could use that. My resolve and purpose returned to me. If I was stuck here, then I would make it count.

I sucked in a breath, swallowed down the last of my tears, and looked at my mother with clear, determined eyes. "Then I would like to go to bed, please. I have a fight to win tomorrow."

"That's more like the Eva I remember." My mother frowned. "Although I do not approve of the fighting – not at all ladylike." She linked her arm through mine, and I had to steel myself to not wrench my arm away from her. I had a role to play now. "It's not so bad here; you'll get used to it and endure, and there is the ball to look forward to."

Sure, Mother, everything can be solved by a ball, I thought sarcastically. Although I supposed it might be a good place to do so more reconnaissance – see where the power lay. Hmm… now I had a fight to prepare for, a ball to attend, and a message to Blade and Maxen to somehow send.

As my mother walked me over to a door and into a small bedroom, I hoped Maxen would forgive me for abandoning him. I was getting pretty good at that lately, I thought, disgusted at myself.

My mother pecked my cheek, said, "There's more clothes in the closet. Sweet dreams, darling," and left me alone, pulling the door closed behind her.

My hand trailed up my cheek to the place where she had pressed her lips, but there had been no warmth there; I felt as though they were poisoned barbs instead. I was tempted to scratch at my skin before the figurative tendrils hooked their way in, to bind with Taranis's 'darkness'. I refused to let either it or my mother's madness take root. I was not the sum of their deception. I refused to succumb. I refused to be what they expected.

I was Eva Celestri, and I would finally find my purpose.

Blade came to me in my dreams. It was my vision, expelled from my subconscious, but overlaid with the delicious haze that only dreams can evoke, where you are free to indulge, free to follow your heart and not bleed from the consequences. The vision expanded, changed, and I floated across a dancefloor of clouds dressed in a confection of a gown that shifted and swirled like a thunderstorm. Hands spanned my waist, twirling me around. His face hovered inches from mine, and I lost myself in his loving green gaze. I cupped his face in hands adorned with bejewelled stacked rings and tipped with silver nails, taking my time, memorising every inch of his handsome face. I craved to press my lips to his, but I knew, with a burning in my veins, that if I did, he would vanish – as insubstantial as the mist cloaking us. So I guided us instead into a dance, a slow-stepped rise and fall. The music was our heartbeat, our pace our breath. I wished it would never end.

But it inevitably did.

I awoke with tears soaking my pillow.

I dressed slowly and methodically before braiding my sheet of hair into my favourite training hairstyle: three long braids, one either side of my head and one from my crown. I bunched them together at the nape of my neck and twisted them into a combined knot. Smiling grimly at myself in the mirror, I looked at the trousers I wore – the ones I'd wanted to wear the day before. My mother could have no objections today, I was sure. I paired them with a tight-fitting top – wearing loose clothing was just asking for it to be used as a grip-hold. I strapped my dagger in its sheath to my thigh, tucked one more into my boots, and stooped to rifle in my pack.

I sat back on my heels as I found Maxen's knuckle gloves. He must have inadvertently stowed them in my pack. I allowed myself a moment of sadness as I thought of my friend, before offering up a silent thank you to him. These would definitely come in handy; I slipped them into my back pocket. No need to put them on yet and give Warne a heads-up. I found my retractable staff and grabbed that too. That was where my true strength lay.

I had resolved to win now; I had no intention of letting Warne carry on his persecution of the skilled, and so I would have to play to my strengths.

Unbidden, a memory swamped me: Wen spinning out of reach as I taught her to fight, using dancing as a way to add some much-needed balance and agility to her skills.

I'm smiling because I think I'm getting better at this, she'd said, and I'd replied, *I hope so*, because I hadn't wanted to lose her... and then I'd lost her anyway. Damn it all. I gripped the staff and strode to the door, intending to fuel myself and get down to the arena to warm up.

Sybilla sat at the table, sipping a drink. She watched me approach over the rim of her cup. Lowering it, she gestured at the chair opposite her. "Your mother is getting ready, so now might be the perfect opportunity for us to have a little chat. Get to know each other, as it were."

I had no inclination to get to know her, but humouring her might afford me some vital information about her life here. I sat, poured a cup of the dark drink, and took a sniff.

"It is tea – quite bitter, but has a lovely smoky aftertaste that is quite pleasant," Sybilla said, taking another sip of her own. "You are honoured, Eva, that Taranis has taken an apparent liking to you. You would be wise to accept your place here and not try to cause... ripples."

I set my cup down without drinking and chose my words carefully. "You must allow me some time to adjust. My whole life has been turned on its head. I have no wish to be Taranis's new toy, but I will do what I must to survive. Isn't that what we women in this family do?" I couldn't help the cynical bite that sneaked in at the end; I was tired of everyone telling me how I should behave. Why couldn't I just be me?

Sybilla set her own cup down in its saucer with a snap and gripped my wrist. "We come from a long line of Solian nobles. Despite your Nosian appearance, the blood and its ambition runs in your veins too. Do not forget that." She released me with a smile that was in stark contrast to her frosty eyes. "Now, you will allow Captain Caligo to win this fight. You will act as a demure, biddable female, and accept your role as Princess of Fog."

Everything inside me revolted at the insinuation that all I would ever be was a pretty, empty-headed female who sat at the side of Taranis. Meek and meaningless.

Sybilla must have seen my revulsion. "*Think*, Eva! Do not allow anyone to see your true potential or strengths. How do you think I managed to survive in this place? Not by fighting and railing at every turn. There are other ways to wield your strength. Displaying it out in the open is not the way."

I grabbed one of the pastries and started shredding it on my plate, trying to make sense of her words. Was she truly trying to help me? If I allowed Warne to win, he would be free to walk the streets of Fog, his ego inflated, and his desire to do more of Taranis's bidding would only increase. I certainly didn't want him to be my personal guard, but I had concluded that it might well be a case of keeping your enemies closer. I narrowed my eyes in thought. *Keep your enemies closer...* Coming to a decision, I pasted an obedient smile on my lips and aimed it at my grandmother.

"Very well." Let her think I had capitulated; let them *all* think that. I could bide my time. It wasn't as if I was going anywhere.

I forced myself to eat the pastry and drink the tea as Sybilla sat back in her chair in satisfaction.

"Good morning, darling, Mother." My mother wafted out of the bathroom dressed in a tight-fitting trouser suit in a shade of light grey. Her hair had been pulled to one side and anchored with a clip bejewelled with shards of a dense black gemstone. "Have you eaten?" she asked.

I gestured at my empty plate, and she smiled in a parody of motherly concern. "You will need your strength for today."

Sybilla frowned at her. "Don't be silly, Salomé; she is going to lose, as we discussed last night." She set her cup down and pushed it away, but I saw the look of consternation on my mother's face.

"I know we discussed it, Mother, but I know Eva – she never gives in." Was that a touch of *pride* I heard in her voice? "She's stubborn, just like her father."

Ah, no – not pride, then. But if she thought I was like my father, I would take that. I would rather be like him than her, any day. I only wished I'd realised that days ago.

"She *will* lose." Sybilla stood. "If she knows what is good for her."

My mother shot me a look, something flickering

behind her eyes.

"Don't worry, Mother. I've got this," I said with an arrogant, slightly condescending smile. A smile she should recognise. I'd learnt it from her.

She pursed her lips, then nodded. "Fine. But if you get a bruised face I will not be happy."

Oh yes, Fate forbid I look less than perfect for the ball.

"Shall we go?" I asked innocently, retrieving my staff. They might want me to throw the fight, but I would not go down easy. I would just give them a glimpse of what I was capable of.

Sybilla looked at me sharply, but I simply smiled at her.

"Hmm. Yes, let us go." She took my arm, resting her other on my mother's, and with a swirl of smoke we left behind our rooms.

Seventeen

I opened my eyes and saw we had arrived at a circular arena surrounded by a high wall, beyond which sat tiers of seats. This was no Nosian training yard.

"What is this place?" I murmured, deciding not to ask my mother and Sybilla how they had managed to transport us by smoke. I assumed it was a 'gift' from Taranis, but was interested in how it worked. I put it away to ask at a later, more appropriate time.

Sybilla cast me a disconcerting smile. "Oh, Taranis puts on a bit of sport to keep the citizens entertained."

"Keep them in line, you mean," my mother said, a moue of distaste on her red lips.

"What do you mean?" I asked, dreading the answer.

"Oh, well, let's just say that Taranis obliges the skilled in their desire to use their skills. He lets them use them… on each other."

"What? That's barbaric!" I thought of poor Flint

being forced to use his weather skills to defend himself, and anger filled me, hot and fierce. My mother shrugged in disinterest.

Scanning the room, I watched as the seats slowly filled around us with Fogian citizens. Well, if it was a show they wanted, it was a show they would get, but the only skills I would be using were the ones I had earned and honed. I flicked my wrist, and my staff extended and clicked into place.

"Eva," Sybilla said in warning, and I forced the anger down. I met her eyes coolly.

She nodded and took my mother's arm, directing her to a set of steps leading up to a box above the arena. No doubt Taranis would soon arrive and join them. I waited on the arena floor, wondering when Warne would show his face.

The double doors at the other end of the arena opened, and he sauntered in. He wore tight leather trousers and a long-sleeved top tucked into them. Boots were laced up to his knees, and a sheath was strapped to his thigh. From across the arena, he met my eyes. I tilted my head up and twirled my staff around, enjoying the fleeting faltering look in his green gaze.

The chatter around the room diminished as I sensed that now-familiar tension in the air, and I knew Taranis was about to arrive. I turned my back on Warne, looking up to the box where my mother and Sybilla were sat. There was a misty ripple, and then Taranis was there between them.

He looked down at me, and then beyond to where Warne stood. "You will fight until one yields or is incapacitated. No fatal blows."

Hmm. That gave me a lot of scope for fun and

games. I bowed my head in understanding, then turned. Behind Warne, I noticed that members of the Fog Guard were posted at the doors, but they weren't Taranis's personal guard; these looked to be the boots-on-the-street kind. I took a closer look, and my heart stuttered as I recognised Kane – and Dag.

I expected to see anger on his face, but he stared back impassively until I saw a flicker of something else behind his eyes. He was worried for me. There was no way news of this fight wasn't getting back to Blade and Maxen.

I didn't have time to worry about that. A clang filled the air, and Warne rushed at me with a roar.

Eager much? I neatly side-stepped, and he barrelled past me. Fates, this should be a walk in the park, but I was supposed to throw the damn fight. And I would... later. I spun around as he came at me again, but this time he had reached down into his sheath and pulled out an extending staff of his own.

I grinned.

Our weapons met with a thud. Warne pushed forward, seemingly hoping to get me off-balance, but my ballet lessons had given me exquisite control over my body, and I planted my feet before pulling my staff back and twirling away. My grandmother didn't want me to fight, but I would do it my way. Elegantly and crowd-pleasingly. I wanted to help these people, so I needed them to believe in me.

I whacked my staff against Warne's thigh as he misjudged the distance between us, and he let out a growl.

"Do you want to know why I didn't tell Taranis

about your friend?" he hissed as he circled me.

That threw me, and I faltered. He swiped my legs out from under me; winded, I looked up at him from where I lay flat on my back. "Why?" I wheezed.

He leant over me, using the staff to pin me to the floor. "Leverage," he said with a mocking smile.

I'd underestimated him. Frustration at myself surged through me, and I scissor-kicked my legs, propelling him off me. Briefly, as I lunged backwards away from him, I caught a glimpse of Dag staring, his eyes wide. I forced myself not to react. I didn't want Warne to realise I knew him.

"What do you want?" I demanded as I rushed Warne, who stepped back out of reach.

He watched me for a moment, as if planning his next move. "Tell me where Blade took you, and I'll keep your friend's identity a secret."

He was asking me to choose between Maxen and Blade. Fates above.

"Not going to happen." I used the end of my staff to jab him in the stomach. He doubled over, expelling a large breath, and I stole his legs out from beneath him. Immediately I straddled him on my knees, my staff across his neck. "I'll let you up," I hissed, "but no mention of either Maxen or Blade."

His eyes shot daggers at me as he struggled. I saw the light dimming in his eyes, so I eased the pressure slightly.

"*Agree*," I growled.

His eyes flashed, and something built within them, like tiny electrical flickers. *What the…?*

Suddenly, I was ejected from him as if I'd been shocked by lightning, my staff flying from my hand.

Warne had kicked at me at the same time, so it took me a moment to register what had actually happened. Was he *skilled*?

I blew out a breath and stood on shaky legs to look around the arena, but no one seemed to have noticed anything abnormal. Warne came at me again, this time with fists raised.

I dodged the first blow, but took the second in my ribs. "You're skilled!"

"What are you talking about?" he hissed as I staggered away.

"I saw it… I *felt* it!"

A nervous look crossed his face, and he glanced around the arena. I realised he must be used to hiding his skills. If he was found out he would be locked up, and used as nothing but entertainment fodder.

With another roar he came at me and grappled me, but that was exactly what I wanted. As he leaned in to twist my arm back, I sneered, "You're a traitor. I bet the other skilled would love to get their hands on you."

He met my eyes.

"Leverage," I whispered sweetly, but couldn't help a gasp of pain as he pulled my arm up higher, almost dislodging it from the socket.

With a noise of disgust, he let my arm go, still holding on to me, so he could speak without anyone realising. "I won't mention your friend" – I raised an eyebrow at him – "*or* go after Blade… if you keep your mouth shut."

I shoved my fist into his ribs and watched his eyes dim in pain, smiling in triumph. "Agreed."

He grabbed the twisted knot of hair at the back of my neck and yanked my head back. "But you yield. I have no wish to be your personal guard."

I rolled my eyes. On that we were in agreement.

"Fine," I muttered, but took great delight in bringing up my knee and stopping it only an inch from pain. His eyes widened, but I dropped my knee and called out breathlessly, "I yield!"

He let me go. I dropped to the floor on my hands and knees and kept my head down, keeping up the pretence that I was struggling. I breathed in and out slowly, taking stock. I would have some bruises and my shoulder was burning, but I could have kept going easily. Warne didn't need to know I had planned to throw the fight, but it had all worked out to my advantage. I knew his secret, and he would keep mine.

Dimly, I was aware of the cheering and stamps of feet filling the arena as Warne's triumph was celebrated. Fates if that didn't sting more than my shoulder. I kept my head down for a few more moments. I didn't trust myself not to reveal how disgruntled I was.

When I did rise, I made sure to do so facing Dag. I needed him to see my face, needed him to see I was truly all right – otherwise I had an inkling that Maxen and Blade would try and force their way in, despite the danger to themselves.

I stood and rolled my shoulders back with the merest of winces, catching Dag's eye as I put a hand up to my shoulder. I gave him the tiniest nod, hoping he would understand. Belatedly, I realised that Kane had caught it too. His eyes narrowed between us, and I turned away.

I found myself face to face with Taranis.

"You fought well," he said, his dark eyes lingering on mine, "but I am pleased to see that my guard has indeed been trained thoroughly. Captain?"

I let out a sigh of relief as he turned his attention from me to Warne. He didn't seem to suspect that I had deliberately lost the fight, or that Warne and I had been discussing matters other than how much we wanted to hurt the other.

"You have been promoted to a member of *my* personal guard. You shall be working in the Tower. I have need for more loyal guards such as yourself," Taranis said imperiously, evidently believing he was bestowing a great honour onto Warne.

I had to hide a snort as Warne's eyes widened in dismay. Apparently I hadn't been the only one who had made assumptions about exactly what reward he would be given. He had obviously hoped for a promotion within the Fog Guard and freedom to lord it over the unassuming citizens – but it seemed that he would get to wear a neat little uniform instead and spend his days watching closed doors and decorating the great hall's perimeter. He should have elected to become my personal guard. At least I would have made it interesting.

He caught my eye, and I *almost* hid my delighted grin. He couldn't react; Taranis was waiting for his response.

"I am honoured, my lord Taranis." He bowed his head.

"Indeed. Your father will be very proud of you. Now, go and get cleaned up and report for duty this evening at the ball."

"The ball is tonight?" I blurted out.

Taranis turned to me, his cold face impassive. "Yes. I have invited the upper echelons of Fog. You shall see what it is to be favoured by a Fate such as I."

The words fell heavily around me as his dark eyes probed mine. I didn't want to be favoured by him. I wanted the cool stillness of Nos; I wanted the moonbeams to caress my skin. I wanted to beg Arianrhod to tell me that my existence was not in vain, that I was *her* daughter, a daughter of Nos, not born of the darkness of the Fate before me.

I felt myself falling into his eyes. He had claimed me, and I would never get the chance to speak to Arianrhod. The connection had been severed, and the loose tendrils sought something else to anchor themselves to.

I pulled out of his thrall, and the tendrils snapped back.

"I look forward to it," I said, and saw a flicker of surprise cross Taranis's face.

"Then I shall see you, Salomé, and Sybilla later." He inclined his head and vanished.

I sagged. Warne and I stared at each other for a moment before he turned on his heel and stalked away, Kane and Dag pushing open the double doors for him. Dag spared me one quick look, then he and Kane followed Warne out.

"What was that? I told you not to reveal your full strength." At Sybilla's outraged voice, I spun to face her while the room emptied of spectators.

I laughed in spite of myself. "You think that" – I gestured around the arena and at myself – "was me at my full strength?"

"Disrespectful, foolish girl," Sybilla hissed. My

mother slid smoothly between us, her hands up in a placatory gesture.

I lost my patience. Stepping around my mother, I snapped back, "I had to make it look *believable*. What did you expect me to do, cower at his feet? Cry and beg?"

"Yes! You should have given them" – she threw a hand out to the now-empty stands – "what they expected to see. A pampered Nosian young lady terrified to be in Fog, but grateful for Taranis's leniency."

"Well, Captain Caligo still won. I don't see the problem." I shrugged, then winced at the burn in my shoulder.

"Because, *granddaughter* dear, Taranis was testing you. Seeing what you could do, looking for weaknesses, chinks in your armour... ways to perhaps use you." Sybilla's blue eyes flashed. My mother was watching the back-and-forth with eyes cloaked in apprehension. "You should have yielded straight away. Now, he thinks you will always try and fight if backed into a corner."

"I'm no match for a *Fate*." I pointed out, not understanding her point.

"But you could inspire others with your tenacity. Give them hope. It only takes one," Sybilla said.

All it takes is one spark... My mind flickered with possibilities. Could I inspire the people? Could I light a fire beneath them? Sybilla had unintentionally given me information that I could use.

It was all starting to come together. Free will was important, Taranis feared the skilled, and I could be a beacon of hope. Yes, it might only take one spark, but I couldn't do it alone. A flame needed fuel.

I blinked as Sybilla took my arm. "You will present a demure face at the ball tonight. You will show your support for Taranis, and will not under any circumstances mention your desire to return to Nos."

"Why not?"

"Because you do not want to put yourself in a position where Taranis offers you a deal." Sybilla smiled tightly. "You might just find you are willing to take it." I scoffed, but she shook my arm. "You have no idea what you might be capable of doing, or agreeing to, when it comes to the people you love."

I didn't, for one moment, believe that she or my mother were capable of real love, but I believed the truth behind her words. I'd seen the aftermath of what they had done in the name of their supposed love.

I just hoped I would never have to find out what *I* might be capable of doing.

Eighteen

Sybilla took us back up to our suite of rooms.

"I'm going to take a bath," I said, but my mother followed me into the bathroom and slammed the door behind us.

She met my eyes with a livid gaze. "Eva, could you *please* not antagonise my mother? She is liable to take it out on me!"

I turned on the hot tap and peeled off my clothes.

"Are you even li…" She trailed off as she stared at my torso, now covered in a multicoloured bloom of bruises. "What even possesses you to take delight in an activity where you end up like this?"

"Because it's fun, and—" *It was the only way to get you to pay attention to me.* Old habits died hard, it seemed. All the dance recitals and official events where I'd been on my best behaviour, and she'd never even raised a smile or a word of praise… but fight until I was black and blue, and I got her full attention. Then she would spend hours in my room, slathering on lotions and creams, demanding Alys 'fix' me, so that I would be back to the beautiful miniature version of Salomé Celestri: a Nosian extension of herself.

With a huff of disgust at how easily we'd slipped back into our old roles, I stomped to the door and opened it. "Don't worry, I didn't get any on my face," I said sweetly.

"You are impossible. Clean yourself up, but don't take all day. We all have to beautify ourselves." My mother swished past me.

Gratefully, I closed the door after her and turned the lock.

I soaked my bruised body until I felt slightly better. Physical pain didn't bother me; it was the emotional pain I resisted. At least I had bought Blade and Maxen some time. It was a stroke of luck that Warne hated me to the extent that he'd allowed his emotions to get the better of himself and reveal the secret he hid. Now I held something over him. I would keep his secret, and in turn no one would be after Blade and Maxen. I just had to find a way to contact them.

I pondered on that. It seemed guards were allowed in the arena. If I could get down there and get a message to Dag next time he was on duty, that might work. But how would I do it? If only I had the magic that Taranis had bestowed upon my mother and Sybilla – then I could *poof* in and out.

I would have to earn that right. The ball tonight might present an opportunity for that. With that thought at the forefront of my mind, I pulled myself out of the bath.

I had left my hair in its braids and didn't bother to

wash it again; I would leave it loose in the soft waves that would result from the plaits. Wrapped in a towelling cloth, I exited the bathroom, and – ignoring Sybilla and my mother, who were lounging in front of the fireplace in the armchairs – made my way into my bedroom and pulled open the closet.

I rifled through the dresses and found one that was a grey so dark it was almost black. It reminded me of the dress Wen had worn at the Fate's Day Eve ball. When I had done a spectacular job of almost ruining everything *again*.

I sat down, hugging the dress to me. It was made out of layers and layers of a gossamer net and sparkled like the stars through the mist. I would wear it, I decided. Wear it and be a better version of me – better than the one I had been at that ball.

Oh, Wen. I need you *now. Your strength, your perseverance, your love despite it all.* I curled up in a ball on the bed, still in the towelling cloth, the dress falling in a heap to the floor. It billowed out like a cloud, and I closed my eyes.

I had a sudden urge to hide away, so I did in the only place possible. Slumber.

"Head up, Eva. Goodness, what *has* happened to your posture?" As we arrived in the great hall, my mother pressed her hand on my spine to straighten it. I bit back the hiss of pain and the acidic retort that perhaps having an almost dislocated shoulder and bruised ribs did not aid good posture.

The dress was strapless, leaving my neck and shoulders bare. It covered most of my bruises, except for the one on my shoulder, but I'd hidden that one with my sideswept swathe of hair. I'd paid particular attention to my makeup, lining my grey eyes with a dark glittery sweep and slicking a plum-coloured lip gloss onto my lips. The full skirt of the gown brushed the top of my silver stilettos. It was the closest I could get to Nosian fashion without it being a pointed statement. Inside... inside I was dreaming of dancing beneath star-strewn skies with the man I lo—

I stumbled on my heels. Where had that thought come from? There was no man. There could be no... *love.*

My mother shot me a look at my clumsiness as we headed to the raised dais. We were the first to arrive, but a handful of Taranis's personal guard were already stationed around the room.

It had been decorated with floaty strips of pale grey silken fabric billowing from the ceiling, and large urns of strange, shimmery, white-grey flowers with spiky vines trailing from them were positioned around the edge of a dancefloor. A group of musicians was setting up on a platform nearby. The semi-circular table and chairs that had been in the room previously had been removed, and smaller clusters of chairs and tables were dotted around the perimeter. Each table had a tall slim candle in a pewter holder, throwing off an intimate light.

As I took my seat, my eye landed on a particular glowering guard. I waggled a lazy hand at Warne, and his lips tightened. I hoped this wouldn't be the only entertainment I would find tonight.

My mother noticed my mocking wave. "Eva, do not deign to interact with the help. You are above them. We shall find you a suitable consort amongst the guests."

"*Consort?* No way, Mother." Was she out of her mind? I'd barely arrived, and she was already bartering me away. If I *were* to take a consort, I would choose my own, and he wouldn't be found within the Tower. My thoughts trailed away to a pair of arresting green eyes and a flirtatious smile. *Stop torturing yourself, Eva.* "This is not Nos – I am not some bargaining chip for you to use to further your social standing. We're in Fog!"

"I am well aware of where we are. We will all have to make sacrifices if we are to survive here." She spoke through gritted teeth frozen into a welcoming smile as guests began to filter through the doors.

"You would do well to heed your mother, Eva. We may be in a different realm, but the rules of the game are still the same." Sybilla inclined her head at a couple passing by.

"This isn't a game," I hissed.

"No? Are we not but pawns on the gameboard the Fates set up? They have been making their moves and counter-moves for millennia."

"Well, I wish Arianrhod and Belenos would take out their opponent," I muttered, but too low for either of them to hear me.

The music started up a lively tune, and without warning this time, Taranis suddenly stood on the dais before us. *That was close.* A second earlier, and he might have heard me.

He turned to me and held out a hand. "Daughter?" he said, a mocking lift to his eyebrow.

I swallowed and my mother gripped my arm, her

nails digging into my skin. The painful incentive mobilised me into action. I stood in a graceful, fluid motion, accepting his hand. I had to fight against the visceral reaction deep within my soul which told me to get away from him. Far away.

Taranis led me through the guests, many of whom had looks of adulation on their faces as he passed them by. It made me sick to my stomach, but I put on a pretty smile and allowed him to escort me onto the dancefloor. He took me in hold, and as the music swelled around us, we danced. I tried to keep my gaze just above his shoulder. I didn't want to fall into his dark, fathomless eyes again.

"Are you recovered from your injuries?" he asked as he spun me around in a dizzying circle.

"Oh, yes, thank you," I said breathlessly.

"As I said before, you fought well. But I am curious as to why you did... fight?"

I looked into his eyes at that. "My lord?"

"I sense a stubbornness in you. One that tells me you won't be intimidated... and I wonder if that applies to everyone you encounter? That no matter the size or *power* of your opponent, you will not yield."

"But I did yield," I said, a prickle of unease seeping down my spine, as if ice-cold fog poured from the fingertips clasping my uninjured shoulder.

"But *did* you?"

"I said the words. I yielded."

"Words, yes, but your actions told me a different story. You see, Eva Celestri, we Fates are very good at hearing what isn't said, at unpicking the lies in the body language while the mouth professes truth. You are a mystery: one I intend to unravel. And I shall have your whole bestowed lifetime to do so – perhaps a mere snap of the fingers for me, but an eternity for you." He spun me around again, his other hand tightening on my waist, his fingernails aggravating a bruise.

I hissed in pain, and he smiled.

"I'm no mystery. I simply came to save my mother, but I see now that she should be here," I said.

He narrowed his eyes. "You believe she *should* be punished?"

"This is hardly punishment," I said lightly, looking around.

For a second the room dimmed. Lightning sparked around Taranis; fog spewed up around us, wherein shadowy figures waited. *Shadowwraiths*, I thought with a shudder. I held my breath as they moved infinitesimally closer. My grip on Taranis tightened and he let out a low laugh, but I could not see him; I could only orientate myself by the feel of his form beneath my fingers.

I gasped, and suddenly everything barrelled back in. He smiled a cold, cruel smile. "Punishment hovers on the edge of my will. Remember that." He spun me away from him. "Now go and enjoy yourself."

He glided from the dancefloor. The moment he left, couples took to the floor. I stood uncertainly on the edge, watching Fogians dancing in slinky dresses or suits comprised of cropped jackets and tapered trousers in shimmering hues of charcoal, pale-grey and silvery-white. As they blurred around me, I nibbled on my lip. I didn't know what my next move was supposed to be.

"Would you like to dance?"

Awareness flowed over me, and everything within my body stood to attention. I knew that voice — recognised the way it rippled over me, caressing and soothing my soul. But I couldn't turn around. If I turned around, he would vanish. He couldn't truly be here. It would be impossible.

"Eva."

"You're not here. You can't be."

A hand brushed mine, and I spun around.

"You *shouldn't* be here," I said in a whisper. I stared at Blade, and he gave me a tender smile.

"Neither should you." His hair had been pulled back into a long tail, and he wore tight grey trousers and a silky fog-grey shirt that moulded to his chest. The jangling nerves left over from the dance with Taranis smoothed out by merely looking at him.

"How did you get in?" I asked quietly, throwing a wary look around at the guards manning the walls.

He pulled me into his arms and set us dancing, my breath catching in my chest at his proximity. "I wangled an invitation."

"Don't be flippant," I said. "How?"

He smiled, and it did nothing to help my breathing. "Warne. Whatever happened during your fight—" He broke off to frown at me, indicating that we would be revisiting that later. "Well, it made him stop hunting me down like a ratroach bug. I gave him back his precious bow and quiver, and in turn he helped me get in here."

"You couldn't resist another dance with me?" Now it was my turn to be flippant. A little frisson of happiness rippled through me that he had come to me.

He spun me around, and his gaze steadied on mine.

"I would risk everything to be with you," he said, his voice intense.

As before with Taranis, the ballroom seemed to fade away, but this was fuelled by a different emotion to fear – one where we could just lose ourselves in each other's eyes and the motion of the dance. My dream came back, until I couldn't separate what was wishful thinking and what was reality. I cupped his face, and in that long moment I forgot I was surrounded by Taranis's acolytes and guards. It was just Blade and me.

His hand tightened on my shoulder beneath my hair, and I flinched. His eyes darkened as he brushed my hair aside and stared at the bruise.

"I'm fine," I said hurriedly, but anger still flashed across his features.

"I should kill him for putting his hands on you. But I've seen what you can do... no doubt he's equally as bruised, if not more."

I grinned. "Of course. It was worth it." My voice turned husky as he met my eyes again.

I had no idea why I was acting like this. Where had my resolve gone? Yet the danger made it all the more crucial that I simply enjoy this moment. Because if this was all I was to have, this one moment of pretending that we could, together, be something more than we were apart, then I would take it.

I gave myself to the dance and laid my head on his shoulder. I could have stayed like that for eternity.

But of course, it wasn't to be. Instead, a very unwanted, but familiar voice, made me falter in his arms. "And just who is this handsome young man?"

Why could I not have just one moment?

Please, I thought. *Don't spoil this for me too.*

Nineteen

Blade released me, and we stepped apart. I shot him a warning look, but he looked over my shoulder with a friendly smile on his face.

"My lady." He bowed to my mother, whose avid gaze, I noted as I turned with a deep breath to face her, raked over him.

"Mother."

She didn't even spare me a glance; her eyes were all for Blade. I could see her calculating look and knew it did not bode well, for me or Blade. "Won't you introduce me to your new friend, Eva?"

Damn. I couldn't use his actual name, surely?

"Master Stone, my lady," Blade said smoothly, and I bit my lip.

"You would do perfectly," my mother said, giving me an approving look.

"For what?" I said, dreading her answer.

"For your consort, of course. He is handsome, looks strong, and obviously he is of good standing if he has been invited." Was I mistaken, or did I detect a mocking look in her eyes?

I looked past her to the dais where Taranis and Sybilla sat, but both of their gazes were locked on us, standing at the edge of the dance floor. They had all no doubt seen our intimate dance. Fates, had I revealed too much?

Reacting instinctively, I laughed. "Don't be silly, Mother," I said, not looking at Blade – I could *not* look at him. "He's not my type at all."

My mother searched my face, but I put on the mask that concealed the true me, and she raised one perfectly arched eyebrow.

"Hmm. Well, you had better pick someone soon, or I shall." She waggled a hand at Blade before turning on her impossibly high heels and sauntering away.

Fates above. I looked at Blade, but his face was an impassive mask too.

"I had to save you," I said helplessly, and a chink of emotion broke through.

"You can deny it all you want – to yourself, to others, to the whole of the realms – but I hope you realise it before it's too late," he said cryptically, and turned to leave.

"Wait! I have information."

"Not here," he whispered. "Meet me out on the terrace in ten minutes."

"The terrace?"

He jerked a head behind him, and I saw a pair of glass double doors that I hadn't noticed previously. I nodded. He gave me one long look, then turned on his heel and vanished amongst the dancers.

I went the opposite way, heading for a table that had been set with refreshments. I picked up a tall, narrow flute and took a discreet sniff. It smelled like some kind of fruit punch. I hoped there was no alcohol in it, as I was in no position to add to my poor decisions that night. My stupid mouth had already said words I couldn't take back. I hoped Blade knew that I hadn't meant what I'd said. Of course he was my type; my blood burned with the knowledge that he was my *only* type. But I could never act on it. I would never allow him to be used as a pawn in this hideous game.

I sipped the drink cautiously, but it merely refreshed me, so I continued to drink it, avoiding the interested glances thrown my way by smartly dressed young men. They were here because they were champions of Taranis, and even if any had piqued my interest, that fact alone would have deterred me. As it stood, I feared my heart was no longer my own to command.

As soon as I judged enough time had passed, I glanced at the dais. It was surrounded by a group, shielding me from sight, so I slipped around the edge of the dance floor and headed for the terrace doors.

"Joining your boyfriend, are you?" a snide voice said. Warne was now stationed to the right of the doors.

"Don't be crass, Captain Caligo, I am merely overheated," I said as haughtily as I could manage.

His lips twisted in disbelief, but I merely carried on through the doors and kept walking across the tiled floor.

The terrace was actually a wide balcony, surrounded by tall plants in pots along its metal railings. I walked to the far end and stared out over Fog. The grand hall must have been halfway up the Tower, as I could see over the perimeter wall and beyond to the circular rows of buildings and streets of the city.

The back of my neck tingled, and I knew Blade had joined me.

"Is Max all right?"

"He's understandably angry, Eva," he said, leaning on the railing next to me but keeping in the shadow of one of the plants.

"I had to go. Or at least I thought I did at the time," I said.

"But you don't now?"

I turned to look at him. "I made a mistake in thinking my mother could be saved, *wanted* to be saved, but I'm still glad I came. I can be of use to your cause here. Did you know he makes the skilled fight each other in the arena?"

Blade nodded grimly. "Why do you think I do this – we do this?" His hand moved closer to mine on the railing, and my skin began to tingle even though millimetres still separated us. "But I don't want you to put yourself in danger, Eva. This… isn't your fight."

I moved my hand to his and covered it. He jerked beneath my touch. "I just made it my fight."

He stared at me, and the air between us began to thrum. His other hand snaked up to bury itself in my hair, and I couldn't move. I should have pulled away; I knew I should, but I couldn't. My traitorous body and heart worked in tandem to thwart my common sense, and as for my resolve? It melted away once I fell into his green-eyed gaze.

As if one, we moved towards each other, our lips a whisper apart.

"I knew he was your type, you sly girl."

I jerked backwards, my eyes wide. *No, no, no –* this could not be happening. I stood in front of Blade as if I could protect him, but I knew things had moved beyond that. Giving into my emotions had only led to pain. Why had I not heeded my own warnings? I wasn't sly; I was stupid and naïve.

"Come with me, both of you," my mother commanded.

"No."

My mother's blue gaze turned glacial. "No?"

"Not this time, Mother. Just let him go. Find someone else to torment."

She tried for an innocent expression. "Torment, darling? Oh no – I merely want to make you happy! To make your life here filled with fun and excitement."

I stared at her. Was this what she thought my life should be – an echo of hers? Find a man to manipulate, stand with those in power, and go to an endless stream of balls and parties, all beneath the haze of that month's favoured drink?

"I want more than that, Mother. I want purpose. I want to know I did some good, and not just lived an empty, vapid life."

She narrowed her eyes. "You forget yourself, daughter. *I* moulded you. *I* shaped you, not your father – me!"

"And what have I become?" I stepped forward and squared up to her. "I am nothing. I have nothing... thanks to you."

I sensed Blade move behind me, his hand brushing my back. *You have me*, the touch seemed to say, and oh, how I wanted to believe it. But I dared not. I could never have anything that was truly mine. Not without my mother's blessing. Why did her blessings always seem like a curse?

A moment of frozen silence fell between us, until with one violent move, my mother slapped me hard across the face. My head snapped back. I didn't even feel the sting of her nails raking across my cheek; I was too numb. Blade pulled me away and placed himself between us.

My mother smiled a slow, shrewd smile. "So it's like that is it? Perhaps you won't do after all."

Why, because he sees you for what you are? Because he wouldn't be easily manipulated?

"Just let him go," I said wearily.

"I won't leave you here," Blade said through clenched teeth, and I groaned.

"Thank you, Master Stone," I said pointedly, "but it was just a silly misunderstanding between mother and daughter."

My mother trilled out a laugh. "Oh, my darling, I taught you well."

"Don't call me darling," I snapped.

"What, then, shall I call you?" My mother spoke slowly and maliciously. "Daughter of darkness? Child who owes her very existence to Taranis?" She flicked her eyes to Blade, and I felt all the blood drain from my face. "The Fate who now deems her the princess of his realm?"

"No…" I trailed off as Blade turned stunned eyes on me. "That's not true. I am a daughter of Nos, born of a Twin Realms' Union!"

"But not a true Fated Union, *darling*..." My mother pursed her lips as she looked at me with false sympathy.

Tears streamed down my face. Why was she doing this? I reached out to Blade, but he stepped back, holding up a hand as if trying to process my mother's words. The heart that had been trying so hard to beat to his rhythm stuttered at the thought that he might truly believe I was all part of Taranis's master plan.

"I had no part in it, Mother. It was all you – you, your sister, and your mother. Wen and I were innocent babies, born into a treachery of *your* doing." My fight came back to me. If I was going to lose whatever tentative bond Blade and I had been building, then he should at least know the truth. I looked him in the eye, willing him to understand. "Yes, Taranis orchestrated my parents' Union, but they *are* of the Twin Realms. *I* am of the Twin Realms, and whatever darkness is perceived in me, it's *her* doing. From her evil heart, and hers alone. I chose to turn from it." I stepped to his side, and whispered so that only he could hear. "I chose it when I met you. Now I have a purpose."

"What are you muttering?" my mother demanded, and yanked me away from Blade, who was now looking at me with pity in his eyes.

I didn't want his pity. I wanted something *more*. My blood sang with the words, but I did not recognise the language. I was too frightened to translate them into ones I could understand, because I knew what it would mean for me and for Blade.

We could never enjoy it, because my mother would never allow me to have something that *she* had never had. I could never amount to *more* than her. I was supposed to be her imitation, not her improvement.

"Enough of this," my mother said. "I'm tired of your tantrums and woe-is-me attitude, Eva. We're here, in Fog, and you had better make the best of it, or—"

Whatever else she was about to say got cut off in a shout from inside the great hall. Blade and I exchanged a look and hurried to the terrace doors, my mother tottering after us.

I froze in the doorway as I saw two guards wrestling a young man towards the dais, where Taranis and Sybilla sat. Even from this distance, I could see he had black hair. I shot a terrified look at Blade.

"Is that *Maxen*?" my mother said, rounding us. She wasted no time in pushing through the crowd and making her way over to the dais.

"Oh dear… that's your friend, isn't it?" Warne observed from beside me. I shot him a warning look, and he backed away.

"If you're going to leave, now's the time to do so," I said stiffly to Blade. I felt as though our burgeoning connection had been severed.

He frowned. "I don't abandon my friends." I winced. He shot me a frustrated look. "Sorry, I didn't mean—"

"Don't worry. Apparently we both have a habit of saying things we don't mean," I said with a twist of my lips.

I didn't wait for his reply or to see if he followed me before striding over to the dais, my eyes on Maxen and his bruised face. Had he been caught, or given himself up?

"Ah, here she is. Perhaps you can shed some light on why we have *another* young Nosian in our midst?" Taranis beckoned me up onto the dais to stand beside him.

"Oh, but it is obvious, my lord Taranis. Maxen is a good friend of Eva's; he must have followed her down. He always was very protective." My mother smiled at Maxen, who stared back, but his eyes flicked to mine, and I couldn't help the exasperated look that filled my face.

"Is that so?" Taranis stared speculatively from me to Maxen, as if trying to read our expressions. "Well, I do admire bravery and determination, however misguided. The Celestri ladies are my permanent guests, young man. They have no need of your chivalry." He sent a mocking look around the crowd, who laughed sycophantically.

"Oh, and it seems she has a new protector, my lord." My mother curled her hand around Taranis's arm, and pointed to Blade, who had made his way through the crowd.

"Indeed. Well, what are we to do?" Taranis made a show of sincerely pondering his question.

Excitement lit my mother's eyes, and nausea roiled through my stomach.

"How about a game, daughter?" Taranis drawled.

I tensed. The air had filled with a static crackling pressure. Why had Blade not left? Why had Maxen allowed himself to be caught? Now we were all in an impossible position.

"A g-game?" I stalled.

Taranis pulled away from my mother and clapped

his hands. "The ball is over."

Immediately, the room began to empty of guests. Soon it was just Taranis, Sybilla, my mother, Maxen, Blade and I, along with the guards that held Maxen and the ones stationed around the room.

"Now, where were we?" Taranis took a seat and indicated that my mother do the same. That left me standing on the dais, with Maxen and Blade behind me. I didn't like the direction this 'game' was taking. "I think we should play a game of choose-one."

I blinked. "Pardon?"

"Choose. One."

"I don't understand," I said, sweat starting to bead along my brow.

"It is quite simple. Choose between your Nosian friend, or your Fogian protector."

"I can't," I whispered, pressure building behind my breastbone. Taranis placed a hand up to his ear, so I repeated louder, "I *can't*."

"Well, isn't that interesting?" He let out a resigned sigh. "In that case, perhaps *I* should." He stood, gesturing the guards back with a wave of his hand, and strode to the edge of the dais. His fathomless black eyes swivelled between my friend and the one I hoped could have been something more.

"No!" I shouted.

Twenty

"Ah, so you *have* made your choice?" Taranis turned back to me with a satisfied smile.

I swallowed down my disgust at the situation, but I couldn't show what I was truly feeling. Now was the time for the performance of my life.

I looked at Maxen and hoped with all my heart that he understood why I was going to do what I was about to do.

"There's no choice to make," I said with as much disdain as I could manage. "I told Maxen not to follow me, but like a little puppy, he did."

His un-swollen eye fixed on my face.

"Why not send him back to Nos? Now *that* would be true torture for him." I gave a laugh, and my mother looked at me approvingly. "That way he would have to see Lady Ceridwen and Lord Malakai every single day. Be ruled by them."

I couldn't even look at Blade. I knew I would see disappointment and censure on his face, and it would break me, break the façade I was trying so hard to cultivate.

"She does make an excellent point, my lord Taranis. I never knew why Maxen and Lord Malakai always fought after little goody-goody Wen, when they had my beautiful Eva before them." My mother turned a speculative look on Maxen. "Perhaps that's why you came after her, Master Mercurius – because you realised Eva was the better option all along. I don't know what it is about those Moonshade women and why men hanker after them."

Distaste, dark and acrid, danced along my tongue. She let out her tinkling laugh, the one that I had always admired, but now it sounded harsh and false. Just like the rest of her.

"So you think I should send him back to Nos to face emotional torture there?" Taranis said, looking excited by the prospect.

I turned away from Maxen's gaze. I had to save him. I should never have let him come down here with me. My mother hadn't changed. She was never going to change, and she would never be free. But he could, and this was the only way.

"Come home with me, Eva," Maxen ground out.

Even in the face of his hurt and anguish at the vitriol my mother and I had just tossed his way, he still wanted to help me. But I was beyond help now. I had to see through what I had started down here. *He* still had a chance.

"Do not push your luck, boy. I have considered Eva's suggestion, and I am inclined to agree with it. I have no notion to anger Arianrhod over my part in *physically* tormenting one of her own, and so you shall return to Nos – but if I ever see you in Fog again, I shall not be so lenient."

Maxen straightened, his eyes on me, and for one moment I let my true emotions bleed through the mask. I hoped he saw and understood that I didn't mean any of it, but I also hoped he would find peace in Nos, somehow. He deserved happiness.

Taranis clicked his fingers. With a swirl of fog, Maxen was gone. I sagged in relief, but Taranis's next words froze my blood.

"And now, what to do about you?" He tapped one long finger to his chin as he surveyed Blade.

No, please don't hurt him, I thought desperately. I had hoped that with Maxen gone, Taranis would tire of his little game.

"Why not let her have a little fun with him, my lord Taranis, and keep her biddable." My mother smirked in my direction, and in that moment I hated her with everything I had. "The trick with Eva is to keep her plied with toys and treats, and she'll be on her *best* behaviour. Why not let him live for now, until she tires of him – and she will. The other thing about Eva is that she gets bored very quickly."

I looked at Blade, but I couldn't read his face.

"Is this what you want, Daughter of Fog… is *he* who you want?" Taranis stepped between us, so I could only see his eyes.

With every fibre of my soul. I almost spoke the words aloud, as if Taranis was compelling them out of me. I almost pushed him aside in my desire to get to Blade and shield him from these evil monstrosities.

A vision bloomed in Taranis's eyes until I was falling into it, caught in strong, loving arms. But the eyes… the eyes were all wrong when I stared into

211

them. A haze covered their beautiful green irises, and there was only surface adoration, no depth of meaning, no true emotion. *No*. This was not what I wanted. I wanted the truth, not the lie that Taranis could make happen with one click of his fingers.

With a supreme strength of will, I wrenched myself from the charade. But it wasn't a charade. I came back to the present, to the great hall, to find Blade's arms actually encircling me, the same haze in his eyes.

"No. Not like this," I groaned as Blade smiled adoringly at me.

"A gift. Now go." Taranis snapped his fingers, and when the mist cleared, Blade and I were in the suite of rooms I shared with my mother and Sybilla.

No, not a gift, I thought. A curse.

I pulled out of Blade's arms and walked over to the window, my gown whispering across the floor. This was the second ball I'd been to that had ended in disaster. I stared unseeing out of the window, across the low green light of Fog.

Blade joined me, his hand trailing down my arm, and I turned to him angrily.

"Why can't you fight it?" I whispered, close to tears. "Fight it, Blade, *please*."

He ignored my words and continued his slow trailing down towards my fingers, linking his through mine.

"Maybe I don't want to fight it," he said slowly.

His eyes snapped up to mine, and for the briefest of flashes the haze cleared, and I saw the truth there. This wasn't just an act of compulsion; it was a revelation of what he felt beneath his surface. Taranis's thrall had only enhanced what was already there; something real, something that would span eternity... if I let it.

I was undone. I stumbled back at the intensity, at the knowledge he had handed me. They could not know, they could *never* know, or they would use it against him… against us.

"Blade," I said, creating a distance between us. I couldn't concentrate when he looked at me like I was the only person in the realm. The only person for him. *No, focus, Eva.* "We must save your people. You must break free of this compulsion. If you're nothing but my consort, how can you save anyone else?"

"I don't care about anyone else." The haze was back.

I took hold of his arms and, gripping tightly, gave a little shake. "What about Niara? What about Grenda and Flint? Don't they matter? What if Arianne shows signs of being skilled? Will you stand by and allow her to be persecuted, all because of this faux desire for one person?"

"It's not fake," he said, outrage tinging his tone. I knew it wasn't, but I had to get some real reaction out of him, not this simpering devotion. "I lo—" he began, but I couldn't bear him to make such a declaration under duress.

I clamped my hand over his mouth. "No, Blade!" I shoved him away and marched over to the bathroom.

I locked myself in and slid down the door to curl up on the floor. What was I to do now? Maxen was gone, Blade was gone in any real sense, my mother had revealed her true monstrous colours, and I was nothing but Taranis's puppet.

As Blade knocked on the door, calling for me, I

scrunched my eyes closed. *Arianrhod*, I prayed, hand over my heart. *I need your help, your guidance. Help me; show me I am your daughter, that your starlight is within me… I'm drowning…*

Breath-stealing sobs wracked my body, and I cried until I was light-headed. I actually felt myself floating away, and I welcomed it. Embraced it.

"Eva… Eva Celestri…"

The soft voice stirred me, and I opened my eyes. I stood in the caves in Nos before the statues of Belenos and Arianrhod. A full, glorious moon shone down through the open roof, its benevolent moonbeams caressing Arianrhod's serene face. I fell to my knees, palms upwards.

"Mother," I whispered. "Help me." But the statue's face remained still and beautiful.

My heart dropped. I didn't have the large Moonstone, the one needed to call her forth. So why was I here, suspended between dream and reality? What was the purpose of it? There was a splash behind me, and I turned.

My father and Wen emerged from the cave's pool.

My heart swelled at the sight of them. Forgetting everything that had occurred, I stumbled to my feet and rushed toward them. But they stepped through me, as insubstantial as mist. Or was it I that was nothing but smoke and mirrors? I looked down at my skin and saw that it was almost transparent. Was I a hidden witness to something that was happening now, or a mere echo of what had been?

I glided over to where Wen and my father stood before Arianrhod, and where they had slotted the Moonstone at her feet. They waited poised, as did I, and I watched in wonder as Arianrhod awakened. They all conversed, but to me the voices were muted and indistinct. I couldn't make out the words, but I knew whatever they were, they were devastating to Wen – *my sister*. Her legs gave out from underneath her, and my – *our* – father had to catch her. I had never seen so much emotion upon his face as when he glared up at the Moon Fate. Torn between curiosity and frustration, I waited, trying to fathom why I was being permitted to see this.

Their conversation continued until Arianrhod's face fell still. I wilted, but suddenly she was back again. A few words broke through to my ears this time, and I could have sworn her gaze flicked for a moment onto me. "What you and your Fated Partner do... will ripple across *all* of the realms... Choose wisely."

The words seemed to echo around the caves, and around my head, until they were absorbed into my veins and moved around my body to the beat of my heart. *Fated Partner... Fated Partner... Fated Partner.*

I put my hands up to my head and stared at my father. He was trying to comfort Wen, but the words had obviously rattled her too. She dived into the pool, and for one still, silent moment it was just my father and me. I stepped into his eyeline, believing for one moment that it was me his anguished gaze fell upon. *Comfort me,* my heart pleaded.

But I came back to my senses lying on the cold, tiled bathroom floor in the suite in Fog, alone with only the echo of the words.

What you and your Fated Partner do... will ripple across all of the realms... Choose wisely.

I sat up, knuckling the tears from my eyes. Arianrhod had heard my plea; she had gifted me something without actually telling me directly. Those words were not only meant for past Wen – because something deep down in my soul told me that what I had just witnessed was a memory, absorbed into the caves and activated by Arianrhod herself – but they were also relevant to me in this time.

With a renewed sense of determination, I stood. I wouldn't dwell on the Fated Partner element; I didn't have that luxury, or the bravery, to open my eyes to that possibility, but I would focus on the final part… Ripple across *all* of the realms. *Choose wisely.* My path was still the same. I would do whatever it took to save these people, because in saving them and freeing them from Taranis's tyranny and his Shadowwraith pets, I would free my own people too. Wen's people.

But first I had to free Blade.

I opened the door, and he fell in at my feet. He must have been sitting against the other side of the door, while I had been curled up against my side of it. The mirroring was not lost on me. I stepped back and allowed him room to gain his feet.

He advanced, but I stayed him with my hand. "You wish to please me, yes?" I asked firmly.

"Of course," he said, his eyes dull.

"Then go back to your base." I walked past him, hoping my perceived coldness would snap him out of whatever hold was over him. My mother had suggested I be allowed to keep him until I grew bored of him; well, if I affected boredom, would it break? I had to hope so. If not, well, there were other ways to have him removed.

I tried the suite door, and found to my relief that it was unlocked. I peered out. Seeing that the coast was clear, I beckoned Blade after me, and he followed obediently. *Still enthralled.* We descended the circular staircase down to the next level and kept going. I was intent on finding Warne. He'd got Blade in; he could get him out.

We reached the level of the great hall and I hesitated outside, peering in through the double door's windows. The dais sat empty, and I wondered where Taranis, my mother and Sybilla were. But I was not about to let the opportunity pass me by. I pushed open the door, whispering for Blade to stay hidden, and the two guards who remained in the hall looked up at me.

"Where is Captain Caligo?" I asked imperiously.

They exchanged a look. One said, "He's on break, on the lower level."

I nodded my thanks and left, closing the door behind me. We descended the main curved staircase that led to the lower level of the Tower: a wide entrance hall with many doors leading off it. I made Blade wait in an alcove, then tried the first door, finding a room that looked to be full of guards' uniforms. A second door yielded a command room of sorts.

"What are you doing in here?" an older, moustached guard snapped as he looked up from a desk.

"I'm just exploring the Tower," I said sweetly. "If I'm to be making my home here, I need to know where everything is."

He stood and marched over. "You do not need

to know anything about *this* room," he said, and closed the door in my face.

How rude. I pursed my lips. Third time lucky?

I pushed open the door and found a room dominated by a long wooden table and benches. Guards sat and ate, or played what appeared to be a game using small round stones. Silence fell as one by one the guards noticed me framed in the doorway.

Warne looked up, and I saw the ire in his eyes as he set his fork down slowly. "I'll deal with her," he announced, and stood.

I backed out of the room; he followed me out, closing the door behind him.

"What do you want?" he asked wearily.

"I need you to get him out." I jerked a shoulder, and Blade came forward, his eyes glazed over.

Warne took one look and burst out laughing. "Oh, how the mighty have fallen!"

I was very proud at how I restrained myself from smacking the laughter off his face.

"Get him to safety, Warne, or your little secret will be revealed," I hissed. His eyes narrowed at me. I didn't enjoy manipulating him, but I'd do whatever it took.

Was it my imagination, or did Blade's eyes sharpen again for an instant? But he gazed back at me with that simpering expression, and I shrugged it off.

"Go with Warne, now," I told him. "I'll find you again, I promise." I tried to keep my tone firm and not betray any of what I was feeling. I needed him not to latch onto a thread of weakness.

"No. I won't leave you," Blade stated, and Warne rolled his eyes.

"Warne, now," I pleaded, and turned away. "I don't

care how you do it, just get him out of here. Say you found him after the ball, too drunk to leave. Whatever it takes!"

Warne gave a shrug. He took out a knuckle glove and put it on with slow, measured moments. *Oh, he's really enjoying this.* With one final look at me, Warne ploughed his fist into Blade's cheekbone. I winced.

I made myself watch as the haze lifted from Blade's eyes for one blinding moment, and then his eyes closed as his head snapped back. Warne caught him, threw one of Blade's arms over his shoulder, and half-carried him out of the Tower.

Fates. I had really sunk to the depths of what I would do for the people I cared about. Sybilla was right.

A metallic taste filled my mouth as I turned on my heel, ready to start the long ascent back up to my rooms. I needed to plan.

Twenty
One

I had just stepped onto the first stair when I heard faint shouts and screams coming from a door set further back beneath the staircase.

My heart in my mouth, I hesitated. I really was pushing my luck, but... The guards seemed to be having a break; Taranis, my mother and Sybilla were strangely absent. Maybe this was my opportunity to discover what lurked in the depths of the Tower.

I headed for the door. Inside, a guard stood on a wide platform encircled with metal railings, a staircase leading down. He looked up and held out his sword. The point stopped inches from my throat.

Really? I thought with a sigh. This was getting tiresome. I feigned fear, stumbling back, but at the last moment I dropped and swiped out my leg from beneath my voluminous skirts. The guard fell as he lost his balance, his sword clattering to the floor.

"Thank you," I said, and picked the weapon up. Returning the favour, I aimed it at him. He scrabbled backwards. Green light flickered overhead, illuminating his annoyed face.

"You can't be down here," he panted. "Taranis will have my head."

"I don't think that's the most pressing problem," I pointed out, lifting the sword fractionally higher. "What is this place?" Screams and more desperate shouts filtered up from beneath us; I peered over the metal railings. The stairs seemed to go on and on.

The guard swallowed. "It's where he keeps the skilled."

"Your own people," I said, the words accusing and low, and he had the good grace to look ashamed.

"You don't understand," he spat out. "You weren't born here. They're unnatural, and Taranis says they're a threat to us. All of us."

My anger licked through my blood. "The only threat is to Taranis, and he knows it. Grow a backbone, man. What if one of them was your mother, or your sister... or the person you loved. What then?"

His eyes flicked away from me. In that instant I knew, and it horrified me, turning the anger to grief. "There *are* people you know, people you care about down there, aren't there?"

"I *cared* about, yes. But no more. They are dead to me." He turned his eyes back on me, and I saw the truth there. He really didn't care anymore.

I stumbled, the sword slipping in my slick palm. "They're no threat to *you*." Did I really think I could convince him of that? I shook my head, knowing I was wasting my time with him.

I had learned everything I could about the Tower.

Now it was time for action.

"Take off your boots," I said, and the guard raised an eyebrow. "*Please*," I added sweetly, gripping the sword more firmly and pointing it at him. Reluctantly, he did as I asked and tossed them over to me. "And now your uniform."

"What? No way!"

I aimed the sword lower, and he hurried to undo his jacket. Finally, he stood in his undergarments.

"Turn around," I ordered. He glared at me before obeying.

I toed off my heels and pulled on his trousers one-handed beneath my gown, before ripping the gossamer skirt away, leaving the top part. I shrugged into the jacket, keeping an eye on the guard, and zipped it up. Finally, I stepped into his too-big boots and laced them up tightly. I bundled up my skirt and heels and tucked them behind the door.

"Now, how long do we have before you're relieved, and are there any more guards below?"

He turned, scowling. "About ten minutes, and no. Anyone would be a fool to try and break into Taranis's Tower."

Well, I was no fool – reckless, yes, but fool, no – and I wouldn't exactly be breaking *into* it. "Lead the way, then."

In his socks, the guard started down the metal staircase, his own sword at his back offering incentive. The shouts from below had ceased as they heard our descent. I listened for a change in his breathing, indicating he was readying to ambush me, but it didn't change until we got to the bottom. I almost didn't discern the shift, I was so distracted by the rows and rows of cage-like cells running the length of the cavernous room.

He made a sudden turn, ducking low, and at the shouts ringing out from the nearest cells, I just managed to evade his low punch. With a sound of disgust, I used the sword's hilt to knock him out. He crumpled to the floor and didn't move. I knelt and checked his breathing, before turning him onto his side. I had no wish to kill anyone, however deplorable and misguided their ideals. I hoped Blade, I, and the others could evoke a change in that perception of the skilled.

"Nice, lady," a young voice said, and I looked up to meet a pair of bright green eyes peering at me through the bars of the nearest cell.

"Tell me, where are the sewerage tunnels?" I said urgently.

The boy frowned. "Everything seems to run away over there." He pointed.

Thankfully, the area was well lit with tall versions of those glowing white-green stones. No doubt the guards wanted to see the torment on their prisoners' faces, I thought sourly.

I made my way along the cells, meeting the startled gazes sent my way with reassuring smiles until I got to a grate. I pulled it up and looked down with a shudder. It would be a disgusting journey, but it was the only way I could get them out. I gauged that ten minutes had already passed, but no new guard had appeared, so the first one must have lying about that. Still, I had no time to waste.

I made my way back to the first cell. "I'm Eva. What's your name?"

"Roarke," the boy said with an impish smile.

"Do you know where the keys are to the cells? I'm guessing you can't use your skills to get out?" I said, keeping one ear on the metal staircase for the sounds of any booted footsteps.

"Nah. The cells bind us – wouldn't want us living up to what they fear and attacking them," he said. "He'll have one key, and another guard will have another. It takes two to open that cabinet over there for the master keys."

I turned and noted a metal cabinet attached to the stone wall. Patting down the guard's jacket I wore, I located a key on a small metal keyring attached to a chain looped inside the breast pocket. Now I just needed the other one.

As if on cue, I heard the ring of the staircase and a voice yelling down. "Peeter?"

I met Roarke's eyes and placed a finger to my lips; he nodded and gave me a wink. I checked the guard – Peeter, I assumed – but he appeared to still be out cold. Not taking any chances, I dragged him into the shadows and waited there, sword against his chest.

As the other guard descended onto the last stairwell, I slipped underneath it and waited until his legs were level with my arm. I reached through the gap and pulled his leg as he lifted it. With a yell, he toppled forward and landed on the stone floor. He tried to push himself up with a groan, but I was already there, straddling him, the sword at his back.

"Hello," I said, and he twisted his head around.

"You! I saw you in the break room. I thought Caligo was supposed to deal with you."

"He had more pressing matters to deal with," I said.

"Now, key, please."

"You are mad. Have you any idea what Taranis will do?" the guard grunted, trying to push himself up.

I dug my knees in and he stilled. "Key. Please," I repeated, and he huffed out a breath.

"I can't get it if you're sitting on me."

I eased up. As he reached inside his jacket, Peeter gave a groan. Damn.

"What did you do to Peeter?" the guard asked, pulling the key out.

I snatched it off him. "He'll be fine. Now, I'll be needing your boots, thank you."

I backed away, keeping him within reach, so that I stationed myself between him and the slowly-coming-around Peeter. The guard pulled off his boots and made to toss them over.

"Pull out the laces," I instructed. Comprehension dawned in his eyes. "Roarke, how are you at knots?"

"The best, lady," he chirped.

"Excellent." I looked at the guard. "Shuffle yourself backwards and put your hands through the cage."

With hatred burning in his eyes, the guard moved back on his behind and did as I ordered.

"Use one of the laces to tie him to the cell, Roarke, and toss the other lace over," I said. As Roarke worked, I noticed more and more interested eyes moving towards the bars of the cells.

Roarke quickly tied up the guard. At the man's hiss of breath, I deduced the boy had done it tightly. He tossed over the other long lace, and I made quick work of securing Peeter. He glared at me with dazed eyes.

"Do you want to get out of here, Roarke, and back home to your family?" I asked.

The boy nodded. "I don't have a home or a family, I'm an orphan, but I *do* want to get out of here." I fought to keep the pity out of my eyes; he didn't need that. "Not everyone will want to leave though, lady, they'll be too scared."

I didn't want to leave anyone behind, but I needed to be the spark. Hopefully, the inferno would follow. I nodded, then turned to unlock the cabinet.

"You're making a huge mistake," the guard muttered.

"The only mistake I've made is not using one of Peeter's socks to gag you," I retorted, and was rewarded by Roarke's giggle.

With a grin on my face, I pulled out the master keys and unlocked Roarke's cell. He and the other occupants quickly slid out. "Get to the grate," I told them. The two young men and elderly man nodded and moved away, but Roarke stayed by my side. I shot him a look.

"Let me help," he insisted. Touched, I smiled at him.

While I unlocked the cells, he pulled the doors open and urged people on. Another guard was likely to arrive soon, but the cells seemed to go on and on. How many people had Taranis taken?

Most seemed to be happy to leave, but some who Roarke told me had been there a long time shied back against their makeshift beds. One older lady who stared at me with frightened eyes visibly cowered when she looked at me.

"Darkness," she whispered. I faltered, but her hand snaked up to stroke over my hair. "It's like a sky I once saw, full of glittering darkness."

"Come with us, and you may see it again. But we have to stop Taranis first."

"That's all that will come with us, lady," Roarke said softly, joining us. "We'd best go if we don't want to be caught."

I gently took the older woman's hand. "Come with us, please."

She looked deep into my eyes, her own green ones searching. After a moment, she nodded, and Roarke and I helped her up.

Roarke called to the ones left in the cells as we passed them. "Come with us now! Don't be afraid. You've spent you whole lives in fear. Now is the time to take back your power." I looked over at him, feeling inspired. So young, but so wise.

Some tentatively trailed after us, like soft ghosts. We reached the grate, and I helped the woman down into the arms of men who waited there.

"Go on, Roarke, follow the tunnels. Find a way out," I urged after the last person had left.

"No, lady, not until you leave. You risked everything to save us." His eyes glowed with respect, and I stared back along the rows of cells at the ones left behind. What would become of them?

"I'm just Eva," I whispered, suddenly feeling helpless and so terribly small.

Roarke shook his head. "Lady," he said adamantly. "After you."

"But what will happen to them?"

"You can only open the door to the cage. It is up to the bird if it takes flight. Sometimes the bird prefers the safety of the known to the fear of the unknown."

I looked back at Roarke in confusion. His eyes had glazed over, as if he was speaking words that were not his own.

He scrubbed a hand over his face and gave me a sheepish grin. "My powers must be returning."

I looked down into the tunnel. "Are there those who can sense things – like a location, for instance?"

Roarke nodded.

With my mouth like sawdust, I slipped into the tunnel, Roarke after me, and we slid the grate down. I hoped Taranis wouldn't punish those who had elected to stay as his 'guests'.

"Farin, the lady needs you," Roarke called down the tunnel, and from the sea of green eyes, I saw one figure move forwards.

A young man stood before me. "How can I help?"

"I know of a place in the tunnels where you'll all be safe, but I don't know the exact way."

Farin took my hands. "Close your eyes," he said, "and think of this place."

I did as he asked. I had to shove my thoughts of Blade aside to concentrate on his base, and not what would happen when I saw him again.

"I have it," Farin said after a few seconds, and I blinked my eyes open.

"Then lead on."

He sloshed his way through the tunnels to the head of the group of a hundred or so skilled.

I saw more of them taking advantage of their powers returning to them, now they were no longer bound by their cells, as light glowed from many hands as we moved on. My heart hammered in my chest; I cast anxious looks backwards, fully expecting Taranis to suddenly whirl through the tunnels and obliterate us all.

A small hand found its way into mine, and I looked down at Roarke. He squeezed my fingers comfortingly, and I gave him a grateful smile.

"Thank you, Lady Eva," he said.

Tears sprang up in my eyes, and I had to blink rapidly to clear my vision. "Don't thank me," I whispered. "We haven't reached safety yet."

We took a turn, and I noted that the tunnels were cleaner and more familiar. We were close to the base. My heart gave a leap of relief. It didn't matter if Blade wasn't happy to see me; all that mattered was that I had brought his people, and amongst them hopefully Flint's parents. Getting them to safety was what mattered.

We stopped outside the door of the base. I pushed my way through the crowd to the door and gave the knock I remembered Blade giving. I took a deep breath as the spyhole was pulled back.

My breath caught as Dag peered back at me, his expressive eyes wide.

"Uh, Blade," he called over his shoulder. "We have visitors."

Twenty
Two

The door was wrenched open, and Blade stood in my eyeline. He strode to me. With a squeak, I backed up.

"Hey, mister, leave the lady alone!" Roarke muscled in between us. Blade shot him a look, but relaxed.

"Don't worry, little mate, I wouldn't hurt her." His eyes took on that vague, loving look, and my heart sank. Was he still under Taranis's thrall, even now?

Roarke frowned, but I smiled at him reassuringly. "Help everyone inside, Roarke. You're my second-in-command."

The boy's eyes lit up in his grubby face. I still couldn't tell what colour his hair was, it was so matted and caked in dirt.

Roarke and Dag helped everyone inside, and after a few minutes it was just me and Blade on the threshold of his base. He took my arm, and heat shot through the jacket. Together, we entered the base and he locked the door.

"Before we deal with how in Fog you managed to

free all of these people, do I have you to thank for this?" He gestured at his bruised cheekbone.

I swallowed and gave a nervous laugh. "Sorry. You were under Taranis's spell, and I had to break you free. So I enlisted Warne."

"Warne?" His eyes cleared. "I remember bits and pieces — what secret do you have on him?"

I studied his face, but he seemed back to his normal self. "He has skills. When we were fighting, he shocked me — like a mini lightning strike."

"What? That little traitor!" Blade exclaimed, his eyes flashing. "I suppose it's useful to have over him, but it disgusts me how many people he took in, and how much he enjoyed it."

"I agree, but he was obviously terrified of his secret being revealed. He had to keep up appearances." I knew all about putting on a front. "He'll have to make a choice one day; let's hope it's the right one."

"Hmm. Now, how about you tell me all about what happened after I was unceremoniously ejected from the Tower?" He eyed my Fog Guard uniform. "I take it you haven't enlisted."

I smiled at his attempt at humour. We sat at the top of the stairs and looked down across the room at those I had rescued, being cared for by Blade's people. I could tell he felt frustration at not having been able to assist me, but his enthrallment wouldn't have been broken if I hadn't sent him away. I hoped he could see that.

Briefly, I recapped all that had happened, not liking the emotions playing across Blade's face. When I told him about waiting for the second guard he dropped his head in his hands, but I carried on, not leaving anything out.

He lifted his head, and his green eyes raked over my face. He had changed from his smart ball clothes, but he looked as handsome as ever.

Without warning, he put a hand to the back of my head and said, "You are amazing." My skin fizzed at his touch, but I couldn't say anything. "Reckless, daring, but amazing."

I pulled away and dropped my gaze, remembering what I had said to Maxen and how I had dismissed Blade to my mother.

He took my chin and carefully pulled it up so I met his gaze again. "You did what you had to, said what you had to. I see that; Max will see it too."

I shook my head in his grip. "You don't understand what happened before we came down here. Max and I were different people then. I acted like an awful, spoiled, pampered princess. I have to pay the price of that, but Max didn't deserve any of it, and now he has to re-live it. Fates, I'm not amazing, Blade, not even close. I'm an awful friend, awful daughter, and an awful sis..." I couldn't even say it, but it was true. Wen deserved a better sister.

Blade caught what I had been about to say. "You have a sister?"

I pulled out of his grip and stared unseeing at Dag, handing out cups of water. "Don't worry, she isn't Salomé Celestri's daughter – the realms only need one of those."

"Don't do that," Blade said.

"What?"

"For such a 'spoiled, pampered princess', you put

yourself down a lot."

"You have no idea what I've done. Yes, I have a sister. My father and his true Fated Partner had a daughter, born a few months after me – Wen. She's the cause of Maxen's heartache, because she's Fated to another." The words tasted like sawdust on my tongue.

"But I don't understand. What did you do?"

I met his eyes. He would soon see me for who I really was. "I... I *abandoned* my sister, just when we discovered what we were to each other, to come down here to rescue the woman who tried to *kill* her." I added the final, damning detail. "All because... I was jealous. She had her Fated Partner, a loving mother, *my* father... everything I had always wanted. A true family." My voice turned husky as a tear worked its way down my cheek.

Blade caught it on his fingertip. His arm slid around my shoulders and pulled me close. "You're only mortal, Eva. You can be excused for reacting extremely to an extreme circumstance. When you go back to Nos, you can have your true family. They'll welcome you with open arms, I'm certain of it."

But what about you? I wanted to ask. What about this thing that was brewing between us? If I left to find my true family, I might be leaving something equally as important behind. I was brave when it came to fighting, but emotions? There, I was a coward.

"I don't know, Blade. They're truly good people, all true Nosians – Arianrhod's light shines through them. I wouldn't want to taint that."

"You wouldn't *taint* their family, Eva Celestri, you

would enhance it. I see no darkness in you. Don't let Taranis work his mind tricks on you and have you doubt yourself. Doubt who you truly are."

"What was it like... when he compelled you?" I whispered.

"Like I was trapped inside my mind, and what I wanted to say, how I wanted to act, was being guided by another's hand."

"So it was all Taranis?"

Blade captured my gaze. "I thought I wasn't your type."

I flushed. "I had to distract my mother."

"So... I am?"

Damn. The man was good. I laughed, all my tension flowing out of me. In an easy, companionable silence, we looked down into the room.

"So what happens now?" I asked. "Surely Taranis will be after us."

"We should be safe here. He never leaves the Tower."

I gaped. "What, ever?"

"Why do you think your Fates have their Fate's Day? It's the only day they can become corporeal and set foot upon your Twin Realms. The same is true for Taranis."

My mind tried to work through this revelation. "So how can he appear at will in his Tower? Is it not technically manifestation?"

Blade nodded. "Do you remember when we first met and I was adamant about Taranis not getting his hands on you – I said something about him loving having three generations of you?"

A shiver worked its way down my spine. "Yes?" I

said slowly.

Blade scrubbed a hand over his face. "He uses your grandmother and mother as tethers."

I didn't like the sound of that, but I recalled my mother and Sybilla having the ability to travel via the mysterious fog. Was it all connected? "Tethers?"

"To the mortal plain. With your grandmother, his visits were few and far between, leaving his Council and the Fog Guard to run things, but when your mother arrived, he's been able to come down from his pinnacle more regularly. I believe he was grooming you to make the choice to commit yourself to him; another woman of your bloodline would enhance the tethers he had already created."

"I'm going to be sick," I muttered. "How did you figure all this out?"

"Grenda," Blade said. "She showed me some things – things that didn't make sense until your arrival. Why do you think I was waiting for you?"

"So it wasn't a coincidence you were there below the bridge that night? You were waiting for..." I trailed off, our gazes locking.

"You. I've been waiting a long time for you, Eva Celestri."

I believed him. And I, in turn, felt as though I had been waiting for *this* moment. My head swam dizzily. I, Eva Celestri, daughter of the most infamous Fated Rulers in the Twin Realms, had been waiting an eternity to sit in a secret base in the bowels of Fog with a non-noble-born man who was more noble than any I had ever encountered. *This* was where I was supposed to be.

Dare I say it? Dare I be brave, just this once?

Who knew what the morning would bring – whether we would all be discovered and rounded up.

I had stepped to the cusp of my decision when a hammering on the door behind us made us stare at it. Blade sprang into action, hurrying to the door and pulling back the spyhole.

"Niara? Flint!" He wrenched open the door. "What are you doing here? I thought you were going to lie low, with Kane on your case?"

Niara shook her head impatiently. "There's no time. Grenda had a vision. We came to warn you—" She broke off as a rumbling roar sounded down the tunnel.

Flint's eyes widened and he spun around, hands up. I just had a glimpse of a wall of water barrelling down the tunnels before Blade hauled me back and grabbed Niara, who screamed.

"Flint!"

I flinched, bracing myself to be swept away by the tumult, but it never came. I opened my eyes and blinked in shock. Flint stood in the doorway, his hands still up, the wall of water frozen into a swirling, cloudy wave.

A man and a woman rushed past from behind me. "Flint!" they cried, coming to stand beside him.

"Mum, Dad!" Flint shrieked, and through the tension on his face, I saw tears of happiness spring free. Overcome, I blinked back my own tears as I took in their reunion.

"Let us take over now, son," the man said, and took one of Flint's hands, while the woman took the other.

I stared at the wall of ice, and a wisp of a memory came back to me. *What does he want from me? A declaration, a promise? Well, he'll be waiting until Fog freezes over before I reveal what's in my heart…*

Until Fog froze over.

I stared up at Blade. As if he could sense my thoughts, hear my heart beating louder – for him – he moved closer. "Are you all right?"

I gave him a tremulous smile. Flint and his parents pushed their hands out, and the wall of murky ice became crystal clear before exploding in tiny, iridescent flakes of fluffy snow. They billowed around us.

Under the cover of the white swirls, I leaned forward and pressed my lips to Blade's.

He jerked beneath my touch, but it didn't take him long to respond. My soul sighed, and deep inside me I heard a click – a tiny key turning in a lock. The darkness I'd perceived in myself receded, replaced by something far more powerful and alluring. I had surrendered, but it felt more like winning. The knowledge within me glowed. I was cresting on a wave of a thousand stars. I was completed.

We broke apart to Niara saying, "About time." But all I could see was a pair of green eyes, looking as dazed as I felt. We stood in a flurry of powder-soft snow.

"We'll revisit this later," Blade whispered.

"Blade! How did you get my parents out?" Flint said, hurrying over to wrap his arms around Blade's waist.

Blade grinned at me over the top of the boy's head. "You have Eva to thank for it, Flint. It was all her."

Flint let him go and barrelled at me, the force of

his hug almost knocking me over. I squeezed him back tightly, feeling close to tears again.

The man and woman joined us, their eyes shining. "We never got the chance to thank you in the tunnels, but sincerely, you have our eternal gratitude for reuniting us with our boy," the man said. "I am Caelum and this is my wife, Tora."

Flint let me go, and I smiled at his parents. "Eva. I've had the pleasure of meeting your mother, Grenda," I told Tora.

Tora's green eyes twinkled. Her short, pale grey hair was matted and lank, but she radiated happiness. "I am sure she was as equally pleased to meet you, Miss Eva. How can we ever thank you?"

I flushed, suddenly awkward in the face of praise for merely doing the right thing. Blade came to my rescue. Squeezing my hand, he said, "Let's get everyone cleaned up, fed and comfortable, and we can plan our next steps."

I nodded as he locked the door. I suspected the truth of our departure had reached Taranis, and he had retaliated by sending a flood down the tunnels. I assumed it wouldn't be the last of his attempts at revenge.

Niara linked arms with me, and we made our way down the staircase with Flint, his parents and Blade following.

"Woah, Flint, that was immense," Dag said, joining us. "You saved us all."

Now it was Flint's turn to blush. "I've been practicing," he said with a shrug.

Dag ruffled his hair, and his gaze landed on me. I took a deep breath and unlinked my arm from Niara's.

"Can I have a word, Dag?"

He gave a half-shrug. With Blade giving me an encouraging smile, I drew him over to one side so we could talk in private.

"I have no excuses for what I did, Dag. I acted impulsively, single-mindedly, and I used your good nature. I'm so sorry." It had been exactly the kind of manipulation my mother would use, and the thought that I had so easily fallen into that persona made my skin crawl. But going to the Tower had served a many-purposed goal, and for that I would not be sorry. Still, I hated that had meant Dag had been collateral damage.

Dag stared at me, his expressive eyes thoughtful. "I watched you fight; you were fearless. You rescued people that are not your own. You put a smile on Blade's face. You did all this." He gestured around the room. "I forgive the means needed to achieve it."

"Oh, Dag," I said, holding out my hand for him to clasp wrists in friendship. "You and my sister would get on so well. She's such a good person too."

The words had just slipped out of my mouth, but I let them sit out in the open, testing them, feeling them. I had a *sister*.

I just hoped she would forgive me too.

Twenty
Three

I sat on one of the sofas, clean – thanks to the Weather-Wards for creating an abundance of rain for everyone to wash in – and wearing a pair of Niara's trousers and boots and a tunic of Blade's, borrowed from the clothes they kept at the base.

Most of the rescued were sleeping on makeshift beds on the floor. Roarke and Flint had made firm friends, and they, along with the other few youngsters I had rescued, were bunking down in Blade's room. I hoped Roarke would find a home, but for now he was safe here.

Blade joined me and handed me a cup of herbal tea. "Can't sleep?" He and one of the Seers had been on door duty, but had just swapped with Dag and another Seer. We hoped to avoid another surprise attack.

I shook my head before taking a sip of the tea. I looked at him over the rim of the cup, and my stomach twirled at the look he gave me in return. This was the first time we'd been alone since I had accepted what I felt for him. *Since the kiss.* I hadn't dug too deeply about what it meant, but Arianrhod's vision kept sliding into my mind every time I had tried to lie down and close my eyes.

What you and your Fated Partner do…

I straightened and set the cup down on the side table. I couldn't tell him about the vision; I wouldn't put that kind of pressure on him. It would take the choice away from him if he thought that he and I had been ordained. I would not compel anyone to feel something for me they wouldn't otherwise choose to feel. My mother had done that with my father, and Taranis had done that to Blade. I would *never* do it.

And the other reason I didn't want to tell him was that I didn't want him to think that *I* believed it. I had yet to come to terms with the whole Fated Partners deal; from my experience, it was a union hard won, and I didn't know if I was up to the emotional battle. *But, oh, it would be a prize worth winning,* my heart whispered.

Blade's hand gripped mine, and he turned it over to trace the lines on my palm. "There are some who say that these lines can show your future. This one" – he trailed the line across the top of my palm – "is your heart line." He pressed his palm to mine.

What was he saying? That I held his heart in my hand? My own heart started to thud slowly as he lifted our combined hands, turning them so he could press a kiss on the back of my hand, his eyes still on mine.

My breath hitched. "Blade, I—"

"We'll take it slow," he said. "Tomorrow is not promised, but for every tomorrow there is, I will be here waiting." He let go of my hand. "Try and get some sleep."

He stood and walked away, and I felt as if the stars had blinked out from the sky. I settled down on the sofa, my gaze on Blade as he joined a few of his group who were huddled together talking.

My eyes slowly drifted closed as I thought of tomorrow and all the possible tomorrows we could share. If we were lucky enough.

"When is she going to wake up?"

I smiled to myself before I opened my eyes and saw Roarke and Flint hovering beside the sofa. One held a plate, the other a cup.

"Good morning," I said.

"Morning, lady," Roarke said, and offered me the plate. On it was a piece of slightly burnt toast and a handful of berries. He smiled proudly at me.

"Why, thank you," I said, sitting up and taking the plate. "This looks delicious." I rested my eyes on him, taking in his mid-grey hair, now clean and shining and braided into one long tail down his back. The top he wore was too big on his skinny frame, but given time and the right food he would fill out.

"I made you tea," Flint said, not wanting to be outdone, and I took it with my other hand.

"Thank you, Flint."

He dimpled out a smile.

The boys left me to my breakfast. I nibbled and drank while I surveyed the activity before me. I couldn't immediately see Blade, but somehow it was as if I sensed him and knew he was nearby.

He stepped out of his room, pulling a fresh top

down over his torso, and his eyes snapped to mine. His long hair was loose and damp. I nearly choked on my tea. *Fates, Eva, get a grip on yourself.* I forced my eyes down and slowly finished my tea.

"Good morning."

I looked up and he stood before me. I itched to run my fingers through his hair, but instead I smiled and said, "Good morning. Did you manage to get some sleep?"

"I did. You?"

I nodded mutely. The air hummed between us, and I thought we might implode if we didn't put tension into action. We were surrounded by over a hundred people but it felt as though we were alone. I wished we were.

Blade reached down and pulled me up. Our bodies brushed and I took an indrawn breath. He smiled a slow smile. "Later," he promised.

He threaded his fingers through mine and pulled me over to the long table, where most had congregated.

A middle-aged man with dark grey hair in a coil around his head stopped Blade as we approached. "While I'm happy to be out of there, what's the plan? We can't hide down here forever – it's just another kind of prison."

"You're right," Blade said, squeezing my hand before letting go. He took the head of the table, so I hovered to his right. He looked around at everyone, and the chatter around the table ceased.

I saw now why he had left his hair loose and chosen casual clothes. He had made himself approachable – just one of them, the people. They wouldn't see an authority figure, one to control them, but instead someone who would work *with* them to find a viable solution. My respect for him grew another level.

"It's time we took back our realm. Together. Taranis can't leave his Tower – not until the next Fate's Day. He relies on the Council and the Fog Guard to take people *to* him. We must unite our people, stop his power before he can wield it on us," he announced.

"But can we risk it?" a young woman asked, fear shining in her pale green eyes. "If we step foot onto the streets of Fog, we're liable to be snatched up by the Guard or attacked by his pets."

"It is a risk," Blade conceded, "but we've been given a chance. Eva gave you a chance. She's not even from Fog, and she risked everything to set you all free. What do you think Taranis would have done if she'd been caught?" He looked at me, and I saw a brief flash of terror in his gaze.

All eyes fell on me, and I stepped forward. "Blade is right. I'm not from here, but Taranis's oppression is felt even in the Twin Realms. The threat of his Shadowwraiths have long been held over our heads. No, he cannot leave his Tower, but he has found a way to unleash them on our Realm." I stopped, something occurring to me. Perhaps he had been using Sabra as his tether to the Twin Realms – she had, after all, made a deal with him. Hopefully now that had been broken, the Twin Realms would be free of that threat, but I couldn't be sure. "I've given you all a chance, but what we do now will affect more people than just us. Bravery is a choice, and so is doing the right thing."

"Easy for you to say. You can return to your realm,

while we stay here and suffer any consequences!" the older man who had first spoken pointed out.

I sensed Blade's gaze on my face. Did he think I would turn and run if things went wrong? I moved my hand over to where his rested on the table and lightly brushed his little finger. His twitched back, and I sighed in relief.

"I will fight with you." I looked around the table slowly until I landed on Blade. "I will fight *for* you." His face told me everything I needed to know; *he* would fight for them, for us... for our tomorrows.

"I believe the lady," Roarke piped up, earning chuckles from a few people. "I will fight too," he added earnestly.

I focused on Roarke. "You, as my second-in-command, shall be in charge of keeping all the children safe."

His face fell. "I can't fight?"

I rounded the table and crouched down beside him. "Keeping everyone safe is another kind of fighting." I leaned in to whisper, "I don't trust anyone else to do it – it's a big responsibility."

His little chest puffed out, and a proud smile crept across his face. I smiled back at him and went back to join Blade.

"So how are we going to do this?" Niara asked.

"We need to rally the people," Blade said. "I want volunteers to go to strategic parts of the city. Show them that you are free, that you *broke free* of the Tower, and that Taranis did not *break you*. Inspire them to fight back when the Guard come."

"What about the Shadowwraiths?" someone called out.

Blade gave them his slow smile. "Leave that to me."

I looked at him curiously. I knew we didn't have enough of the light weapons to stay a sustained Shadowwraith attack.

"Now, those who are able and willing, fuel up and speak to Dag, Niara and Elianna. They will assign locations. Then we'll come together before the Tower, once we have enough people. Taranis will have to listen then."

I hadn't noticed Elianna previously – she had kept to the background – but now my eyes sought her out. She gazed back at me with something like contempt. While I didn't see us being friends, hopefully we could find a way to work together.

She pushed back from the chair and stepped to one side with Dag and Niara.

"Problem?" Blade said, coming to join me.

"No," I said lightly, not wanting to speak ill of his friend. Pulling him aside, I whispered my most pressing concern. "We don't have enough of the moonflower essence. How are we going to protect people from the Shadowwraiths?"

"Ah, well, as to that. Now, don't get angry, but Maxen's departure to Nos wasn't exactly unplanned."

I narrowed my eyes. "*What?*"

Blade held up his hands. "Your friend is just as stubborn as you are. Is it a Nosian trait or something?"

"Stop stalling," I said through gritted teeth.

"All right." He grinned. "After you left, Max was determined to follow you. Initially I talked him out of it, but then we started putting a plan together. We anticipated that Taranis wouldn't hurt Max; he wouldn't want to anger your Fate. So what would he do with him? We banked on him sending him home, back to Nos. Taranis's will would be the quickest way to get Maxen there."

"And what if Taranis had locked him up?" I was staggered, unable to believe their whole plan had hinged on anticipating a Fate's moves.

Blade shrugged. "We had a back-up plan... you."

I pursed my lips. "Well, of course I would have helped Max escape, but Taranis could easily have hurt *you*. He almost did!" I said, recalling the thrall he had put Blade under.

"That was no hardship, love," Blade said, his eyes softening.

"Don't," I said with a shudder. "That was not how I want..."

"What?"

You.

"Never mind." I blushed. "Let's return to your crazy plan. So, you'd hoped Max would get sent back to Nos, and then what?" Poor Maxen – not only had he had to listen to my harsh words about being tormented by going back to Nos, he had *volunteered* to do so. Once again putting his needs behind everyone else's.

"He was going to find your father and the healer, and get a stockpile of the weapon made up."

"Alys. Her name is Alys," I said softly. I wondered what she and my father would think when Maxen barrelled back into their lives with a tale of Shadowwraiths, a repressed people and a tyrannical Fate.

"Ok. Alys," Blade said, brushing a hand along my arm.

I knew there would come a time when I would have to tell him the whole story, but that time wasn't now. We had more pressing problems to work out. "So how would Max get this massive supply of weapons back down here? Taranis warned him off ever coming back to Fog."

"The how I left to Max's discretion, but I still have a few loyal people stationed in the Guard. They'll ensure he gets back through, and now we have more skilled free, we'll find a Glamour-Shield to change him."

I blew out a breath. "All right. So your absolutely crazy plan worked. You must have had destiny on your side."

"Oh, so you believe in it now?"

"What, destiny?" Did I believe? Had everything been leading up to this, or had I just simply pulled the right strand? Or... did all strands lead to Blade? Perhaps whichever one I had pulled would not have made a difference. Perhaps I would still be here, feeling what I felt, and working with him to help his people. Was that what Grenda had meant – that I would have to make the right choice? A shiver of foreboding trickled down my spine. Perhaps that choice was still to come.

"Hey, I was only teasing," Blade said, and I refocused on him.

"I know." I forced a smile, but he still looked at me with concern. "I'm fine," I told him. "Let's get ready for rallying the people."

He ran a hand through his hair, and I looked sharply at him. "Don't even waste your breath telling me that I should stay here. You saw how that played out last time. I made this my fight, remember?"

He took both my hands in his, and that familiar heat

zinged up my arms. "You did. I wasn't even going to suggest it."

"You weren't?"

He kissed one hand slowly, and then the other. "Nope."

The fight left me. "Oh."

"You, Eva Celestri, are our spark. That first star shimmering through the gloom, giving us hope."

Speechless, I gazed at him, lost in his eyes.

"Come on." He released my hands and gestured me over to the group. "It's time to shine."

Twenty Four

I followed Dag down the tunnels, along with a group of skilled volunteers. Niara, Elianna, and Blade were heading their own groups and had already split off. Each group had a moonflower essence weapon, just in case, but I hoped we wouldn't need them… not yet. Dag and I headed for one of the inner circles of the city, while the others would try the outer circle. We had plans to meet up at the centre where the Tower stood.

My lips still tingled from where Blade had yanked me into a shadowy tunnel and seared them with a burning kiss that spoke of not only tomorrow, but forever. Without thinking, my fingertips trailed up to touch my mouth.

"Eva?" Dag said, and I dropped my hand.

"Are we there?" I asked, moving to his side.

He nodded and pushed open a grate, sliding it up and across. Carefully, he pulled himself up, and thanks to one of the skilled shielding us, we slipped unseen into the alleyway. Dag beckoned us on, and we slipped into what looked like a shopping district.

Dag looked at me with a grin and darted over to a statue. My lips twisted wryly as I saw it was of Taranis. *How perfect,* I thought as Dag climbed up onto the podium.

People milling about stopped as he put fingers up to his lips and whistled.

"Get down from there, Dagatar Diamond!" a voice croaked. "You'll have the Guard after you."

"Let them come!" Dag shouted. "It's time we showed them we won't be persecuted any longer!"

I slipped from the alleyway, my hood up, and the skilled trailed after me. We ranged ourselves around the bottom of the statue, below Dag. One by one, the skilled lowered their own hoods and showed their faces.

"Is that Farin? I thought he was taken in…"

"And Sela, she went two months past…" The voices rippled through the growing crowd.

"What's going on? You'll bring Taranis's wrath down on us all!"

"He thought he could take them in, make them fight each other – their own people – and you all just stood by and let that happen? What if it was *your* child? *Your* husband?" Dag clung to the statue, and his clear voice carried across the street. "Now is the time for us all to come together. There are more groups assembling as we speak. Who will march with us to the Tower? Show Taranis that this is *our* realm!"

I watched the emotions play across the faces in the crowd. Most were fearful, but some were hopeful, some angry.

I lowered my hood, and the murmurs stopped.

Someone said, "It's a Nosian. What are you doing here, girl?"

"Standing with you all. Standing *for* you all," I said clearly. "If you allow Taranis to carry on, he'll only get worse. Soon it won't just be those with a skill – it will be you." I pointed into the crowd. "Or your child. His type of arrogant power will only grow. This is just a game to him. Do not let him win." I strode forward. "Come with us. Take back *your* power."

"Will you protect us if we are attacked?"

I gestured behind me. "We will, and so many more besides. Join us. Fight beside us."

Shouts rose up from the crowd. Some stepped forward; others balked and fled.

Dag looked down at me from his perch and nodded. "Let's go," he said in determined tones, dropping down beside me.

Together with the skilled and the group we'd convinced to come with us, we walked on through the streets, not hiding now. As a patrol of two guards stepped out from a side street, I thought for a second I saw a familiar face in the shadows beside us, but it must have been someone else; we had left Roarke behind at the base.

The guards stopped dead, hands on their swords. "What's all this?" the shorter one asked.

"Either get out of our way, or join us," Dag said.

"Join you?" the guard scoffed.

I grabbed the extendable staff I had got from the base and flicked it open. "The choice is yours."

The two guards looked at the crowd before them, hesitated, then threw their swords down before turning and running. Two members of the crowd scooped up the swords as we passed them and kept going.

Similar events happened with more guards we passed, but a few joined us with smiles, clapping Dag on the back, so I guessed they'd been part of Blade's group already.

We continued until we got near the centre of the city. There would be a heavier presence of guards there, so we slowed, and one of our guards went on ahead to scout.

He came back after a moment. "I saw Blade and Niara with their groups. The time is now."

What had happened to Elianna? She must have been delayed. I hoped her group hadn't run into any bloodthirsty guards.

We merged with Blade and Niara's groups as they surged from either side, and we all made our way to the Tower's perimeter gates. I forced my way over to Blade, who gave me that flashing grin. Niara and Dag joined us, and together we stood at the front.

"Niara!" Kane strode forward from his position at the gates. "What are you doing?" He shot a glare at Blade. "Your influence, I presume?"

"No, Kane." Niara stepped between them. "It's *all* of us. We've all decided that enough is enough. We're not going to hide any longer."

Emotion rippled across Kane's face. "Niara, if you carry on down this path, I'll have no choice but to take you in. Please don't make me take you in." His voice cracked.

"Then join us, Kane. Do it for Niara. Do it for Brienne and Arianne, so they can live a life without fear." Blade gripped Kane's shoulder.

"I *am* doing this for them," Kane said grimly.

"It's the only way I can protect my sister, and my wife and child – by playing the game his way."

"Well, the rules have changed," I said, though not without compassion, stepping forwards to join them. "It's no longer an equal match. Taranis is abusing his Fated powers. He does not adhere to the rules set out between him, Belenos and Arianrhod, and his realm grows dark because of it."

Kane stared at me, obviously recognising me from the arena, while more guards moved up behind him.

One sneered. "Go home, Lady of Nos! You know nothing about us, or our realm!"

I smiled sadly and stepped aside, so I could turn and speak not only to the guards but the people we had brought, too. I raised my voice.

"I know you love. I know you care about each other. I know you would do anything for your families. I've seen it... I've seen it and envied the ease with which you do so, but more than that, I see your strength. You all keep going, despite everything." I let my gaze shift across all the faces: some now friends, some strangers, but all equally as important. "You are not simply the forgotten realm that scars the land beneath Nos and Sol. You are the twilight hours, the shadow across the moon, the haze before the dawn. You are the beauty of everything that is different and unique, and I see you." I looked at Blade. "I see you."

He stepped towards me – but before he reached me, a hand materialised from a cloud of fog and yanked me across the courtyard.

"Pretty words, darling."

"Mother!" I pulled out of her grip, feeling the sting of her nails on my wrist. We faced each other. Her blue eyes were murky, but I recognised the look on her face. It told me she was displeased with me. *Very* displeased.

"Why did you have to go and spoil it all?" She pouted. "Taranis had big plans for us all. We could have been a *family*." Livid now, she lunged at me, and a grey plume of Taranis's power burst from her.

A small figure darted between us. "No! You do not hurt the lady!"

"Roarke, *no!*" I screamed, but I was too late. The smoke hit Roarke's small frame, and he buckled at my feet. "No, no, no," I moaned, and bent to cradle his unconscious form in my arms.

Shouts and running feet surrounded us, but my mother put her hand on my shoulder and shifted us away.

"He's just a child," I shouted, the minute she removed her hand and the smoke cleared. She had pulled us into an alley, out of sight.

"Stop being so dramatic, Eva." She stared down dispassionately at us.

Roarke groaned in my arms. Why had I even thought she would care? She'd taken Wen as a baby and left her on the Celestial Bridge to *die*.

"I need a healer!" I shouted, looking around the alley, but I had no way of knowing how far away we were from the Tower's courtyard. I wondered why my mother hadn't taken me directly there to face my punishment.

"Eva, listen to me," she said, eerily calm now, her rage seemingly dissipated. "I have been ordered to take you back to Taranis, but he is angry, very angry; you must capitulate to him. You must."

"I would rather die," I hissed.

"Then you will, you stupid girl." A whisper of the rage returned. "Let the brat go, or I will be forced to take him too… to Taranis."

I staggered to my feet, the boy still in my arms. I looked her dead in the eye, and for the first time in my life, I completely refused her demands. "No. I'm taking Roarke to find help."

"No?" Her eyes narrowed. "I am your mother. You will do as I say!"

"Those days are over. They ended when you tried to murder my sister – I just didn't see it then." I turned and stalked out of the alleyway.

I didn't for one moment believe she would let me get very far; I probably only had a few seconds while the shock immobilised her. But I had to get Roarke to someone who could help him.

In the courtyard, a fight had broken out amongst our people and the Fog Guard still loyal to Taranis.

"Help!" I cried. "I need a healer!" My voice came out as a hoarse shout, barely discernible over the noise of the fight. To my utter relief, Elianna pushed her way out of the crowd and saw me. "Thank the Fates. Get Blade – Roarke is hurt."

Elianna took him out of my arms, but then her eyes narrowed on something behind me. She gave me a sly smile. "Sorry."

Before I could react, she lifted her booted foot and kicked me hard.

Shocked, I flew backwards and was enveloped by my mother's fog. Elianna had betrayed her people – or did she simply hate *me*? Nausea roiled, dark and greasy, in my stomach as I landed on my hands and knees behind the Tower's gates. Through them, I could see the fight intensifying. Shadowwraiths stepped from a thick blanket of fog.

No! I was trapped behind the gates, separated from those I had come to care for. Where was Blade? My heart thundering in my throat, I remembered the moonflower essence in my pocket. I feigned being winded while my mother tutted impatiently next to me.

I surreptitiously removed the bottle, but just as I was going to un-stopper it, an intense bright light lit up the area beyond the gates. The Shadowwraiths shrank back. I gasped as I glimpsed someone – an extremely familiar someone – standing in the centre of it. It couldn't possibly be... What was *she* doing down here?

I scrabbled to my feet and sprinted to the gates. "*Wen!*" I screamed, gripping the bars.

She turned to look at me, looking impossibly beautiful and poised, her cloud of black and silver curls pulled back into a thick braid, a sword in her hand. Her silver eyes pierced mine from across the courtyard, and I saw what I had been searching my whole life for. Unconditional love.

"Eva!" she cried, and then she was running towards me – my *sister* was running towards me.

"Ugh, how inconvenient. What is she doing here? And is that" – my mother made a noise of disgust – "*Alys?*"

Alys was here? Then that meant... As my mother's hand gripped my shoulder once again, Wen mere feet away from the gates, my gaze rested on a tall figure striding behind her. My father. My father had come too.

But they were too late. My mother shifted us away, and I landed with a thud at Taranis's fog-shrouded feet.

I couldn't believe that what I had wanted for so long was outside, beyond my reach, while I was trapped once again in the Tower. I hoped with everything I had that Blade, his people, and my family could work together, and somehow convince the others to unite and fight back against Taranis's rule.

I knew now what I must do. It was clear as the Nosian skies. I had to try and distract Taranis for as long as I could, while working out a way to break his tether to my mother and Sybilla, so I could send him back up to his lair.

I didn't know if it was even possible, but it was the only plan I had now. And my only chance at getting out unscathed.

Twenty Five

I was roughly flipped over and yanked to my feet. Taranis impaled me with one long fingernail. It drove deep into my shoulder, and I screamed in pain as cold dampness seeped into the wound. He pushed his face close to mine.

"That is *nothing* compared to what I could do to you," he hissed. "I could fill your very soul with the creeping darkness. I could send you to the place where my wraiths wait. They would consume every minute morsel of your starlight."

Starlight? I blinked at him, and he stepped back.

"Salomé, speak to your daughter, please."

Good – so I was no longer considered *his* daughter, no longer a princess of Fog.

My mother moved from Sybilla's side and gripped my arm to drag me away. "Stop this now. You're being a stubborn, spoilt little girl. Not everything can go the way you want it to. Make the choice, give yourself over to Taranis's will, and he will spare you. Perhaps he'll even spare your little friends."

"This isn't about *me*, Mother. Can't you see that?" I stared at her. "This is so much bigger than that."

She smiled a slow, cunning smile. "That is absolutely correct. Once Taranis is powerful enough, he will be able to finally overthrow those other two vain Fates, and rule the Twin Realms too, just as dear Sabra planned. With four women of the same blood united, strengthening and tying him to the mortal realm, he will be *unstoppable*. And we shall be royalty!"

I staggered backwards. So that was why Taranis had taken her – not to punish her or Sabra, but to enact the next stage of his plan. And in taking her, he'd ensured I would follow too. I wouldn't have followed for Sabra, but for my own mother? Oh, Fates. I *had* fallen neatly into his trap.

A still, deadly calm overcame me. My life seemed to flash before my eyes: me sparring with my father, silly grins on our faces; Wen, Maxen and I relaxing below the star-strewn skies of Nos; my mothling, Aruna, stealing frostberries while she thought I was not looking; Alys always being there to listen to my problems when I needed; my training mentor Meuric being impressed with my abilities; my friend Larissa and I going through our dance moves… Nos shifted into Fog, and I was captured by a pair of green eyes and enveloped by strong, muscled arms. My heart broke, piece by tiny piece, as I realised that my final performance had come. The only way I could delay Taranis's plan was to, indeed, make a choice.

A choice to save those I loved, and give them some more time.

I mirrored my mother's smile, and she faltered, then

smiled back. "I'm ready to join you," I told her.

"Oh, darling, you won't be sorry. It's so delicious, the darkness. And you can *poof* anywhere within the vicinity of Taranis. You'll love it." My mother threaded her arm through mine and led me over to where Sybilla waited.

"So, you have made the right decision," she commented. I just kept the fake smile on my face.

Taranis rose from his throne and gestured the three of us over. He searched my face, but I wasn't the mistress of evoking a mask for nothing. Seemingly satisfied, he stood before us. Sybilla took my right hand, my mother the left.

A strange lightness came over me, and I could have believed that I had actually detached from my body and I was floating somewhere high above us. So high, I could reach out and trail a hand through the stars... *What you will do will ripple out through all the realms...*

I swallowed down the tears that threatened and retained my stoic, impassive face. *Oh, Blade, we never even had a chance.*

Taranis took Sybilla's hand, and was just reaching for my mother's when the great hall doors burst open. My mother and grandmother kept their grip firmly on me, but I turned and watched in disbelief as Blade, Maxen, Wen, Kai, my father, Alys, an unfamiliar blonde girl, Dag, Niara and *Kane* raced in – weapons raised, a large crowd behind them.

Blade's eyes locked onto mine, and I tried to tell him everything I wanted to say to him, everything I wanted to say every day for all of our tomorrows, in that one look.

My mother let out a delighted cackle. "Oh, look, darling, your father has come to witness your metamorphosis. How charming." Her voice turned harsh. "He betrayed you, Eva, just like he betrayed me. Use that knowledge and embrace the darkness." She shot a glance over at Taranis and nodded.

I dragged my gaze from Blade over to my father. All I saw there was love – love for *me*. I wanted to correct my mother, to rail at her that it was *she* who had betrayed us, but I had tugged on this particular strand and now I had to see it through. I shuttered my gaze. I had to save them.

"Eva, no!" Blade shouted. He must have seen the resigned grief come across my face.

I sensed the movement from the crowd, from him, from my family, but Taranis gripped my mother's hand. A blanket of fog erupted between us and those who would try to save me.

I gasped as pain engulfed me, mingled with a suffocating sensation as fog poured up my nostrils, into my mouth, and blinded my vision. It worked its way slowly into every tiny cell, every beat of my heart, every drop of blood, smothering and penetrating the very essence of *me*. I resisted the urge to fight it, to repulse it, for I knew I had to take in every last drop of it into myself.

I perceived the sharpness of my mother and the hard edges of Sybilla, and, tenuous pull by tenuous pull, I drew their borrowed dark energy in too, so incrementally that I hoped they wouldn't notice what I was doing. They were so caught up in the exultation of the extra power now being poured from Taranis into me to combine us all that they weren't aware – not until

I had pulled every last tendril of it into myself, into the very core of my mind, my being. I didn't know if my body would be able to survive three times the amount of power. But I had to do it, had to break the tethers between Taranis, my mother and Sybilla – even if it consumed me.

My body convulsed, and for one glorious moment I was darkness itself. I revelled in it, like a purring cat. I could see myself, how powerful I could be; with one flick of my finger, people would kneel before me. I could have anything, *be* anything, and I would never be alone or betrayed again!

That is not you, Eva Celestri. Those are your mother's thoughts, working their tricks on you. Remember who you are.

The serene voice penetrated my thoughts, and I commanded control of my weakening body to battle through the dark fog and search for its owner. *There.* A glittering, luminous presence stepped from the murky shadows and bestowed a benevolent smile on me.

"You perceive a darkness in yourself, but you must understand one thing." Arianrhod paused, and I felt the ghostly touch of a gentle hand on my arm. "Without the darkness… you cannot see the stars." I looked at the vision of her, hope blooming somewhere deep through the fog in my heart. "You *are* a child of Nos; the flicker of a newborn star grew in your heart the moment you were born."

She stared at me. "Do what you were born to do. *Shine.*"

I inhaled. Arianrhod's vision receded, and that was when I felt it – the fervent probing of my mother and Sybilla, trying to claw the power I'd stolen from them back into themselves. Searching within myself, I located the tiny flicker of the star Arianrhod had told me was all mine. I teased the tiny spark until it flickered like a flame and grew and grew.

My mother was strong, but Sybilla, it seemed, wanted it more... so I gave it to her.

With an almighty push, my light erupted. Every drop of the fog was expelled in one supreme rush, pooling back into an unprepared Sybilla. I felt her painful shock, just before the connection shattered violently.

"*No*," Taranis roared as I came back to myself. "It is too much for one mortal to take in one go!"

Sybilla wrenched out of my grip as she crashed to the floor. Her hair had turned grey, and her eyes were black pits like Taranis's. *That would have happened to me, if not for Arianrhod.*

"*Mother*," my own mother screamed, dropping my hand to rush to Sybilla's side. I backed away, equal parts horrified and satisfied by what I had done. Taranis's tether to my mother was broken, but Sybilla still feebly held on, and whatever was within her was keeping Taranis anchored.

She shuddered with the force of it all, but I could see it was overpowering her, weakening her, as it had me. Taranis turned livid black pools upon me and took a menacing step towards me, but I no longer felt afraid. I had a glow within me now – one that was all mine.

The fog curtain flickered and then parted temporarily, and in that lull Blade leapt through and gripped my hand tightly in his. He searched my eyes.

"You're glowing," he said in awe, and despite the danger of Taranis's wrath, he seared my lips with a fierce kiss.

Shine. Our connection lit me up, and I felt as though I could call forth Arianrhod herself. A different kind of tether: a mutual one.

"Well done, clever daughter."

The soothing voice came again, but this time from outside of my mind. Blade and I pulled apart, though he kept his hand in mine. Arianrhod was *there*, standing between Taranis, Blade and I.

She smiled at me, her eyes luminous, and lifted a graceful hand upwards. She sent up a glittering shower of light; a resulting shimmer arced down, and Belenos was beside her, his fiery mane of hair lighting up the whole room. The blanket of fog dissipated, and I saw my beloved friends and family and the Fog citizens, still in the room. Relieved eyes ran over me and Blade, and I smiled.

"How dare you? This is *my* realm," Taranis blustered. My mother's sobs turned into incoherent mumblings as she shook Sybilla, who had stopped shuddering and lay still, her chest moving slowly up and down.

"You did not show our realms the same courtesy, so forgive us if we arrive uninvited," Arianrhod said in her soft voice.

"Oh, but we *were* invited, Ari, dear." Belenos turned his bright gaze on me, and I inclined my head in acknowledgement.

"What? But how?" Taranis stormed, shooting me a livid glare.

Arianrhod joined me and Blade and laid a gentle hand on my arm. "You thought you had outsmarted us by orchestrating an Un-Fated match, but we have long known that this day would come. In your shortsighted arrogance, you forgot one teeny, tiny detail." Her voice firmed, and she shared a look with Belenos. "*We* guide the Twin Realms and all who dwell within them. Did you really think we would not know that the Pairing was wrong, somehow? And that when we sensed a child being created – a child both of Nos and Sol – did we not step in and ensure she was of our light, and not of your darkness?" I felt her pride like moonbeams over my skin. "She is born of both night where the stars flicker, and of the sun that is but a star. She glows with truth; she saw beneath your lies… and she will eclipse you."

"She has *already* eclipsed you." Belenos gestured to Sybilla and at the dark residue seeping from her – too much for her body to contain – and slowly, insidiously, creeping back to its master.

Taranis looked down in distaste and shuddered as his dark fog was absorbed back into himself. He shot me a look. Did he sense the depth of my hatred for him? Could he feel it, like spiked, star-shaped barbs, as it poured back into him? I hoped so. I lifted my chin.

To my surprise, he returned it with an incline of his head. "You were a worthy opponent, Eva, daughter of darkness, daughter of starlight. I cede this round to you." He vanished in a swirl of smoke.

My mother slumped beside the shell of Sybilla, the pair of them appearing to be in a numb kind of stasis.

"Taranis is now untethered. He has been forced back to his lair, and you shall be safe from his wraiths," Belenos boomed. "But be warned, it is only until the next Fate's Day. That day, he will become corporeal and be able to move freely around his whole realm. No doubt he will spend his time plotting and scheming.

There are some who will remain loyal to him, and will have ways of communicating with him, just as you in the Twin Realms do with your Moonstone and Sunstone."

"Indeed. You" – Arianrhod bestowed a luminous smile on me and Blade – "shall have to work hard to unite your people before his next onslaught."

"*Our* people?" I said with a shy smile at Blade, who gazed steadily back at me.

"Oh, daughter, look within your heart. Embrace what you know is the truth." *What you and your Fated Partner do… will ripple across all of the realms… Choose wisely.*

I smiled at her then, finally understanding what it all meant. *Accepting* what it all meant. I looked at Blade. "Later," I mouthed, and his eyes lit with an answering promise.

Belenos had turned to survey the crowd waiting before them, most gazing at him and Arianrhod with awed expressions. "There are some unusual mortals here, Ari. I sense they have more of the *other* in them."

I stiffened, knowing he meant the skilled.

Arianrhod's gaze passed over my family, and her smile turned beatific as she took in a beaming Wen and Kai – the latter's arm slung over her shoulder – then my father and Alys, clutching hands, before a slightly speculative glance settled on a tense-faced Maxen and the blonde-haired girl. Perhaps I had imagined it, as she moved on and nodded.

"They are special. I sense Taranis had something to do with it."

Gasps and murmurs rumbled through the crowd,

and I felt Blade tense beside me.

"Oh, you have no need to fear us," Arianrhod continued. "You are blessed, unique. I believe Taranis once again miscalculated. He thought he was imbuing his people with skills he could utilise, perhaps against the people of *our* realms. He did not fear you all. He was not rounding you up because he felt you were a danger to himself… in truth, he feared Belenos and I finding out *about* you, and so wanted to hide you until he had figured out how to use you against us. But in doing so, he created enemies of you. Knowing how to treat the mortals of his realm was never his strong suit.

"In gifting you these skills, he broke one of our most fundamental vows. We three laid them out together. Gifts, skills, powers, can and do occur naturally in mortals, but we are not to directly interfere in their creation. Our job is to guide our mortals *if* they request it." She smiled at me. "Although we can protect one of our own if another Fate threatens them. We each have our realms, and you are our children to protect. Taranis has behaved abhorrently to you all. We will not add to that by removing the skills that have become intrinsic parts of you. But" – she gave us a warning look, her eyes firming briefly – "we will step in if our people are threatened by them."

Taranis had threatened *my* existence, thinking I would be born of his darkness, but Arianrhod had stepped in to protect me. It was appalling that Taranis didn't respect his own people enough, but hopefully now they would see they were better off without him, and could see they had nothing to fear from the Twin Realms or their benevolent Fates.

"You're right! We must work together to ensure our

safety and freedom!" someone called from the crowd, and I saw it was Tora.

Arianrhod and Belenos smiled in satisfaction at each other. "I believe that is our cue to leave, Ari," Belenos said.

She nodded and lightly touched him. He smiled respectfully around at us all, then disappeared in a sparkling glow.

Arianrhod looked at me. "You must release me," she said. "I was able to come this time, but tethering is dangerous in its continuity. So I suggest that if you need me in the future, to call me in the old-fashioned way. You know where the caves are, of course?" She gave an elegant wink, and I recalled the vision I'd had of her and Wen and my father in the caves, where she had bestowed upon me a secret message.

"I know where they are," I said with a smile.

I closed my eyes and located the shimmering link between us. I carefully separated it, and with her whispered "Goodbye, daughter of the Three Realms" echoing in my mind, I opened my eyes to stare into Blade's eyes.

Into my Fated Partner's eyes.

Twenty Six

"I told you... you are amazing." Blade threw his arms around me and lifted me off my feet, finishing with a long kiss. Cheers and whistles vaguely reached my ears, rushing back in as we pulled apart.

A pointed cough behind me made me turn slowly.

"Um, hi, Dad," I said, and Blade snapped to attention.

"Sir," he added.

I let my gaze trail over to an amused Wen, who stood just behind my father, the biggest smile on her face.

"*Eva*," my father said, and suddenly I was wrapped in his arms, his comforting scent surrounding me. "Oh, my precious, brave girl."

I almost buckled in his arms. How could I ever have doubted his love for me? He hadn't swapped it over to Wen; it had simply increased to include her. I had been so blind.

At motion and a scream of rage behind me, I whirled to try and pull my father out of the path of my livid mother. Propelled by her anger, she launched herself forward in a burst, grabbed the dagger from Blade's thigh, and thrust it towards my father's heart.

"No!" I screamed, and kicked her hand away at the same time as Maxen rushed in. The blonde girl was suddenly there, yanking Maxen back, and the blade narrowly missed impaling him. Instead it cut along his torso, and he let out a yell.

Alys rushed in to join the blonde girl and together they caught Maxen as he fell, while I, Blade, my father, Wen and Kai all subdued my mother. Wen wrestled the dagger from her hand, a look of intense satisfaction on her face, while the rest of us pinned her bucking, writhing body.

"You'll all pay for this!" she howled, tears of outrage squeezing from her eyes.

"We have already," my father said grimly. "Now we're free." He pulled her up, and locked around.

"Allow me, sir," Blade said, and removed a length of rope from inside his jacket.

My father nodded and pointedly turned his back while Blade and I secured my mother to the chair that had once been her throne of sorts. Sybilla, a vacant expression on her face, was given the same treatment. She appeared harmless now, but I didn't think it wise to take the risk.

I stepped back, distaste burning my mouth. These women were supposed to be my family, but they didn't know the meaning of the word. I turned my back on them too, and faced my *real* family.

I hurried to Maxen's side and took in his white face, before catching Alys's eye and offering her a tentative smile. She carried on applying a poultice to

Maxen's wound, but her eyes had warmed. The blonde girl hovered over Maxen, and I noticed that he wouldn't meet her gaze.

"I'm sorry I left you. I'm sorry for what I said to you," I said, taking Maxen's hand and giving it a squeeze. "And I'm sorry that, in coming once again to my rescue, you got hurt."

He winced as Alys started to bind his wound. "Don't worry about it, Eev, I understand the reason behind it."

I threw a furtive look over my shoulder at Wen watching us, a wary expression on her face. Kai turned from speaking to my father to draw her into his arms.

I spoke quietly to Maxen. "You're a far better person than I am. How did you cope with…?" I trailed off.

Alys stood and gave us some privacy. The blonde girl trailed after her, a worried look on her face.

"*They* are the least of my worries," Maxen said cryptically. Perhaps he had resolved to put whatever he had felt for Wen away, but I was still amazed at his stoicism. "Can you do me one favour?"

Anything, I thought, after all he had done for me. "Yes, what?"

"Keep her away from me."

"Who?" I followed his gaze as he stared at the pretty blonde-haired girl who had joined Wen and Kai. "But who is she?" I refrained from adding, *she just saved your life, by the way.*

"Tesni," he said in unreadable tones. "Lord Malakai's *sister.*"

"Oh. *Ohhh,*" I said, recalling her from the bridge, when she had tried to halt proceedings on Fate's Day. Now I knew why. She had wanted to stop her brother and his Fated Partner from killing each other. I took in

Maxen's face and wanted to press the issue, but didn't dare. His face had taken on an impenetrable, stony expression.

"I'll do my best," I promised, and stood.

Dag and Niara came in and helped Maxen to sit up, offering him some water. I exchanged smiles with them and went in search of Blade, needing to speak with him before having a much-needed reunion with Wen.

I found him with Kane, who said, "I was just telling Blade that we've rescued the remaining skilled from the dungeons. They'll all be fine. Roarke will be too; the healers got to him in time. Elianna confessed her actions. She wanted to pay you back for what you did to Warne."

"Warne?" I said, feeling torn between relief that Roarke and the remaining prisoners were all right, and outrage at Elianna's misguided attempt at revenge. "You mean she and him…"

Kane nodded. "It appears so. She's in love with him, but thought nothing could ever come of it because of her being in a secret rebel group and him being in the Guard. But they're out there now, talking. It seems Warne has had a change of heart as to where his loyalties lie." He shrugged. "In light of that, I just want to say – you were right. I will stand with you and Blade."

He bowed and left us. I stared after him in bemusement.

"He's a good guy," I mused. "But I shall be having a little chat with Elianna at some point."

Blade nodded grimly. "You and me both, but yes, Kane is a good man. He just needed a bit of motivation, and your speech worked wonders." He smiled and ran a hand over my cheek. "I see you," he whispered.

I closed my eyes, and he dropped his forehead to mine. We stood like that for what felt an eternity. I could feel our connection growing as our heartbeats started beating in sync. Our breathing slowed and matched, and with a clarity felt deep in my soul, I knew I had found everything I had ever dreamed of.

"I believe."

"In what?" Blade said, a smile in his voice.

In you, in us, in the power of family, that there will be many more tomorrows...

"In Fated Partners."

At the hushed declaration, I felt his heartbeat speed up again. He lifted his head, and I rose my eyes to his.

"Is that so?" he said, lightly, but I heard the hope pushing through. "And in whose particularly?"

I lifted his hand, palm up, and pressed mine to it, connecting our heart lines. "*Ours*," I whispered. "I love you, Bladen Stone."

His eyes swam with emotion. After a long breath, he said, "I've waited an eternity for you to say that, Eva Celestri."

"And I will *continue* to say it for eternity. But let's start with tomorrow."

"To tomorrow, my love, and every day after that." He claimed my lips in a soft, infinitely tender kiss that ignited the star within me until it gleamed. In that kiss we pledged ourselves to each other, and everyone around us bore witness to another Fated Partner Union being declared.

Undeniable. Irrefutable. The truth shining amongst

all the lies that I had told myself. I *was* worthy of love, and I would bask in its light every chance I got.

Wen and I sat together, knees bumping, on the wide staircase that led down from the great hall. Preparations were being made for my mother and Sybilla to be taken back to Sol and imprisoned there. They were deemed too much of a risk to stay within Taranis's realm and reach.

"So, Blade, huh?" Wen said with an eyebrow waggle.

I giggled, delighting in this new, confident version of her. She had truly come into her own, and I could see what the love of a true partner could do. I had that fortunate experience to look forward to myself.

"He wore me down," I said with one of my old arrogant smiles, and she gave me an elbow nudge.

We looked at each other and burst out laughing. The laughter faded away as our gazes sobered.

"Wen, I——" I began, but she focused a stern expression on me.

"Don't you dare apologise, Eva Celestri. You had *every* right to act as you did, and I do not blame you even one teeny tiny bit for trying to save your mother. You had to try; I understand that. We all react in unexpected ways to unexpected events. I'm not proud of how *I* acted, either." She frowned, lost in painful memories. "When I discovered Alys was my true mother after the Fate's Day Eve ball, I ran away, too mired in the grief of her apparent abandonment. Then you came and found me. I *knew* you were my sister then, but I was too afraid, too ashamed, to tell you. I didn't want to lose you."

Tears sprang up in my eyes as I remembered us outside the caves. I had comforted Wen, and in that suspended moment I had been the sister she needed, though I didn't know it. I would never regret that, or chastise her for not telling me. She'd acted the only way she thought she could, and so had I.

"You could never truly lose me, Wen. You know me – I just needed time to calm down. Our fights always blow over."

She laid her head on my shoulder. "I doubted it, I'll admit, for a time. I was scared you had gone to Fog and would never return. Every day, Kai and your father—"

"*Your* father too," I reminded her, and she let out a long breath of relief, as if I'd given her permission to own it.

"Yes, *our* father had to talk me out of coming after you. He knew we had to tread carefully and not cause a war between the realms, but really, I think he understood you *needed* to do this. But I would have come. I would have flown down on Lunara and scooped you up. Still, I see now that you had to come here… you had to meet your Fated Partner." Her tone softened.

"Wait, back up. Fly down on *Lunara?*"

Wen lifted her head, her silver eyes – the exact same as my father's! How I hadn't put two and two together before was beyond me – widening. "Oh, yes, you weren't there when your mother push— ah, anyway, Lunara had a metamorphosis. She's changed and, well, *grown.*"

"Well, that's unexpected."

"It's taken some getting used to. Kai and I are planning a frostberry farm just to keep up with demand." A contented look stole across her face.

"You're really happy, aren't you?"

She took my hand and gave it a pointed squeeze. "Now I am."

I reciprocated with a squeeze of my own. "So are you and Max all right, now?" I wondered how they had all worked together to get down here without him and Kai coming to blows.

She gave a little shrug. "We all brokered a kind of truce. For you. We knew time was of the essence and put it all to one side. I hope, given time…" She trailed off.

"I am sure it will all work out as it's supposed to," I said, serene in my newfound acceptance of destiny and entwined lives.

"Are you coming back to Nos? We all miss you. Kari hasn't been able to create a single new dress since you left, and Larissa has even given up dancing. She said it's not the same without you at the studio. Meuric will no doubt be itching to get back to the training yard – we've left him in charge."

Though I felt the pull of our Nosian friends, something – no, *someone* – pulled me here too. My nerves snapped to attention as I sensed Blade behind me. "I think I'll stick around here for a little while," I said, turning so my eyes settled on his. "At least, until things are back to a degree of normality." I felt Wen's disappointment. "Don't worry, sis, now we're all free to move amongst the realms without fear of Shadowwraith attacks we can visit regularly, and you can come down here. You're my sister! I'll always need you."

Wen threw her arms around me and clutched me.

I gripped her tightly, feeling at peace.

"Your father is looking for you," Blade said, and Wen and I broke apart with enquiring looks at him. "Uh, for Eva," he clarified with a sheepish grin.

Wen and I looked at each other and burst out laughing again. My sister rose, gave Blade a smile, and moved back into the hall.

Blade helped me up. "Come on, I'll take you to him. He's busy putting his head together with Kane's. They're quite similar, it seems, in their views of what is best for the realms."

I liked the sound of that. My father had been an excellent ruler of the Twin Realms and was no doubt steering Wen and Kai in the right direction, and now he was helping Fog too. My heart felt as though it could burst with happiness.

Blade steered me through clusters of citizens and guards; some faces I recognised, others not, but we still exchanged mutually respectful smiles and nods. I noted that a wall of guards, headed by Dag, surrounded the dais, preventing my mother and Sybilla from looking out, and also keeping me and anyone else from having to look upon them. I appreciated that.

My father looked up as I approached, and a wide smile lit his face. Without words, I rushed into his arms.

This time we weren't interrupted by a raging, bitter woman. He held me tight. "I am so proud of you," he whispered into my hair. He pulled back and looked into my eyes. "And I approve of your Partner too. He was relentless in rallying his people to get the gates open and storm the Tower to save you. I've never seen such focus, or love." His eyes crinkled as he smiled. "Well, perhaps with Wen and Kai too. It seems both my daughters chose well."

"We had good role models," I said as Alys stepped behind him. I finally understood that they had done their best, and they had always ensured their respective daughters felt loved, even if they couldn't express the truth of it fully. But now, they – we – were all free to do so. I held out my hand. "Alys," I said, that one word holding a wealth of emotion.

With a muffled cry, she took my hand and pulled me close. We hugged, laughing and crying at the same time. My father's strong, comforting arms encircled us, and soon we were joined by another pair of arms as Wen snuggled in. I had finally found my family.

After a moment, we broke apart and shared smiles. I could hardly believe what had happened in less than a week.

"I take it you'll be staying here for now?" my father asked. His look encompassed Blade as he joined us. "I've been over a few ideas with Kane, and I feel confident that you can all take it from here."

I gripped Blade's hand. "Yes, but we'll be back to visit. I want Blade to see Nos, and I miss Aruna, but for now we need to set Fog to rights."

Blade smiled at me, then looked respectfully at my father. "We'll have to round up the Council and a few who are still loyal to Taranis and see what we can do to work with them, but I suspect they'll go to ground."

My father nodded. "Running a realm is no easy feat, but I believe you, *both* of you, are more than capable. The Twin Realms will always be here to assist you in any way possible."

"The Three Realms," I said slowly, and everyone looked at me. "That's what Arianrhod called them."

"The Three Realms. I like it," Wen said. "We're all connected now."

Kai came up behind her with his sister, Tesni. I'd thought there would be an awkwardness between me and Kai, but he gave me an easy, friendly smile, which I gratefully returned.

I met Tesni's eyes, and for one pensive moment they swirled mesmerically. "We are all connected now," she said in a strange voice, and then her eyes cleared.

Kai looked at her sharply as she put a hand up to her head. "I told you it would be too much for you, surrounded by all these people," he whispered to her.

"I'm all right. Don't make such a fuss," Tesni said, and I saw the frustration bloom in her bright blue eyes. "I'm where I'm meant to be."

I looked at Blade, and murmured, "Perhaps Grenda could help her?" I sensed something *other* about Tesni. Had she *known* she would save Maxen, so that was why she came?

"Great idea," he said. "Why don't we go over to Grenda's? I'm sure she's eager to be reunited with Flint, Tora and Caelum."

"While I would love to meet more of your friends, I must get Maxen back to Nos to recover, and deal with the pressing problem of returning a certain pair to their new abode," my father said. I grimaced. I did not envy him that particular journey.

"Take as many men as you need," Blade said, and my father nodded gratefully.

"Do you have to go straight back?" I asked Wen.

She looked at Kai and Tesni, who shrugged. "We can stay for a short while," Wen said.

"Perfect. I'd like to introduce you to Grenda — she's a Seer." I noticed that Tesni's eyes became more alert. Yes, that had been a good call.

"Visit soon," my father said. I was once again wrapped up in his arms, and Alys pressed a kiss to my forehead.

"Indeed," she said in her soft voice.

"I will. *We* will," I promised.

I said a quick goodbye to a bandaged Maxen, who looked like he couldn't wait to get away. I wondered if he wanted to escape Kai and Wen... or Kai's sister. There was something there that needed unpacking, but it could wait until he was healed. My father and Alys took their leave of the others before they and Maxen followed a group of guards who were manoeuvring a docile Sybilla and my seething mother out.

I didn't even spare her a glance.

Dag and Niara joined us, along with Flint, his parents and a pale Roarke. I gave the boy a gentle hug and a whispered thank you.

"You saved me, lady. I just wanted to protect you," he said earnestly.

"You did, Roarke. I'll never forget it." I pressed a kiss to his forehead.

"I'm going home with Flint's family," he told me. I smiled mistily, so happy that he had found a family of his own. I marvelled at the symmetry of it. Families could be made, families could be chosen, but sometimes they chose you.

Blade left Kane in charge, and we all left the reclaimed Tower. In the courtyard, Blade held me back, letting the others go ahead, to take me in his arms. I stared into his green eyes.

"You would live here?" he asked. "With me?"

"I would live anywhere with you," I murmured softly. "We have a tradition in the Twin Realms where the Fated Rulers alternate which realm they live in. Wen and Kai will make their home in Sol when they are ready to rule, which, with my father's help, should be soon." I ran a hand over his braided hair. "Perhaps we should start a new tradition – one for us. Make our base here, but visit Nos and Sol often. I have a feeling we'll need to keep the bonds between the Three Realms strong, especially in readiness for the next Fate's Day and Taranis's return."

Blade nodded. "That sounds like an excellent idea. I've always wanted to see a shooting star; I've heard they light up the skies in Nos." He took my lips in a blazing kiss before pulling back to stare at me. "But then again... I think I've already seen one."

"Is that so?" I said with a slow smile. "We'd better go to Nos just to be certain."

"I have never been more certain about anything in my life," he said, then pressed his lips to mine gently, reverently.

Neither had I. I was absolutely certain that he was the only choice worth making.

Epilogue

The joyous reunion party at Grenda's spilled over into Niara's flat, so while Tesni stayed behind to speak to Grenda and Tora and Caelum settled Flint and Roarke down for the night, the rest of us decamped to the Glamour-Shield's apartment.

"So, when do I get to see *your* house?" I asked Blade, one eye on Kai, who had downed a second Fog whiskey, trying to keep up with Dag. I didn't envy Wen the coming adrenaline rush. But she didn't seem too bothered; she was currently marvelling at her abundance of now completely silver curls, courtesy of Niara. Kai seemed to appreciate them too, from the way he gazed at her from over the rim of his cup.

Blade turned to me with a smile, one eyebrow raised. "Whenever you like, love. I could take you there in the morning after we see your sister and friends off?"

"I'd like that," I said. "Perhaps you could blur us

there?"

"Blur?" he asked, amused.

"Yes. You sometimes move extraordinarily fast – it's almost like a blur." I studied his face for a reaction, and he dipped his head before meeting my eyes.

"I do have a *bit* of skill," he acknowledged. "My mother had it too. My da likes to remind me of it in his more vitriolic moments, but the way he saw it, it was an abomination. So I've mostly kept it hidden – but no longer, thanks to you." He took my hand and pressed a kiss to my palm.

I moved my hand over to cup his face. "I'm sorry about your mother," I told him.

He closed his eyes and let out a sigh. "Thank you," he said, pulling me into his arms.

There was a tentative knock on the door; reluctantly, we broke apart and Blade went to open it. Tesni stood framed in the doorway, looking uncertain.

She took in the room, and her blue eyes rested on mine. Seeing the question in them, I went to join her. "Is everything all right?"

"Not really," she said. A shout of laughter burst out from behind me and she flinched. "Sorry – I pick up on others' emotions, and I'm already a bit fraught."

With a look at Blade, I took her hand and we moved out into the corridor, Blade closing the door.

"Perhaps you would be more settled with five minutes' quiet," he suggested.

Tesni smiled gratefully. "Would you come with me? I'd like to speak to you both about something."

"Sure," I said, and followed her and Blade out in the stairwell, remembering how I'd escaped here myself not that long ago after seeing Grenda's vision. I felt Blade's gaze on me and knew he was recalling that charged moment too.

Tesni leaned against the railing and moistened her lips. I wondered if Grenda had showed her something disconcerting; it seemed these visions were unnerving to the best of us. I hoped Maxen was doing all right back in Nos and had got over his own shock.

"Grenda has offered to mentor me," she said.

"That's great news," I told her, relieved that it seemed she had escaped an unwanted vision. She nodded slowly. "Are you not happy about the offer?"

"Oh, I am, don't get me wrong. I've spent my whole life battling these feelings – sometimes they're frightening, other times nonsensical, but they're getting stronger, and I know I need help to control them and make sense of them." She broke off, her eyes clouding. "It's just... I'll have to spend a lot of time in Fog, and I've never been away from Sol for long. Away from my family for long."

Ah. "Tesni, I get it." Taking the initiative, I placed a hand on her arm, trying to imbue the touch with comfort. When she didn't flinch away, I continued, "When I first arrived I felt lost, but when you're surrounded by good people – people who only want the best for you – then you find a second home. A second family."

She raised her large blue eyes, hope shining in them. She nodded. "Very well, then. If it's all right with you two, I'll be spending a lot of time here."

"Of course – all are welcome. We need the Three Realms to be united." Blade smiled at her.

"United," Tesni said slowly, and her eyes glazed over. "*If he does not embrace our shared future by next Fate's Day, it shall spell the end of the Three Realms, and only one shall remain standing.*"

She swayed, and Blade caught her. He looked at me over her shoulder, his eyes grim. My heart began to beat strangely.

"Who is *he*, Tesni?" I whispered. But I had already begun to suspect. *Keep her away from me...*

She shuddered out a breath. "My Fated Partner," she whispered, and my heart stuttered. "I'm sorry. I need to be alone." She pushed out of Blade's hold and ran back along the corridor, away from us.

A feeling of foreboding settled over me, threatening to smother me. *The end of the Three Realms?* Surely it wasn't possible. Not when we had barely begun to unite them. Blade took me in his arms as I shivered uncontrollably, thinking of what new threats were to come. Belenos had warned us Taranis wouldn't cease his plotting while he waited for next Fate's Day – who knew what his dark mind would come up with?

Blade pressed a kiss to my head, and I closed my eyes. The destiny of the Three Realms now balanced on a perilous knife-edge of uncertainty. And the hand that held that knife? He had already been through so much; it wasn't fair for this to be asked of him now. But it seemed it all hinged on him looking into his heart and embracing what he saw there...

Or else we were all doomed.

TO BE CONTINUED...

About the Author

E. G. Tudor is an award-winning multi-genre author from the beautiful South Wales coast in the UK, where she lives with her husband, children, and crazy dog.
Her books always have a dash of magic in them, offering pure escapism to her readers.
You can connect with her via her Twitter:
@E_G_Tudor
or Instagram:
@from_the_shelf_of_e_g_tudor
@through_the_fairy_door_books

Thank you for picking up this book. If you enjoyed it please leave a review.

Other Books

UPPER YA FANTASY ROMANCE

E. G. TUDOR

WHERE *Fate* WHISPERS

THROUGH THE FAIRY DOOR

MIDDLE GRADE FANTASY

ESTELLE GRACE TUDOR

OCTAVIA BLOOM AND THE MISSING KEY
BEATRICE BLOOM AND THE STAR CRYSTAL
MARTHA BLOOM AND THE GLASS COMPASS
FELICITY BLOOM AND THE GOLDEN ARROW
OTTO BLOOM AND THE ENCHANTED COIN

Regency
Meets
Fantasy

ADULT FANTASY ROMANCE

ESTELLA G. FOGG

MASQUERADE FALL

THE LEGEND OF ANGELHAVEN

THE SWORD AND THE STONE HEART